The Arabian Nightmare was first published on November 30th 1983 by Dedalus, as part of its first list. It is now regarded as a masterpiece and one of the great works of 20th century fiction.

Here are a few comments:

'*The Arabian Nightmare* is an engaging and distinctive blend of the seductive and the disturbing, its atmosphere constantly shifting from sumptuously learned orientalising to grotesque erotic adventure and dry anarchic humour. As a feat of erudite philosophic fantasy it bears comparison with Eco's *The Name of the Rose*.'
– *Peter Miller in City Limits*

'It is like *Vathek* rewritten by Castaneda'.
– *Heathcote Williams*

'A masterpiece of historical fantasy and fetid imagination.'
– *Mark Sanderson in Time Out*

'It is a long time since a work of fantasy has delighted me so much.'
– *E. Klessman in the Frankfurt Allgemeine Zeitung*

'Quite horrendously assured. His ultimate defence against any charge of frivolity is the sheer weight of talent in the book.'
– *Ros Kaveney in The New Statesman*

Robert Irwin

The Arabian Nightmare

Dedalus

To Helen

Published by Dedalus Ltd, Langford Lodge, St Judith's Lane,
Sawtry, Cambs, PE17 5XE

ISBN 1 873982 05 4

Distributed in Canada by Marginal Distribution, Unit 103, 277 George Street North,
Peterborough, Ontario, KJ9 3G9

Publishing History
First published by Dedalus in 1983
First Viking edition 1987
First Penguin edition 1988
New Dedalus edition 1992

Printed in England by Billings Book Plan, Hylton Road, Worcester, WR2 5JU

A C.I.P. listing for this title is available on request.

Robert Irwin was born in 1946. He read Modern History at Oxford and taught Medieval History at the University of St Andrews. He also lectured on Arabic and Middle Eastern History at the universities of London, Cambridge and Oxford. Since retiring from teaching, he has spent much of his time asleep, which he regards as hard work.

He has published two other novels – *The Limits of Vision* and *The Mysteries of Algiers* – and one work of non-fiction, *The Middle East in the Middle Ages*. He is currently finishing his fourth novel *Pale Princes*, a fantasy set against the English Wars of the Roses.

Dreams come from the night.
Where do they go?
Everywhere.
What do you dream with?
With the mouth.
Where is the dream?
In the night.

A seven-year-old child interviewed in
The Child's Conception of the World, by
Jean Piaget, published by Routledge &
Kegan Paul, 1929

Contents

The Way into Cairo

For a long time I used to go to bed early. Though the art of reading is not widespread in these parts, I confess myself to be a devotee of the practice and, in particular, of reading in bed. It is peculiarly pleasant, I have found, to lie with the book propped up against the knees and, feeling the lids grow heavy, to drift off to sleep, to drift off in such a way that in the morning it seems unclear where the burden of the book ended and my own dreams began. A narrative of the manners and customs of some exotic people is particularly suitable for such a purpose.

For a long time too I have meditated writing a guidebook to these parts, or a romance, a guidebook cast in the form of a romance, or a romance cast in the form of a guidebook, in any case a narrative designed to be read in bed. The writing of a book in which the heroes and villains of the adventure should tour the territory I wished to describe would be a feat difficult but not impossible of achievement. I no longer go to bed early, and when I do unaccountable fears keep me awake, but, as I lie in the cold and the dark, the form my narrative must take becomes clearer.

The city of Alexandria is relatively well known to Western travellers and readers. Cairo is different, and in the Cairo I know, more than in any other place, the stranger needs a guide, for, though the city's principal monuments are obvious to the eye, its diversions are transitory and less easy to find, and though the inhabitants may welcome the foreigner with a smile, beware, for they are all charlatans and liars. They will cheat you if they can. I can help you there.

Moreover, I shall show how a city appears not only by day but also by night, and I have wished to show how it features in the dreams and aspirations of its inhabitants. Else this guide were but a dead thing.

It should be hot now, but I find it very cold . . .

18 JUNE 1486

'Cairo.' The dragoman pointed ahead with obvious pride, though the city had been visible for over an hour now. For over an hour too the way had been lined by bedouin and turkoman tents and the occasional huckster's stall. In a few moments they would be passing through the suburbs of Bulaq and entering through the al-Kantara Gate. Its heavy slitted and castellated masonry was a fraud or, at most, a symbol of defence, for it defended nothing. Its decayed walls were almost engulfed by shanty dwellings and shops which leaned on them for support. Behind them soared a forest of minarets, domes and square towers.

'Cairo – that is, Babylon, the Great Whore, the many-gated city, from out of which the armies of Mohamedanism ride out to bring pestilence and the sword to Christian lands. It is there that the Black Pope of the Saracens keeps his court and knots his net to encompass the destruction of Christendom, and from there that he directs his army of assassins, heretics and poisoners to our destruction. Jerusalem, Acre, Famagusta – how many cities have fallen to his armies and how many shall before you will bestir yourselves? How many have not been taken into captivity in Egypt and, like the Children of Israel, labour for Pharaoh? It is an evil city, in the Devil's power and powerful with the Devil's might, for many are gone down into Egypt and not come back. Soldiers of Christ, we call upon you . . .'

Balian pondered the crusading sermon he had heard Fra Girolamo give in Ferrara three years back. Cairo looked peaceful and inviting and quite unlike the Scarlet City of so

12

many tracts and sermons. It basked tranquilly in the yellow sun of late afternoon.

The dragoman had galloped ahead to negotiate at the guardpost before the gate. Later in the evening the entry toll would be evenly divided among the party. The dragoman had been taken on by the group in Alexandria not so much as a guide, for the way from Alexandria to Cairo was hardly in doubt, but to negotiate on behalf of the group for food, lodgings and the infernally frequent tolls on the road. Few among the group had more than the slightest smattering of Arabic. They had come together by chance, drawn into a party to protect themselves from the depredations of brigands and the arbitrariness of Mamluke officials (very much the same thing). Fear had kept them together on the road for three days, but a wide variety of purposes drew them to Cairo. There was a contingent of about a dozen Venetian merchants, temporary residents of Alexandria and evidently familiar with the route. There was also a painter sent by the Senate of the Serene Republic, as a compliment to the Sultan, to spend the summer painting the Sultan's concubines. There was a German engineer looking for a job, preferably to do with irrigation or harbour works. There was another Englishman who gave his name as Michael Vane but vouchsafed no other information. A couple of Armenian merchants, a delegation of Anatolian Turks, a Syrian priest and about a score of French and Italians who were pilgrims like himself filled out the group.

Balian, speculating whether Vane was on pilgrimage too as they passed through the gate, was so preoccupied that he almost failed to note the Mamlukes at the gate, only about thirty but better equipped and better disciplined than those they had seen so far. As they passed into the city they entered a world of stench and darkness. Balian liked it. It reminded him of his native Norwich. They rode slowly through the almost visible clouds of odour, compounded of urine, spices and rotting straw. Shopkeepers sat on stone platforms in front of their stocks, silent on the whole, regarding the infidel caravan moodily. Above the shopfronts the upper storeys of the houses swung out on great stone corbels, and from these upper storeys in turn projected wooden balconies and lattice-frame boxes, so that the sun, so brilliant outside the gates, was now nearly eclipsed. Below the ground squelched nastily under the hooves of their mules; above swung Turkish lanterns, dripping bags of muslin and great bronze talismans. Everywhere, threaded or nailed on to or between buildings, one saw the Hand of Fatima (a baleful eye staring from her palm), a magic square or the Seal of Solomon. From above again, inside the buildings, behind the wooden lattices, came the shrieks of women mocking the Europeans, while in the street itself Arab children jostled the convoy and made incomprehensible signs with their hands. The Europeans picked their way through all this with great care. They came as supplicants and existed on sufferance.

The atmosphere in the group relaxed perceptibly as they entered the caravanserai. It was already three-quarters full of foreigners. Flagons of wine were ostentatiously in evidence in the courtyards, and in one of the upper arcades two Franciscans had erected an open-air chapel. Mules were noisily unpacked; merchandise was registered with agents of the Muhtasib; the best places in the arcades were fought for. Balian found himself a place with the Venetians in a corner of one of the lower arcades, unrolled his blanket and slid off to sleep.

When he awoke it was deep night, but the scene in the courtyard was as lively as ever. Most of the Venetians were below, arguing furiously with the Muhtasib. The Muhtasib stood immovable, flanked by two huge Turks who carried lanterns on great staves. Black slaves staggered under trunks of merchandise that were being fought over. A party of men was unsuccessfully trying to persuade a camel to leave by the same gate that it had come in by. A sheep was being roasted in the centre of the compound. One Franciscan lay face-down, spreadeagled in front of the altar. The other was talking to some of Balian's fellow pilgrims. As Balian stood up, they saw him and beckoned him to join them. He came down, feeling as he did so his head swim with the heavy night heat

14

and the vestigial rhythm of so many days and nights travelling.

'Bad news.' The words came to him in both French and Italian as he approached the party. He chose to listen to the Frenchman.

'The friar has been telling us. There will be no visas tomorrow. The Dawadar's office is closed, and it is impossible to be received in audience by any of the Sultan's officers. There is a three-day holiday to celebrate the circumcision of the Sultan's grandson, which will take place on Friday. And there is more: the fee for the visa has been increased, and the road to Mount Sinai is now very unsafe.'

Then the friar spoke. 'Of late even the Holy Monastery of St Catherine has been threatened not only by bedouins but also by the Sultan's soldiers. They say that the pilgrims are not bringing any money with them.'

Balian concealed his pleasure. A delay and an enforced sojourn in Cairo would not, in fact, suit him badly. He revelled in a sense of double identity, for he did not come to Egypt solely as a pilgrim. Since taking the vow, over a year ago in England, to go to St Catherine's in the Sinai Desert and thence to the Holy Land, he had received a commission at the French court. He was to use his pilgrim guise to travel through the Mamluke lands as a spy, observing the numbers of the Mamluke soldiery, the strength of their fortifications and other features of interest. The Mamluke government in Cairo was thought to be afraid of the Ottoman Turks in the north and preparing for war in Syria. It was said that a great conspiracy was on foot in Cairo, or was this fantasy? Rumours from the east perplexed the Christian kings. The vagueness of the task he was entrusted with extended the scope of his speculations.

'I shall cut through the contradiction and confusion to discover the truth.'

Daydreams of hunts through underground sewers, hidden gateways, poisoned candle fumes and mysterious signals with scented handkerchiefs filled his mind; in his mind's eye he stood at the centre of a web of intrigue, plot and counter-plot. Reluctantly he drifted back to reality. The friar was explaining that tomorrow the circumcision festivities would begin. Tomorrow, at the hippodrome, the élite of the Mamluke regiments would parade before the Sultan and the populace of Cairo, and there would be demonstrations of skill both in massed manoeuvres and in individual combats, clearly a useful opportunity for foreign observers to assess the fighting qualities of these slave regiments at their best and a yardstick for Balian to use in future judgements.

The others in the party, cursing and spitting, were not taking it so calmly. The friar had taken advantage of their frustration to preach an impromptu sermon on the obstacles, seen and unseen, that they would face as pilgrims in the months to come. He interrupted this general theme of the earthly journey to a heavenly goal several times to warn them of the obscene dangers of circumcision and tattooing. Balian listened for a while, held fascinated by the friar's exposition of the Church's attitude to self-mutilation, and then turned away wearily and reclimbed the spiral staircase to his sleeping place. The Venetians too, having won their case with the Muhtasib, were settling down for the night.

He awoke again only late in the day, after the sun had beaten its way into the shadows of the arcade. He lay back for a while, struggling unsuccessfully to remember a dream of foreboding, and he listened to the sounds. From all over the city came the cries of the muezzins, rising and falling in disharmonious counterpoint, calling the *zuhr* prayer. Some of the Venetians were noisily playing *tarocchi*. Otherwise the caravanserai was largely empty. Further down the arcade Vane was squatting crosslegged on a mat and staring impassively at the yard below.

Dismayed by how much of the day had already gone, Balian hurried out of the caravanserai, vaguely intending to breakfast at a tavern. It was not until he was outside the gate that he paused, remembering that he was unlikely to find wine outside the walls of the compound.

He halted, undecided, pinpointed by a broad beam of sunlight that thrust its way through the trees and columns into the great square. The entrance of the caravanserai from which he had emerged faced the mosque of Ezbek. The spreading patterns of the branches of the trees and the stalactitic decoration of the squinches and spandrels of the great colonnade of the mosque gave the square, even shafted by bright sunlight, the appearance of a mysterious, crystalline underworld through which pigeons and butterflies drifted uncertainly. Scores of Cairo's poor pressed towards the fountains and basins in the colonnade and, rolling back their sleeves and throwing back their hair, stooped and hunched over the running water to perform the ritual ablutions. Many of the stalls had already closed, as their tenants moved off to the mosque for the noon prayer.

A mangy bear padded by, apparently unattended, and Balian's eye slid sideways, following it, until his vision came to rest on a shop that had remained open. In the entrance, deep in shadow, sat a few Turks and the Venetian painter, who was examining a book. His name was Giancristoforo Doria, Balian remembered. Giancristoforo looked up from the book and beckoned encouragingly, and Balian walked over to join him. The shop was selling a hot, black brew in small porcelain bowls. The Venetian bought him one, soundlessly gesturing to the proprietor, and equally soundlessly passed Balian some dried bread. They watched the last few filter into the mosque. Suddenly Giancristoforo spoke. 'Kahwah,' gesturing at the bitter liquid. 'Their holy men and hermits drink it to stay awake at their devotions, but ordinary people drink it too. It tastes better than the water if you can get used to it.'

Giancristoforo was used to it, for he had been in Turkey a few years previously with another painter on a similar mission. The food, the clothes and the religion bored him in Turkey and in Egypt, and his mission alternately bored and appalled him.

'I hate the Saracen lands, the land of illusion and illusionism, the kingdom of the greasy palm and shifty eye. Their guests are offered an infinite variety of pleasures, but it all must be paid for in the end. One must know one's Arab and be on one's guard if one wants to avoid trouble. They are all out to fleece you.'

'I have been abroad before – France, Italy, Germany.'

'Ah, but this place is different and terrible deceits are practised upon the unwary. Let me give you an example. Do you remember the day of our disembarkation?' (Balian remembered it – the old men sitting on the beach, their rosaries revolving in their fingers, the dusty wind rising, the palms bent almost double under its force.) 'Well, that afternoon I went walking along the sands alone westwards towards the swamps of Mareotis. After some hours of walking I encountered a man and a boy sitting by the edge of the sea. They stopped me and importuned me for money. They clutched at their stomachs and hollowed out their cheeks. Beggars are the curse of these lands, and I refused and was about to walk on when the man stopped me again, pulling at my sleeves, and said that he was so desperate for money that, there and then, he would kill his own son if only I would give him two dinars. I laughed in his face, of course, but no, he was serious. He forced me down on the sand beside them and brought out from his bundle of cloth a pot of ashes, a large coil of rope and a flute. The ashes he smeared on his face and that of the boy. The rope he put before him and he sat behind it with his flute. As he began to play the sky was starting to cloud. The man kept looking at me all the time with an oddly suggestive grin, and he stroked the rope as he played. Suddenly, to my astonishment, the rope quivered and began to rise, at first rather uncertainly, into the air until the greater part stood vertical over its coil and its top was lost in the clouds. Then the man spoke to the boy, threatening him, I supposed, for the boy threw himself at my feet and appealed for my protection. So it seemed, but I did not understand what was happening and did nothing. Then the man chased the boy round and round the coil of the rope until suddenly the boy seized the rope and started shinning up it as fast as he could. The man fished out a knife from his bundle. He stuck it between his teeth and followed the boy up until he too was lost in the clouds. I was alone on the beach again and sat there astounded, looking out to sea. A long time passed. Then I slowly became aware that my doublet was getting wet. I looked up, expecting rain. Indeed it was raining, but the drops that were falling on my doublet were drops of blood. Then there were other things – first a hand, then a leg, one by one all the severed pieces of the boy's body hit the sand. Finally I saw the father come climbing down the rope, bearing the boy's head in his hand. When he had descended, the rope flopped limply around him.

'I felt a mysterious sense of relief on seeing the Arab again and, when he asked for two dinars, I paid it to him without demur. He gathered his things and the fragments of his son's corpse together in a bundle and, when this was done, saluted me and walked off with his bundle towards Alexandria. Dumbstruck I watched him walk away. The following day, however, I saw both the man and his son sitting outside a pastry shop in Alexandria, stuffing themselves with food. It was all a fraud. He had only put me under an enchantment so that I thought I saw him go up the rope to kill his son. The fascination . . .'

Here Balian interrupted and said, pointing at his cup of coffee, 'What did you expect? This stuff costs half a dinar a cup. Should you expect him to murder his own son for only two dinars?'

'That no, perhaps not . . . but I was made a fool of. If I ever saw that illusionist again, I could not answer for the consequences.'

'But you are a painter, and isn't painting too a form of illusionism?'

Giancristoforo was on the edge of anger. 'No, by God! Other artists may perhaps be so damned by their works, but I have never laboured to deceive. All my colours are unnatural, golds and scarlets mostly, and I make no use of perspective, for perspective deceives the eye, and to deceive the eye is to deceive the mind, and that is immoral, like the telling of idle tales. Good art must be founded upon good morals. I can tell you, I have many reservations about my present mission. The Sultan is an infidel and a barbarian. He is like any other Turk but in fancier dress. All Turks look the same. His concubines all look alike. It's difficult to get the bitches to sit still when I don't speak their language, and they are afraid that I am painting images in which to trap their souls.

'I am not trying to trap their souls. I don't believe that Turkish whores have such things. The soul of an infidel sultan may be damned, and yet he has one, but women have no souls. That is why painting their portraits is so difficult, for there is no inner essence to be caught, only a body to be sketched out. So while the body of a man is the Temple of God on Earth, a woman's body is in turn only a deformed reflection of the man's. Believe it. When I painted Bajazet's harem I hated it (hated them, rather) and their rolls of white flesh, reptilian eyes and shivery enticements. I know that I shall hate these Egyptian ones too; they'll be too round and blubbery to model satisfactorily in line and shape. You understand, of course, that I have nothing against women as women? Then there is the problem of the bad light inside the houses and the problem of trying to find the right dyes and oils in the market and there is the heat. Everyone is half asleep while I am trying to do my work.'

He tailed off despondently. Balian had been listening with a straight face. Was the man mad? Or simply a homosexual with an amusingly inappropriate job to perform? Balian's head swam. The heat was rising. The man called Vane emerged from the caravanserai and moved off rapidly down a dark alleyway that led through the markets towards the Citadel. Giancristoforo pointed towards him languidly.

'That man knows a lot about dyes and oils, and he knows Arabic. One can learn a lot from him, but perhaps it's better not to. He is an alchemist, and he has close friends at the Mamluke court. Both things make him dangerous. One of these days, I suspect, he will apostatize, which will be a pity, for he knows a lot about things that we should be prepared against.'

Giancristoforo squinted up at the sky as if pondering his next remark. He never made it, for in an instant two Turks with scimitars raised before them emerged from the darkness at the back of the coffee house, smoothly and silently pinioned his arms and, together with a third Turk who joined them in the square, set off with their captive in the direction Vane had already gone, towards the Citadel.

Balian was too shaken to move at first and then properly cautious. He made no attempt to follow them but, picking up the book left behind by Giancristoforo, walked with studied casualness back to the caravanserai. He told the Venetian traders what had happened, and their leader, the consul from Alexandria, said that a protest would be lodged with the Dawadar on Monday when the offices reopened. But what had happened? Clearly the Turks were officials or soldiers. That could be seen from their selective and smoothly efficient way of acting. Had spies been shadowing Giancristoforo from Alexandria? Was it his remarks about Turkish whores? Or about Vane, the Mamluke's friend? Had he offended against some obscure canon of Arab etiquette? Or had he simply passed the shopkeeper a bad coin at a time when the Mamluke police happened to be passing by?

'We could all disappear like that, every one of us here, and Christendom neither would nor could lift a finger to save us,' a Frenchman remarked thoughtfully.

Later that afternoon, when the Europeans set out to attend the day's festivities, they were still nervous and moved off together under the leadership of the consul, Alvise Trevisano. The hippodrome where the games took place lay at the foot of the Citadel, and it was there that the young Mamluke slaves and their eunuch trainers customarily drilled. Despite his eagerness to see them at manoeuvres, Balian felt too shaken to leave the security of the caravanserai immediately. So he did not accompany the others that afternoon. Instead he climbed up to the roof, taking with him Giancristoforo's book. For some reason he had not mentioned this book to the others.

The book was unimpressive, a score or so of folio pages loosely threaded together. Balian noted with surprise that the title was on the back of the book in a spider's scrawl of Arabic. He opened it. The writing inside was in Arabic too, in the same sort of irregular spider's dance, but in tiny writing between the lines of Arabic someone had attempted a translation into Italian. Frowning with concentration Balian read.

'He said, 'Beware of the Ape!'

He said also, 'Some people say that every skull contains within itself its own sea of dreams and that there are millions upon millions of these tiny oceans. They adduce as proof the fact that if you put your ear against the ear of a friend and listen closely, you may hear the sea beating against the wall of the skull. But how can the finite contain the infinite?'

He said also, 'When we sleep we are learning to come to terms with death.'

He said also, 'One honours the spirits of the dream by sleeping with them, even when they are in disguise.'

He said also, 'Why can we not dream that we are two people? This was a great problem for the Ikhwan al-Safa.'

He said also, 'Large areas of the brain are empty. They have never been crossed by man.'

He said also, 'Sleep is man's most natural state. Long years Adam lay dreaming in the Garden before Eve was drawn from his body and she woke him.'

He said also,' One should take care to forget unimportant dreams. One throws the sprats back into the sea of the Alam al-Mithal.' He said also, 'He who is a coward in his dreams will be one also in his waking life.'

Balian put the book down baffled and irritated. He could not see its purpose. Who had attempted a translation? Giancristoforo? But Giancristoforo claimed to know no Arabic. He drifted on to consider the circumstances of Giancristoforo's arrest. The thought passed through his mind that Giancristoforo had been arrested by mistake for Balian the spy, but he rapidly dismissed it. He moved on to dimmer, dozier thoughts and from these into a siesta. He awoke in a pool of sweat. The party had returned from the hippodrome and the call to the sunset prayer was being given. He sat for a while, feeling bored; his fear had turned to restlessness.

As he came down into the courtyard, he found that another excursion was being proposed, a visit to the Village of Women. The pilgrims were the most enthusiastic, he noted wryly. It had taken the ship five weeks to reach Alexandria, and it had taken them another three days to reach Cairo, nearly six weeks without a woman. Moreover, it could not be a sin to sleep with a Muslim!

The Village of Women lay, in fact, within the walls of the city, in the Ezbekiyya quarter, close by the caravanserai. The quarter in which they were lodged was also the quarter of the entertainers and criminals. Again it was a Venetian who took the lead in conducting them round the brothel area. They picked their way by torchlight up and down the narrow paths that threaded across the quarter.

It was a sombre voyage of exploration that he thought more likely to turn the soul towards self-mortification than to gratify the senses. The houses were lower than in the merchants' quarters, being only one or two storeys high. The walls were mostly painted in garish blues and oranges. Frescoes of dancing naked couples, cobras, vine leaves, djinn, heraldic blazons. Very bizarre, a pantheon of Christian and Eastern saints also made their appearance on the walls: St Josaphat casting away money, St Catherine sprawled and broken on the wheel and, everywhere, St Thais and St Pelagia, the patron saints of Egyptian prostitution. Where on the interior ground floor one would have seen rope, camelot, cinnamon or cotton for sale in the merchants' quarters, here another sort of merchandise was on display: flesh – flesh hideously tattooed with apotropaic emblems, flesh lined and hanging in limp folds, flesh pocked with the marks of pestilence. It sat there on display in the torchlight of the interiors. The women sat there indifferent, making no attempt to tempt some custom. Again Balian was reminded of Giancristoforo's discourse that morning. Yet, curiously, the party of Europeans was getting smaller as, one by one, they slipped away to find satisfaction in the arms of age, ugliness and disease.

Very soon Balian found himself walking alone, sick with revulsion, oppressed by the poverty and squalor. Suddenly he was jerked out of his misery by a hand that shot between his legs. He found himself drawn up against a woman who was almost as tall as he was and dressed in the Turkish style – headscarf, tight velvet waistcoat and striped skirt. Her face was as uncompromising as her direct manner of attracting custom, high cheekbones and the brightness of the eyes emphasized by the swooping lines of kohl around them. A Circassian Turkess? She was remarkably young for the area, in her early thirties, and did not appear to be deformed in any way. She set him free and made suggestive signs with her hands, pointing insistently to her house. In fact, it was hardly a house, for only the corners and the floor were of stone. It was rather a kiosk, a ramshackle construction of fretworked wood. She drew him in and up, behind a blanket that hung from the roof, on to a raised stone platform covered with mats and rugs. Still staring haughtily at him, she threw herself back on these and, pulling up her long skirt, drew up her legs. Roused by her imperious manner and the exotic surroundings, he moved in easily.

It was therefore with some surprise, when it was all over, that he heard the woman say, 'Well, I did not think much of that!'

'You speak English!'

'I learnt the language from your friend.'

'He taught you very well – but who is my friend?'

She looked pleased. 'Vane, of course. You came to Cairo with him.'

'Vane isn't my friend. We have never spoken to one another. I don't even know what he does here in Cairo.'

'Oh, I assumed that he'd brought you back from England

24

to work with him. Forgive my error. But I expect that you will become acquainted with him in time. Most people know Vane; they know his reputation at least.'

'But you were expecting me, lying in wait for me?'

She began to search for something in a little wooden box that she had beside her. 'Oh, yes, foreigners are watched all the time.'

'What did you mean by "I did not think much of that"?'

'I was just expecting more, that's all.'

'What more, in God's name, did you want?'

She produced a thread from the box and ran it through from one nostril to the other. Balian, thoroughly intimidated, watched her cleaning her nostrils. It was some time before she replied.

'People like you suck up the energy of others, sitting, listening and asking questions without ever saying anything for themselves. As to your sexual performance, I had assumed, foolishly I suppose, that all Englishmen were like Vane, or, if not that, then that you might have been taught by him. He has a great reputation here in Cairo as a lover. I could teach you some things, I suppose. *Imsaak* in particular.' She looked at him speculatively. There was an odd glint in her eye.

'What is *imsaak*?'

'*Imsaak* is the art of delaying the climax with as many twists, turns and contortions as possible. It is in this that the real art lies . . . You look exhausted. God knows how you got to Cairo; I wonder if you will be able to raise the energy to leave. Your penis stands erect, but your eyelids flutter. Your body moves, but the serpent within you sleeps.'

She clutched her hands dramatically to her bosom before continuing. 'You have a serpent coiled and sleeping at the base of your spine. It must be sung to and lured to rise until its head is between your eyes and you see the world through its eyes, a body of pure sexual energy. In Christendom copulation is very like sleep, but in Egypt and in Sind it is a science. I could also teach you *karezza* and the rites of sexual exhaustion, but at the moment you are throwing your semen away as if it were water. First we must rouse the serpent.'

'How do you rouse the serpent?'

She raised her finger to her lips. The eyes moved from side to side as if searching the room for spies. 'It cannot be spoken of. It can only be demonstrated. The act of drawing the serpent up the spine is like climbing a rope. He who has understood how to do it and climbed the rope pulls it up after him. I shall initiate you. It will cost you money, but it will be worth it for you to wake from a sleep which is half a death.'

Balian replied as reasonably as he could. 'Our faith teaches us that initiation is not to be found between the legs of a woman, nor pearls in a gutter. If you have knowledge you cannot speak about, then do not speak about it. I have been travelling a long time. Of course I am tired, yet I doubt, lady, if perverted intercourse with you is the remedy. Have you no family? How could someone like you descend to the level of the whore?'

Her long thin tongue travelled slowly round her lips as she considered. It was obvious to Balian that she was mad.

'More of these tiring questions. Oh yes, I have a family. If you are lucky, you will never meet them. But I am no whore. I am a princess. Indeed, my prince approaches, and you should leave quickly. Go now. Shoo! You must hurry, for the streets become dangerous so late. Remember the way back, and be careful not to sleep alone in this city. Now pay me. Two dinars please.'

Balian paid her.

'My name is Zuleyka. We shall meet again.'

He turned and rushed out into the street.

2

Another Way into Cairo

If my audience would like to hear of more wonders like the rope trick they shall, but the rope trick itself can never be explained. By the way, as this is a tale designed to be told at night, it seems appropriate that it should have within it a strong sensual element so as to stimulate what I have heard they call in the West wet dreams, but we shall return to these matters later perhaps . . .

'Cairo.' The guide pointed ahead, a skinny bronzed hand shooting out of his robes. The city grew larger and larger. Balian, who was riding beside the guide, lowered his hood, unable to stare directly into the sun until they came in under the shadow of the walls. Then they passed in through the gate, and now Balian was puzzling at the many unexpected features of the city he saw on every side – the rugs spread out to display the little brass idols of Mahound, Apollyon and Tergavent, the twisted candy-columned doorways, the storks that nested in towers and minarets and drifted across the sky from one to another, the broad staircases that shot up steeply from the main highway closely lined with statues of elephants and men. Children stood on the roofs waving at them.

But where are all the women? thought Balian. Oh yes. Of course, their husbands have hidden them away. I was expected.

Some streets were boarded off, against what it was not clear.

'There have been few Christians who have crossed over to Egypt this year.'

A vivid memory came to mind of the sea this summer, its green surface coated thick with dust. Cobwebs hung from waves which had risen but not broken, and when the occasional wave did fall, sending dirt and discoloured foam splashing upwards, a swarm of buzzing insects rose with it too. The whole horizon had been obscured by the dust that hung in the air.

The children waved but did not say anything. The sound of hooves was muffled on sand. It was very quiet. They rode further into the entrails of the city. The guide and he dismounted. It was difficult to see the guide's face; he might have been veiled. The guide showed him a book and Balian read in it:

He said, 'There are some who hold that talking about it, even thinking about it, is enough to attract it and stimulate its attacks. For this reason we do not name it. But even this may not be enough. Therefore I advised that no one should read this book unless he is already aware of what it is, and let those who know forget if they can.

Balian put the book down on the ground and rose to confront the indistinct figure before him. 'Who are you?'

The reply came easily enough. 'I am here to satisfy your doubts. I mean to satisfy you that you are not me.'

A flash of teeth. Things seemed to shimmer a little in the limp air. Was it all quite real? The silence was deeper yet. Balian and his companion stood motionless in the middle of a great open space. The silence intensified until, paradoxically, it became a buzzing in the ears. Flies and other insects spiralled upwards. Balian's vision had become very fluid. The ground shook slightly. Then he saw that it was life that pulsed in the earth, the bricks and the trees and forced its way upwards in great roaring flames of energy that lengthened into tongues of umber, black and green. The whole universe was burning up around him in ecstasy.

The roaring was inside his head. And blood. He awoke and

it came jetting out of his nostrils. His mouth was full of blood too, some of it overflowing in thin driblets down his chin. He was on the roof of the caravanserai, and a circle of Italians were squatting anxiously around him. He had been talking in his sleep, shouting rather, and clawing the air. Was he ill? Balian indeed did not feel well; his dreams more normally ran on the themes of flashing swords, noble and appealing ladies, 'a message for the Duke' and so forth. He was ill, then, and needed a doctor. The Italians were summoning the other Englishman, Vane, from across the caravanserai. Vane began to pick his way slowly over recumbent bodies. It was early morning.

Vane stripped Balian to the waist, probing and pummelling him, and he questioned him also on his sleep, especially on the details of his dreams. 'I have never seen this before, but it is clear that you have one of the night sicknesses. I am certain that there is nothing wrong with your body; it's not your lungs or your stomach, but it is a disease of sleep that has made you bleed, and it is likely that it will come back again.'

Vane's brows furrowed. 'It is fairly serious. It could be one of the forms that the *lamiae* take. Yes, that is likely when one considers the number of unconsecrated burial grounds in Egypt.' He paused, conscious of the mystery he was creating. Then, 'At least it is not the Arabian Nightmare. I don't think that I can do anything for you on my own. I have some knowledge of physic, especially of the night diseases, but I would not venture an unadvised opinion. But you ought not to spend another night without seeing a physician. There is a master of night medicine, a good one, in the Bulaq quarter of the city. If you will allow me, I will conduct you to him immediately, for I don't think that you have lost much blood and, wherever it is coming from, it seems to have stopped.'

For a while Balian stared blankly up at him, then he began to think. Two people had warned him against Vane, but they were both at least partially insane, so perhaps their warnings amounted to recommendations. Besides, if Vane were a spy and if he had had some responsibility for the arrest of Gian-cristoforo, Balian wanted to know him better.

Michael Vane's appearance certainly provoked curiosity. In his early fifties, he was quite tall but tended to conceal his tallness by walking with a stoop. His head was shaven almost bald like a Muslim *hajji*, his nose was broken, his skin porous and greasy and slightly scarred, yet his face was blasted with a sort of melancholy which made it seem almost attractive. Most extraordinary, he wore in the Cairo summer a coat made of what seemed to be old rat skins and carried a broad-brimmed felt hat. He looked, Balian decided, clever enough and tough enough to be captain of a mercenary company or a king of thieves.

Vane had obviously taken Balian's assent for granted. 'On your feet and be ready to leave very shortly. I for one do not intend to miss the Prince's circumcision this afternoon.'

Balian struggled up and washed himself at the pump, trying to clear his mouth of the unpleasantly dry taste of stale blood. Presently they set out together.

Vane, forging ahead through the crowds, suddenly turned. 'Stick close to me. Even in the daytime some quarters are not safe to cross alone; some are controlled by robbers' guilds and they often work hand in glove with Mamluke guards. It's particularly dangerous for cross-worshipping infidels from overseas.'

Foolhardily, Balian decided to try Vane. 'I know. You have heard doubtless of how the Italian I was having breakfast with yesterday was taken away by the Mamlukes, presumably to prison?'

Vane's grin was positively wolfish. 'Oh, I know. I had him arrested.' He let this sink in. 'I thought I recognized him during the journey down from Alexandria. Then I knew where I had seen him before. It was at the late Sultan Mehmet's court at Constantinople, where he was employed to paint the Sultan's harem. But there were grounds for thinking that the Serene Republic had sent him to the Ottoman court to do more than paint obscene portraits. It was obvious that he had become very friendly with the then prince, now Sultan Baja-zet. Now Venice wishes to consolidate its understanding with the Ottoman Sultan, and it hopes for a joint Turkish–Venetian expedition against Egypt. The time is right for them. Egypt is very vulnerable. Qaitbay is old and sick, whether in the head or body is not clear. Perhaps he would not even be able to lead his army into Syria to encounter the Ottomans. So, believing the painter to be a spy, I informed the Dawadar of my suspicions. My hope is that I have successfully foiled another Venetian plot against the Sultan. But don't tell the others, will you, lad? Because if you do, you and I will both have cause to regret it.'

Although what Vane said was unpleasant and the manner in which he said it was blunt, Balian still gained the impression that Vane was lying. When Balian spoke, he kept his voice low and concealed his anger. 'But isn't the fall of the Sultanate something every Christian must pray for? How else can the Holy Places be redeemed from its control?'

'The Holy Places, the Holy Places! Where are your eyes, lad? The Ottomans threaten Belgrade. After Belgrade, Vienna, then Salzburg and Milan and the call of the muezzin from the rooftops of Paris. The Crusade for the Holy Places is the dream of chivalry, yet it is also a masquerade for the designs of secret people. Don't let yourself be used by the dream and deceived by the masquerade. Nothing is simple, but think on this: who but the Mamlukes can save Christendom from the Ottomans?'

There was silence for a while, as they elbowed and shoved their way through knots of people. Then he spoke again. 'The only pity is that it is such a weak and feeble ally. The Sultan is old. Prices rise and there are bread riots. A man called the Nightingale moves through the city, stirring up trouble, and there are rumours of revolt – of the slaves, or the Copts, or the Bedouin of Upper Egypt – rumours too of a new Messiah. You may feel sorry for the painter, but the situation is much too fragile to run risks.'

By now they were deep in a labyrinth of small streets.

Balian was as much confused by Vane's speech as he was by the geography of the city. His head felt tight with unresolved questions. How was it that an English alchemist had become so involved in Levantine politics? How close were his connections with the Citadel and the Mamluke government? What had he been doing in Constantinople? Why was he taking such an interest in what might be no more than a nosebleed? But Balian asked none of these. Instead, 'What is the Arabian Nightmare?'

'The story – and it is only a story, for those who know it best cannot speak about it – is curious but unclear, leaving one to doubt whether it is a disease or a curse. The Arabian Nightmare is obscene and terrible, monotonous and yet horrific. It comes to its victims every night, yet one of its properties is that it is never remembered in the morning. It is therefore the experiencing of infinite pain without the consciousness that one is doing so. Night after night of apparently endless torment and then in the morning the victim rises and goes about his daily business as if nothing had ever happened, and he looks forward to a good night's sleep at the end of a hard day's work. It is pure suffering, suffering that does not ennoble or teach, pointless suffering that changes nothing. The victim never knows that it is he, though he may well know the story and speculate on it, but there will be people in the market place who will know him by certain signs. There will be talk behind his back, for he has been marked – as a sort of idiot Messiah perhaps. That is the Arabian Nightmare.'

Vane spoke with feeling. Balian wondered if Vane's melancholy was an indication that he believed himself to be a victim of this invisible affliction.

'But, as I was remarking, that clearly is not your problem. You remember your dream. The heat is very prone to affect the vapours in the head and disorder one's dreams. It is best dealt with quickly, for a nightmare like yours, with physical after-effects, if not treated quickly may go, as it were, gangrenous.'

The streets they thrust their way through presented an

increasingly ruinous appearance. Vane explained that whenever a man died a violent death in this city, his house was usually left untenanted and left to fall into ruins and that this was a very violent part of the city.

At length they reached the house (Vane called it the House of Sleep), a large and rather splendid house that towered over its neighbours in the most ruined part of the city that Balian had yet seen.

Vane spoke to the negro at the door and returned rapidly. 'He is away – the Father of Cats has gone on pilgrimage to the tomb of Sidi Idris, but he will be back later and we are urged to call again, perhaps tomorrow. We must hope that you are not visited again tonight, or at least that it does not take a more violent form. You should be watched while you sleep. Well it's a pity, but at least we shall not be late for today's ceremony. We can cut across from here to the hippodrome.'

The preliminary celebrations had already begun, and the tiers were full. They would not have secured a seat at all but that Vane went up and spoke to the Naib al-Jawkandar, Deputy Polo Mallet Bearer of the Sultan, who had them conducted to the enclosure reserved for privileged foreigners, which directly adjoined the Sultan's own pavilion and which commanded the head of the hippodrome. Beside them, in the Sultan's pavilion, a massive baldachin extended itself, capable not only of sheltering the hundreds of courtiers and soldiers who attended the Sultan but also of enclosing within it a small garden of orange trees, rose bushes, fountains and mechanical singing birds in cages.

Qaitbay sat stiffly erect on a raised dais in the centre, a thin, frail old man, sunken-cheeked with wispy hair – incredibly, the source of all power in one of the world's greatest empires. He sat there stiff with pride. But Balian noted the rings under his eyes. Behind, in a ring on the platform, the élite corps of the *khassakiya* extended themselves as a sort of bodyguard, yet their heavy armour could not hide the obvious truth that they did not consider themselves on duty, for all were relaxed; some were fondling one another. Balian had already heard much about the effeminacy of the Turkish Mamluke court and the scandal it gave rise to among the more conservative section of the Arab society in the big cities. To the left of Qaitbay a great screen of pierced wickerwork had been erected, and from there the royal harem could look down upon the games, doubly shielded by the screen and by their veils. Behind the *khassakiya* the royal enclosure was a multi-coloured sea of swaying turbans and conical caps, each denoting some royal office or rank. Vane did his best to identify them – the Dawadar or Bearer of the Royal Inkwell, the Royal Armourer, the Vizier, the Grand Mufti, the Polo Mallet Bearer, the Bearer of the Slipper, the Royal Falconer, the Shaikh of Shaikhs, the Chief Eunuch and so on and on. Among the courtiers flitted willowy pageboys.

In the hippodrome horsemen tilted at the quintain and fired arrows at moving targets. They were followed by dervishes who slashed themselves with swords and ran fiery needles through their cheeks, chanting the names of God all the while, and these were followed in their turn by a team of polo players. It was not until late afternoon, as sunset approached, that the circumcision ceremony proper began. Prince Bahadur, one of Qaitbay's grandsons, was to be circumcised in the company of no fewer than seventy sons of leading Mamluke emirs.

Conducted by a master of ceremonies, these seventy youths rode slowly across the hippodrome, covered in gold and silver and dressed as little girls. Vane explained, 'It shields them from the Evil Eye until the operation has been performed.'

Behind them paraded seventy barbers and seventy barbers' assistants, all chanting praises to the one God. Pageboys ran up and down the length of the procession, bearing strange, unidentifiable objects on long poles. At the far end of the hippodrome tents had been erected, into which the children were conducted. The military orchestra stationed behind the tents began a rhythmic yet halting tune. From the women in the crowds came shrill ululations, which mixed with the rising chants of the dervishes; if the din was intended to drown the screams of the children, it did not succeed. One imagined seventy knives rising and falling, seventy bloody foreskins. The entire hippodrome throbbed and screamed and swayed. The children did not emerge from the tents. From the walls of the Citadel a gun boomed out, a sign that the ceremony was over. The crowds began to disperse.

'Tomorrow we will visit the Father of Cats. Be sure to be at the caravanserai at around the time of the noon prayer tomorrow.'

Vane raised his hand in farewell and disappeared.

There was a delay at the gate.

'The guards are checking everyone. They are looking for the Messiah,' it was explained.

'But how will they know who he is?'

'It's in the book.'

The bony finger pointed and Balian read:

He said, 'the Messiah will be one who has been purified by infinite suffering. Yet he will also be one who has not been weakened by the consciousness of suffering.'

'But don't worry. You are on pilgrimage. We can slip you in by a side gate.'

They passed through and came to the hippodrome. Catherine of Alexandria lay spreadeagled, roped to the great wheel tilted up to face the sun, around her the turbaned and veiled bourgeoisie of Cairo. A Mamluke, whose face was hidden by a chainmail coif, produced a hammer from a sort of metal quiver which he had slung at his waist. He had to watch. An old man was telling him, 'Only meditation on the extremes of pain will prepare you for your future ordeals.' A gap-toothed mouth opened and laughed. 'I usually meditate on being eaten by lions!'

The Mamluke turned to face the Sultan's pavilion now, the head of his hammer resting in the palm of his hand. A trumpet sounded, and the Mamluke wheeled abruptly and brought the hammer down on one of the saint's knee joints. In the shimmering hot air he could hear unnaturally clearly both the splintering of the bones and the hiss that ran through the crowd. The hammer rose and fell again and again, striking Catherine's joints with military precision. The wheel began to spin under the guiding hand of the executioner. Balian felt himself dizzy and dripping with sweat and raised his hand to mop his brow. Only when he did so did he become aware that he was manacled to the old man. He heard a voice saying, 'Now it's your turn.' Then something soft and loathsome seized him from behind.

Zuleyka was shaking him. He was in her kiosk. She was kneeling over him, dressed this time in yellow silks. He felt very groggy.

'A horrid dream.'

'But you are safe here, if nowhere else. A bad dream is like being buggered by an uninvited stranger. It's best forgotten.'

A pause. Something was wrong, he knew it. She was asking him his name. What was his name? He panicked, squirmed and awoke on the roof of the caravanserai. At least he supposed it was a true awakening. Blood was everywhere, welling out of his mouth and jetting out of his nostrils. Vane was shaking him awake with one hand and trying to staunch the nosebleed with a handkerchief in the other.

'It is lucky that you were watched this time. As soon as the bleeding has stopped, we must visit the Father of Cats. I have been sitting over you ever since we got back to the caravanserai.'

Balian struggled to remember.

Vane continued, 'You will not be disappointed in the Father of Cats; I should tell you that I have been a student of his for some time.'

The Father of Cats received them, reclining back into a pile of cushions on the roof of his house. He was expecting them, but the little pilgrimage of the previous day had exhausted him, and he hardly stirred as Vane described the symptoms but let his eyelids droop lower and lower. Bald and emaciated, with a bushy white beard, he slouched with his arms hanging over his knees and his face flung up towards the sky. The face which he briefly turned to study Balian through slitted lids did not reassure the latter; it was curiously smooth, the skin stretched luxuriously over the planes of the face, as if it were silk sheathing the skull. Well-fed cats crawled over his chest and legs, Egyptian cats with narrow wedge-chinned faces, and one slept on his shoulder.

He began to speak to Vane, and Vane interpreted to Balian in unsteady bursts. Diagnosis was slow and punctuated with many questions about Balian's manners, customs and beliefs. The old man seemed almost asleep as he gave his judgement. The infection was one that was easily caught in a country as hot as this, but it was not so easy to cure. A little time was necessary.

'But tomorrow I must see the Dawadar.'

'The day after tomorrow perhaps. He says that you must spend a night or two in his house. Be his guest and his patient.'

'Tomorrow I must go to the Dawadar's office and get a visa to visit St Catherine's in Sinai. I cannot wait around in Cairo.'

'What do you want to go to St Catherine's for? There's nothing there. Dry bones. Dust and sand. Sand and dust and filthy ignorant monks.'

Vane's insistence only made Balian nervous. 'I owe to St Catherine that service. She saved my life at the siege of Artois. I have made a vow to her which as a Christian and a gentleman I must fulfil.'

'Surely there is no need to go to the Dawadar's office for a visa? You are ill and for your pilgrim's vow the intention will suffice. You can visit St Catherine in your sleep, or perhaps she will visit you.'

A slow chill spread over Balian's back. He was now sitting in shadow. The old man had begun to whistle tunelessly to himself, apparently quite withdrawn from the dialogue; his eyeballs were turned upwards, and the whites showed shuddering, the palsied hands shaking before him as if playing an invisible mandolin.

37

Vane continued, 'If you bleed like that every night, you will be dead before you reach Mount Sinai. Only in a big city like Cairo can you find a man like the Father of Cats, who specializes in the diseases of sleep. In the desert the caravan will abandon you; for them you would be only a burden as the victim of the Evil Eye. But my friend the Father of Cats' (and here Vane rather gingerly put his arm round the emaciated shoulders of the old man) 'is not afraid of the Evil Eye and is no charlatan, if that is what you are thinking.'

The Father grinned and Balian decided that they were both charlatans.

Vane continued, 'He knows of, and is master of, recurrent nightmare, insomnia, sleepwalking, catalepsy, catatonia, talking and predicting in one's sleep, nocturnal emissions, enuresis, blasphemous dreams and the eight classes of dreams proscribed by the Ikhwan al-Safa.'

'And what is wrong with me?'

'None of these.'

A studiedly cryptic pair, Vane and the Father were staring at him intently.

'The Father of Cats has asked if you would like to be shown round his place?'

Balian nodded his assent.

'Then let us go down.'

At first Balian could not understand why they wanted to show him round, for there seemed nothing of particular interest to see. The house was large certainly; it towered over its neighbours in the quarter, but one empty room with yellowing plaster walls looked very much like another. Vane explained that they all ate and slept more or less where they felt like it. Only a few of the rooms had any furniture at all and that was of the most vestigial kind – low wooden tables, bolsters scattered at random and, once, a Koran stand. They crossed a cool, dark courtyard lined with cypresses, but it smelt of drains. A heavily shrouded servant girl scuttered past. They visited the coffee-maker's room with its cones of sugar as high as a man; they walked through the great *mandara* –

reception room – with its fountain run dry in the centre of a floor of cracked tiles. As they continued their inspection through empty storerooms and cells of indeterminate purpose, Balian became aware of a faint sense of discomfort; his eyes ached and his heart felt heavy. He thought that he would not like to spend a night in this place. Even in daylight it was a little oppressive. Alabaster windows let in a frowzy, yellowish light which flowed over smoke-stained walls and made faces shimmer and dance in their uncertain illumination. Cockroaches hurried across the floors; the Father of Cats had cast off the appearance he had given at the consultation of being half-dead with exhaustion and took delight in displaying his agility, dancing the insects to death with his bare feet. The harem area they did not see. On the roof herbs were spread out to dry, and an attractive Berber girl padded about, laying out the washing. From the roof Balian was able to look down into the street by which they had entered, and he noted how a man, passing the entrance of the house, spat over his left shoulder; it seemed to be not a gesture of contempt but, perhaps, a ritual of propriation.

It was not until they descended again to the courtyard that Balian began to feel that there were things of interest to be seen. Round a corner, off the courtyard, was the pharmacy, a tiled kiosk with niches set into the walls at close intervals. In the niches, sealed in jars or wrapped in leaves, was ranged an amazing collection of roots, leaves and powders: white hellebore which made men die, suffocated with their vomit; black hellebore which purged in dangerous convulsive spasms; mandragora, the drug of somnolence; garlic for the production of melancholy; *qat* for exciting the nerves; *kola* to produce insomnia; opium for the twilight states; *barsh*, an odorous paste, to be smeared on the teeth; the forty-nine fruits of the *zaqqum* tree; the sudorific cumin; viper's bugloss that expanded the heart; chewing seaweed; balsam; fennel; galingale; asafoetida; ambergris; spider's-web pills; iliaster; aloes; *banj*; and asphodel. Also ostrich feathers, narwhal teeth and hop pillows.

They descended further to the cellars where, the old man explained, the dormitories for the patients were situated. The dormitories were a fantastic sight. From either side of the stairwell a long hall stretched into darkness, beyond the limits of the light shed by the candles set in great bronze candlesticks, the height of a man, which stood in the centre of the hall.

It was still only midday, yet even so a few of the beds were occupied. The restless sleepers, arms akimbo or flopped over the side of the mattress, eyes staring sightlessly at the ceiling or face flung down into the pillow, were attended by the Father's assistants, young men mostly, who would move noiselessly from bed to bed, and, squatting on their haunches or reclining on their sides, would whisper through cupped hands into the ears of the sleepers, sending their dreams this way and that. In the middle of the night the hall would be filled with a susurrus of whispers, wheezes and snores, but mostly a tracery of whispers, dictating the pattern of the night. Huge black slaves moved up and down the hall, bringing and removing bedding. Lice were endemic here. From the darkness at one end came the sound of a lute.

'Your disease is rare. The Father will treat you for nothing.'

'How will he treat me?'

'I do not know. I am only a student of his methods, but I have learnt that the brain secretes thought as the liver secretes bile. It may be that there is a disorder in the secretory process in the ventricles of the head, which in turn produces an excess of the sanguine element in the constitution, which in turn leads to spontaneous bleeding.'

Vane sounded both self-conscious and vague. The old man was conferring with one of his disciples.

'At all events you will not sleep alone tonight. Someone will be watching you. In the morning I will come for you.'

'Me? Sleep here?'

'Why not? This is the safest place in Cairo. It has the patronage of some of the most powerful emirs. In the caravanserai the Venetians may steal your money and the priests may steal your soul, but here you are safe. If you are to stay any length of time in the city, you will need the protection of someone like the Father of Cats and the refuge of a place like the House of Sleep. The city is not safe. There have been murders nightly; there has been talk of riot and revolt; but whatever happens, they will not touch the sleep teacher.'

But suppose he talked in his sleep? Suppose that he revealed in his sleep that he had come to spy? But that was all right, for the Father and his disciples appeared to understand neither English nor Italian. Yet he would lie there unconscious, watched over by aliens, dreaming perhaps in a foreign tongue and would awake, helplessly bleeding, in a foreign cellar. Something else, though, worried him. What was it? Yes, when did the dream about St Catherine and Zuleyka begin? At sunset or earlier? Did he dream it in the caravanserai or in the hippodrome? Did he dream just about St Catherine and Zuleyka or also about the royal circumcision, even about Cairo?

Vane, seeing that he was hesitating, took him by the arm. 'For God's sake, lad, you will kill yourself if you don't receive treatment. Kill yourself or be killed. I said just now that it might be a disorder in the process of secretion in the brain. And so it might be, but why are you afflicted only when you sleep? It is quite possibly a form of sorcery by someone who is trying to poison you in your sleep. Christians, Christians from the West anyhow, are not liked in Cairo, and very likely someone is practising a spell on you.'

'I am not staying here. Thank you nevertheless.' Balian made what he hoped was a polite gesture towards the Father and, without looking back, climbed out of the cellar and made his way out into the street, into the blinding light of day, and lost himself in the crowd.

The crowd was a mindless beast which moved slowly and complained noisily when goaded. It moved at the pace of the slowest, that is to say, at the pace of the very old and the sick. It was said that the greater part of the population of Cairo did not work but begged or resigned itself to dying slowly. Balian struggled against this crowd, vainly willing it to part before him like the Red Sea before Moses, but it looked at him with obstinate dead eyes and shuffled its feet. He saw gangs of old men with linked arms, proceeding majestically along the thoroughfares of the city, carrying all before them, their naked, bony feet kicking up the dust as they moved. He would learn that these crowds were dangerous too; sometimes several processions would converge upon one place, and then people would die in the press.

But Vane and the Father could not follow him through this, and eventually Balian relaxed, letting the crowd carry him where it would, aimlessly in movement, seeing what there was to be seen.

One's eyes could tell one more in this city than in Venice or Norwich: the green turban of a *hajji*, the yellow robe of a Jew, the great double-headed axe and begging bowl of a Bektashi dervish. One's clothes revealed one's faith and one's ambitions.

So he came, desultorily and aimlessly, to encounter Yoll. At a street corner the crowd had halted and gathered round a *qasas*, a storyteller. He sat on a sort of wooden throne deep in the shadow of a corbelled house. An uncomfortable ape on a chain squatted on one of the *qasas*'s shoulders. At the foot of the throne a musician sat hunched, playing the *rebec* softly to the storyteller's words, and a boy served out coffee on a brass tray. Otherwise every eye was focused on the *qasas*. A young woman, unveiled and strikingly beautiful, sat adoringly at his feet. The older men stood or squatted in a circle around him, pushing the children out to the periphery. The circle was a wide one, Balian was amused to note, for gobs of spit flew from the storyteller's mouth. The story was an entrancing one; the wail of the *rebec* rose and fell and the arms of the *qasas* swept and cleft the air, working on his slack-jawed and glass-eyed audience. The storyteller, unusually, was a young man, shock-headed, his face drawn with concentration. Sweat clung to his face, and sand clung to the sweat. He was the dirtiest person Balian had ever seen. He seemed to be utterly lost in his story, yet as Balian approached the group, the *qasas* halted, apparently in mid-sentence, leaving the *rebec* player to continue to play. Holding Balian with his eyes, the *qasas* gestured dramatically at himself with his thumb.

3
Roda Island

A pleasing picture that.

Now, too late of course, I wonder if I have started my tale at the right place. It might have been easier to start by explaining the relationship of Michael Vane to the Father of Cats or, better yet, to begin with the true story of the origins of Fatima the Deathly. And have I mentioned the Ape yet? I cannot remember. For some reason I thought it best to start with the entry of this innocent young man into Cairo. Privately I am not fond of him, and I ask myself what he will think of me. I doubt if I will ever know. Certainly he does not seem to think about other people very much.

Too late to start again, and anyway it is now time to introduce myself . . .

'I am Yoll,' The storyteller spoke Italian with a heavy accent. Stranger yet was his next sentence. 'I have been telling these people your story.'

'My story?'

The crowd turned to regard Balian appreciatively and let him pass through them to stand before the throne of the story-teller. Yoll gestured impatiently. 'Yes, your story. How you came to Cairo on your way to the holy monastery of Mount Sinai. How you saw the arrest of an Italian painter, were attacked by visions in the night of ill omen and fell into the clutches of the Father of Cats and an English alchemist.'

He paused to see if Balian thought that he had got the story right and went on, 'We all know the places and the people. It is a good story. It is easy for somebody like myself, who estimates information at its true value, to reconstruct this tale from a hundred sources in the city. I am Yoll, the only story-teller in all Cairo who makes a living from telling true stories. Sometimes people pay me to tell their story in public places, perhaps in the hope that it may edify the crowds or that it may bring lustre on the family name. At other times I select an individual and honour him or ruin him by telling his story.' He paused. 'Sometimes I am paid not to tell the story.'

'What will happen next in this story?'

Yoll paused again and a big grin spread over his face. 'You will meet a storyteller called Yoll, and he will give you some extremely valuable advice, if you will be good enough to wait a few moments. You will forgive my interest in you, but a good storyteller strives to give his stories some shape, even if they are true ones.'

Without waiting for a reply, Yoll turned back to address his audience. He spoke for what seemed quite a long time, gesturing occasionally at Balian. The audience eyed Balian sympathetically. At length the discourse ceased and the little boy passed among the audience, collecting coins in a velvet bag. Yoll stepped down from his throne, leaving the boy to dismantle it. The *rebec* player had disappeared. The sun had vanished behind a bank of clouds and the wind was rising, sending little dust devils down the street. It was time for the mid-afternoon prayer. The melancholy complaints of the muezzins rang out across the city, 'There is only one God . . .'

Yoll smiled at Balian. 'Will you deign to accept my hospitality? The house is some distance away, but,' and here he affected to lower his voice in a mock whisper, 'there is wine there.'

Balian inclined his head and Yoll waved his arms wildly with pleasure. The house was indeed some distance away, but they did not talk on the way. By the time they reached the house it was late afternoon and, though the sky was still a deep blue, in the dark streets below it was almost night. Shutters were going up in the covered markets and whole areas of the city seemed to be deserted, while others were thronged with people promenading up and down, eyeing one another curiously.

The house Yoll took him to was very small but strikingly comfortable. No walls, floors or windows were visible. Rather, they reclined in a cavern of cushions, carpets and hanging silks; all were somewhat frayed and most had stuffing coming out.

Yoll produced a jug of wine and grinned. 'I need seclusion from the outside world for my great work. The stories I tell in the market place serve only to keep body and soul together. They are a way of earning a living, nothing more. You ask what my great work is?' Balian did not. 'I will tell you. It is really something, as you shall hear. The sultans and emirs have their monuments: the Sultan Hasan Mosque, the Sultan Qalaoun Hospital, the Emir Jaqmaq Fountain. They dominate the streets of our city, and in their shadow the oppressed poor, God's children, must walk in awe. The poor have no monuments. But I, Yoll, am creating one for them.'

Yoll's speech became a torrent. He was, Balian learnt, writing a work, more precisely a compendium of stories, loosely related to one another. 'I shall call it "One Thousand Nights and One Night".' Every night he dictated a portion to a calligrapher friend of his. As Balian listened he became aware of Yoll's extraordinary and twisted cunning, for the stories Yoll was inventing were not just to entertain the poor of the city but also were written in a deliberately unpretentious, muddled and colloquial fashion, designed by Yoll to give the impression that these were actually the creation of the tradesmen and paupers of Cairo.

Yoll was full of compassion for the people of his city. Yet, mingled within the pity, Balian detected a strain of contempt for the tradesmen and their lack of imagination, and a fierce disapproval of their passivity and materialism and, above all, their orderliness. There was nothing orderly about Yoll. 'These poor folk have no voice. They have no dreams, they

46

sit like rag dolls beside their merchandise, but I am becoming their voice and I shall create their dreams for them.'

Yoll followed his vocation with a maniac's intensity. He wanted to submerge his own very strong personality in these tales and to become only a filter for the feelings and hopes, slender though they were, of the street people. To this end, whenever he was not working or dictating, he used to wander through the alleys and squares of the city, backwards and forwards, taking nothing in consciously, taking everything in somehow, floating in the airs of Cairo. He would return to his home on the edge of the Armenian Quarter and let himself drift, with his eyes shut, until images began to dance on his eyelids and a story began to form around them. Yoll's stories came, he claimed, from a twilight area, somewhere between conscious creation and the seethings of pure nonsense. 'Take, for instance, the story of the two Haroun al-Rashids, which I produced a few evenings ago. The story goes like this . . .'

At this point Balian could restrain his impatience no longer and broke in upon the torrent. 'But tell me, how is it that you speak Italian?'

'Boccaccio has long been my inspiration. We like Italians.'

'We? And do you like Englishmen as well?'

Yoll pointed to a corner of the room. While they had been talking a woman had slipped in. It was the woman who had been sitting at the front of the audience.

'Mary the Copt, my sister. Actually we are both Copts, but people call me Dirty Yoll.'

She smiled and sat down. When the smile had gone, it was as if it had never been. She was a sombre, heavy girl who seemed to smoulder with fury – or was it impatience, or suppressed desire? – as she hung on to Yoll's every word. The wine jar was replenished.

Yoll continued, replying to Balian's previous question. 'We shall see. You are the first Englishman I have ever met, apart from Vane.'

'What can you tell me about Vane?'

'Enough, I hope, to persuade you to shun his presence. This

has been a fortunate meeting. I do not like to see people, particularly Christians, fall into the hands of that pair.'

'That pair?'

'Vane and the Father of Cats. I warn you, they take people over, and people who have fallen under their influence are impossible to talk to afterwards. They are guardians of a common secret, or at least that is the impression they seem to wish to give.'

'Has Vane known the Father of Cats a long time?'

'Yes. Vane has been a regular visitor to Cairo for a long time. Sometimes he was resident in the city for years at a stretch and then he used to stay in the House of Sleep. No, there is something very odd about that pair, that bag of old bones and that cutpurse picaroon. Oh yes, when Vane first came to Cairo, he was scarcely more than a petty criminal. He could have been a galley slave for all I know. Certainly he had lived very rough. He didn't comport himself like a *signor* and a scholar or discourse learnedly on physics and metaphysics, as he does now. No, he was a cutpurse, a clever and ambitious cutpurse, but a cutpurse nevertheless. He went to the House of Sleep and the Father of Cats must have seen his potentialities, for he educated him as if he were his own son. Vane studied with him the languages of the civilized world, Arabic, Persian and Hebrew; he learnt manners; and he studied alchemy, medicine, gematria, physics and oneiromancy. Above all he has learnt to serve his masters.'

'You mean –?'

'I am not sure what I mean . . . Vane works for the Sultan and his officers as a spy probably. So, I think, does the Father of Cats. There is a lot of coming and going between the House of Sleep and the Citadel. They must traffic in information. How they come by that information is not easy to see. Maybe it is from clients who come to have their dreams interpreted and their fortunes told?

'You should try to leave the city as soon as possible. The Father of Cats is a dangerous man to know, as a friend or as an enemy. Forgive my insistence on this, but I must tell you that the origins of the Father of Cats are hardly less disreputable than I suspect Vane's to be. Let me tell you a story.'

Yoll drank deeply and continued. 'I heard it many years ago from the lips of the Father of Cats himself, before he became the important person he is now. The Father of Cats was not always master of the House of Sleep. In his youth, when he was new in the city and there were many more skilled in the hidden sciences than he was himself, he subsisted by casting spells and selling potions for small sums of money. He specialized in aphrodisiac potions and emblems, images to lure men into bed. These emblems were very dangerous things to deal in, for he used to paint them on the bodies of his customers. He always ran the risk of having the husbands notice the signs painted on the bodies of their wives and discovering who had put them there, but it was a good trade, for the signs were powerful and came from the Arbatel of Magic. One day a woman, who called herself Fatima, came to him with the usual story about her husband ceasing to desire her, so the Solomonic signs were painted on her navel and the insides of her thighs and between her breasts. He was well paid and she departed. Not long afterwards, one morning, a youth with his throat cut was discovered floating down the Nile. These things happen from time to time, and no one paid any particular attention.

'Then, as the days went by, another body was discovered and another and another, all men and all with their throats cut. It was like a plague epidemic and as it spread from the poor quarters of the town in the north-east to the smarter areas beneath the Citadel and along the river, it began to cause some concern to the government. Vigilante parties were sent out to roam the streets at night. Several times these parties were within an ace of rescuing a victim before the knife fell. Rumour ran wild. Many people said that these were ritual murders committed by the Jews or Copts, and some members of the Jewish community had to leave the city for a while.

'Well, one night the Father of Cats was wandering alone through the Village of Women. Whether he was hoping to gain money there or spend it one can only guess. He was wearing a hooded *jallaba* in the Maghribi style; people say that the Father of Cats came originally from the Atlas Mountains far away in the Western lands. He passed a veiled woman standing on the edge of the village evidently soliciting custom. He walked on and then he turned back for, mysteriously, he felt powerfully attracted. He came closer to her. She unveiled herself. She was smiling as she drew a long silver knife from the folds of her sleeves. Despite seeing this he was fascinated and sexually aroused. He could see that she was going to kill him and yet he could do nothing to pull himself away. Without feeling himself move, he still saw that the gap between them was narrowing.

' "Ah, you would not," he croaked.

'By way of a reply she bared her upper half and there, incredulously, he saw that same aphrodisiac symbol that he had painted between the breasts of that woman Fatima some months previously. Now that the talismanic sign was visible, the unnatural attraction was redoubled. The Father saw that he was on the brink of being destroyed by one of his own lures. As a desperate last gamble, he called out to her, "Ah, unhappy woman, who has done that to you? You are marked for death, since you bear the emblem of Azrael, the Angel of Extinction between your breasts."

'There was a sudden flurry and the woman was gone, running into the darkness of one of the side alleys. He tried to follow her, for he still felt terribly attracted, but she had vanished. The murders ceased that night. Only now again, years later, there are unpleasant stories being told in the *suqs* of Cairo, and some fear that Fatima the Deathly has returned. If she ever existed,' added Yoll thoughtfully. 'The Father of Cats is certainly never to be altogether trusted or believed. It is a good story; I have told it many times.'

'It is a strange story,' said Balian cautiously.

'You do not believe it?'

'I believe that the Father of Cats told it for some purpose.'

'The Father is mad,' Yoll continued inconsequentially.

50

'Sleep is such a pleasant, leisurely pastime. I know little and understand less of what he is doing, but I gather his science makes sleep a test and a peril to his pupils and patients. When I go to sleep, I like to go to sleep. I'll see my visions when I am awake and can appreciate them properly. People go to the House of Sleep looking for something, some spiritual treasure perhaps. People are crazed by fantasies of treasure in this place. The people of Cairo believe that they can find treasure by lying down and going to sleep and maybe the djinn will tell them where it is, or I don't know what. It seems to be that what the Father of Cats offers is the lazy man's way to heaven.'

'Lazy men want to go to heaven like anyone else.'

'Well, they won't find their way to heaven with their eyes shut, dreaming on undigested food. Dreams make people want to sleep; my stories will make people want to stay awake. In fact, they will make sleep unnecessary.'

The torrent was in full flood again. Yoll believed that it should be possible to take dreams away from the dark kingdom over which the Father of Cats reigned and bring them out into the sunlight of happy fantasy. So with ceaseless industry (Balian found it hard to believe that anyone who drank so much could be ceaselessly industrious), with ceaseless industry, he worked to produce tales of porters who married princesses, marvellous isles of Paradise, mothers-in-law turned into mules and treasures available at the twist of a magic ring. The essence of it all was that the extraordinary should suddenly happen to an ordinary man. 'A woman beckons from a strange house. An animal is heard to speak. I am a greater artist than Mutanabbi or Mutazz, but an essential of my art will lie in my art's concealment.'

Balian reflected that perhaps Yoll and the Father of Cats were not so very different in their bizarre schemes and ambitions, but he kept that thought to himself.

Yoll continued, 'In truth, the lives of most people here are so miserable that they can be changed only by a miracle. That is the greater part of what my stories offer them. But of late the real world has been entering into competition with the storyteller.'

'What do you mean?'

'It is hard to say. There are signs, if one can read them. There are these murders nightly, particularly in your quarter, the Ezbekiyya. Then there is your illness. Well, they tell you that it is an illness, but I am not so sure.'

'Neither am I. I think that it's only a nosebleed.'

'Ah, but I think that it may be an omen. Only a week ago a baby was born near the Citadel with two heads and forty arms. Such things are harbingers of coming troubles, fighting and famine and perhaps a new holy –'

But here Yoll was interrupted. From outside there came a loud crashing sound of metal on wood, a recurrent thumping, something pounding on the door. Yoll's face grew wide with fear.

'Who is it?' asked Balian.

'I don't know. They must be looking for you. Vane and the Father of Cats. Or perhaps Mamlukes. But we are not staying to find out.' Yoll leant forward to blow out the candle. 'It would not do for them to discover us together. Hold on to one another and follow me.'

Balian found his hand being clutched by Mary, and he was drawn through layers of hanging silks until they emerged at the foot of a staircase which led up to the roof. They raced up it on tiptoe, trying not to breathe too loudly. It was now deep night. On the roof Yoll turned to face them.

'We should separate here. You go down that way, while I go downstairs now and open the door to our visitors. I think that I shall pretend that I have only just been woken up.' Yoll seemed elated with childish glee. His head shook wildly. 'Mary will take you to Bulbul's. I will join you there as soon as I can.'

He spoke to Mary rapidly in Arabic. Mary's lips parted briefly, but she said not a word. Having scrambled down the side of the house easily, she gestured that Balian should follow at a distance. She walked ahead at a steady pace down one lane after another. The streets were almost deserted except for lamplighters and the occasional soldier. Now and then, from the rare vantage point of an open place, Balian could see the Citadel of Qaitbay, looming over the little mud and wood houses on their left. They were moving away from the areas of Cairo he had become familiar with. Suddenly, coming out of a little alleyway, he found that they were walking alongside the Nile. Its turbid surface moved sinisterly, gleaming in the moonlight. Soon they were crossing a bridge which led to an island in the river.

'Roda.'

There were few buildings on the island and these were mostly clustered on the waterfront. They passed into a wood that was also a cemetery. Balian had to follow close upon Mary's silhouette in order not to lose his way. Soft and cling-ing things caressed his face; the branches of the trees were draped with cloths and rags, the votive offerings of the bereaved. Even at this hour the cemetery was not deserted, for veiled, wraithlike figures, carrying candles, darted among the trees. Mary slowed her pace and took his hand. Her hand was hot. They had come to a clearing and in the clearing was a cluster of houses of mud and wattle of the type Balian had become familiar with in the poorer parts of Cairo. They paused before one of these; this was presumably the house of Bulbul. A man emerged from it and Mary addressed him. She said very little but she spoke so slowly that Balian had ample time to contemplate the figure before him: two glittering bright eyes set deep in the sides of a huge hooked nose, the curve of which was echoed in a wider arc by the curve of his paunch. His tongue darted, lizard-like, from side to side in his mouth as he replied. Then he began to speak also with his hands. Arms spread out expansively (but of course, be my guest), a gesture of salaam to Balian, a hand beckoning them in, eyebrows raised to deprecate the misery of his awful hovel and finally a sharp, lingering stare into Balian's eyes that said more than could be interpreted. They went in. Bulbul almost danced around the room, as he mimed his craft and displayed products of his workmanship to his guests. He was a letter writer and, more than that, a calligrapher. Fists beat his chest, the best in Cairo.

When this charade was finished, he squatted down in a corner to make some tea – another little charade. While he was thus engaged, Mary was making signs with her hands, signifying that they would sleep there that night. Bulbul rejoined them with the tea and a sugar cone, which he proceeded to chip to pieces with a little hammer. Three cups of tea were ceremoniously drunk. Bulbul talked all the time to Mary, ignoring Balian save to pour out more tea and to offer him a piece of cake. Mary said almost nothing.

At length rugs were brought out, and they stretched themselves out to sleep. At least Mary and his host did so, but Balian lay alert, staring at the ceiling, lost in circular thoughts. He had dreamt twice since coming to Cairo, and he feared to dream again. Instead he shifted his weight from limb to limb, as he drowsily considered the warped symmetry of his experiences, dreams and facts all interlocked: two sultans, two beautiful women, two states of consciousness and so forth. Did everything in the universe have its corresponding partner in a pair, a left hand and a right hand? Might he too have his flawed twin? He was finding it difficult to think clearly; his thoughts were slowly turning over as on a spit in the hot night air.

Then there was a scuffling noise in the hut and, shifting his position slightly, Balian became aware of two figures standing over Bulbul, Mary and himself. He felt sick with a panicky sort of butterfly fear as he identified the two silhouettes as those of the Father of Cats and Michael Vane. Vane shielded a candle flame with one hand.

The Father turned to Vane and remarked with studied casualness, 'Insomniacs have an actual terror of falling asleep. They fear lest the problems that threaten them when awake will fall on them and devour them when they are unconscious.' Then, kneeling down and thrusting his face, pestilential with an old man's bad breath, into Balian's, 'But you don't know whether you are asleep or awake, do you? Hello, did you think that we could not find you? Did you think that I confine my teaching to the House of Sleep? Do you think that your new friends can be relied upon? I think it possible that you may be mistaken. If St Catherine and pretty Zuleyka can visit you in your sleep, surely we can too? Vane!'

He snapped his fingers impatiently. Vane produced a glass and the hammer that had been used earlier to break the sugar. He put the glass down on the dried mud floor and brought the hammer smartly down upon it. The glass remained unaltered, still bearing its dregs of tea within it, long enough for Balian to draw his breath in sharply with surprise. Then abruptly it shattered, scattering shards of glass and tea leaves over a wide radius. The sleeping forms of Bulbul and Mary did not stir.

Vane never took his eyes off his face as the Father began to speak again. 'That was your first lesson, how to determine whether you are dreaming or not. The world you are in approximates closely to reality but not closely enough if one applies certain tests. The glass demonstrates that you are dreaming; more to the point, now I come to think of it, I am speaking to you in a language that you can understand. Clearly you are no longer in the world of reality, a world which is governed by the laws of God and logic. No, you are in the Alam al-Mithal, which, being interpreted, is the World of Images or Similitudes. With your co-operation, we hope to teach you to stamp your will on the Alam al-Mithal and, of course, even before that, to diagnose your sickness and discover the root of the bleeding. You should know that if we had not come here first, something much more unpleasant would have.'

Vane meanwhile had knelt down over the other two sleeping forms and whispered into the ears of first one and then the other.

The Father continued, 'I think that we should examine you back at my house, but before we set out for it you must accept my initiation and you must trust us when we say that we desire only to cure and to guide you. Do you trust us?'

'I do.' Balian voiced his acquiescence in a jerky sort of croak. Actually he felt not trust, only pure blind fear of his nocturnal visitors.

'It is good,' said the old man calmly, and with his long nails he scraped some earth from the floor of the hut, gathered it together in his palms. Then, kneeling over Balian, breathing with difficulty, he said, 'Look at me.'

Balian did so, and the old man blew the dust into his eyes.

The old man got up, his breath rasping. 'Come with us,' he said, and they went out into the night. The air was close, heavy, and the indigo sky loomed down on them, almost touching the tops of the minarets. Balian felt as if he was breathing through a straw. Soon they were making their way along the edge of the island. The moon had vanished and in the near-total darkness they were guided by the oily gleam of the water and the slapping sound it made against the mud embankments. Sometimes he stumbled against something soft that moved, one of the thousands of the poor of Cairo who slept in the streets.

'We have to make a detour,' said the Father of Cats apologetically as they passed over the bridge. On the other side they quickened their pace, for the way was better lit. Their path crossed and recrossed those of the night watch and the gypsy lamp-lighters. Three furtive figures, they toiled up under the walls of the Citadel.

'This is the quarter of the Tartar Ruins, and here,' said the Father, 'is someone you should meet.' Vane and Balian followed him into a tent. In the centre of the tent, on a carpet, a figure slumped in a curious posture. Something was wrong, but what it was that disturbed was difficult to make out in the darkness.

'This is Saatih. He is a *kaahin*, a soothsayer, but God has cursed him and is turning his bones to jelly. His head will be the last to go. Naturally you will not meet him in real life; a figure like this exists only in dreams.'

Balian squatted down to take a look and rose up again hastily, swallowing back his rising gorge. The *kaahin* swelled, rolled and bubbled over the mat, moving restlessly this way and that. Only the head with its unwinking eyes remained motionless at the centre. A throaty voice came up from the carpet. 'Welcome to the Alam al-Mithal.'

'Saatih wanted to see you, to know if you might not be the man who suffers the Arabian Nightmare. It appears that you are not,' said the Father.

'God help you if you ever meet his companion, Shikk,' said Vane.

'Prophecy has passed and only dreams remain,' said Saatih.

The Father of Cats knelt down beside him and for a few moments they conferred in low, inaudible tones.

'Saatih was not the reason for coming up here,' said the Father as they re-emerged into the night. 'We are taking you to see the Dawadar in there,' and he pointed to the walls of the Citadel that seemed to hang over them.

'Why the Dawadar? Why now? Anyway wouldn't it be better to see him in the morning when both he and I are awake?' Balian was now distinctly irritated and had determined to put a logical bar in the way of the capricious fancies of the grotesque pair.

'Because we wish to show you to him. He will ask a few questions, that is all,' said the Father firmly.

'Well, I think I am going to wake up,' said Balian.

'You fool! It's terribly dangerous,' shouted Vane as he threw himself upon Balian. The Father, more agile than his years should have allowed, followed. Vane had him by his legs, while the Father clung grimly to Balian's back as they rolled and scrabbled down the path that led from the Citadel.

'You'll have to carry me with you wherever you go,' shouted the Father, but Balian was beginning to pull away from his assailants and from the dust and from the night under the walls of the Citadel.

Yet there was little relief in breaking free from that nightmare. It was difficult to see in the dim and airless space. He seemed to be lying in a tent of hair. He could not move a muscle; he could not breathe. He thought his eyes were open, but it was difficult to be sure. Some great thing, soft yet heavy, pressed upon his chest and arms, suffocating and paralysing him. Only one part of him was not paralysed: his penis. It rose and swelled painfully. The thing lay upon him, close and intimate, evilly intent. Whatever it was, Balian sensed it as being, though physically close, infinitely distant from a human being and a human being's concerns. It lay so close upon him that its interest should have been sexual, yet he conceived of the eyes in its face, if it had a face, as being pits of pure and endless nothingness. Balian began to pray silently. Slowly the pressure began to ease, and Balian became capable of distinctions. They were knees that pressed upon his arms. A woman knelt upon his chest, her feet pressed into his crotch, her hair hanging over his face. She was bending over his face, crooning. Slowly, as Balian grew in consciousness, she mysteriously withdrew. In the space where she had been there was nothing but the shimmering grey pearls of the false dawn.

He was in Zuleyka's kiosk. She slept peacefully beside him. 'Why should anyone come at dawn to kneel upon my chest?' he pondered. 'Perhaps it was the heat.' He lay oiled in sweat. He shook Zuleyka awake.

'Zuleyka, did you kneel upon my chest just now, or did I dream it?'

She looked at him. Her eyes were wide with seriousness. 'Someone was probably following you, when you came back through the Roda Cemetery. You are a fool to enter a cemetery at night.'

'But who was following me and why?'

'I imagine that it was once a woman and that it was

58

trying to collect your semen – not that I left her much.'
Zuleyka laughed lazily, and added, 'The numbers of the
dead increase only slowly and they wish to procreate. Go
back to sleep now.'

'But the walk through the cemetery was only part of my
dream, wasn't it?' Yet as he said this he realized something
else.

4
The Citadel

And where was I while Balian was conducted to Roda Island? Well, having eluded my pursuers – there is always a hue and cry for someone in this city – I retired to a coffee house on the banks of the Nile where I hoped to be alone with my thoughts. As it turned out, that was not to be, but that is another story. What I wish to say now is that it is often necessary for me to withdraw into solitude to compose my thoughts and get the sequence of events straight. If too much happens to me in a day, I become uneasy. Too much material for one of my stories is as bad as too little, and after so much excitement I fear that I will not be able to digest it all and that my sleep will be heavy.

It is obvious from the scenes I have just described that my sister Mary is a very desirable woman. That must surely be clear, but I shall elaborate no further on her charms. I share, in one respect at least, the oriental compunctions of my fellow citizens. I do not think it proper that strangers should eye my sister up and down and guess from her deportment whether she is a virgin or not, or that they should try to estimate from the brightness of her eyes and the turn of her ankle what her bride-price would be. A woman loses her fascination if she ceases to be mysterious. I shall be at pains to see that my sister plays no part at all in the story which remains to be told, if possible . . .

He awoke, almost choking in his own blood. His half smoth-ered shouts drew Bulbul and Mary to his side almost immedi-ately, yet they did nothing but watch as it jetted out through his nostrils and his mouth; they simply waited until it mysteriously stopped. Then they took him out to the clearing, and Mary went away to fetch a pitcher of water to wash away the slowly congealing blood. Bulbul propped him up against the side of the hut. It was daylight, though overcast. The air was intensely humid in the Roda woods; it prickled against the skin. Balian felt sick and dizzy. His initial relief at escaping was rapidly replaced by a feeling of despondent helplessness. He was unable to imagine by what sort of elaborate pantomime he could communicate his experiences to his alien companions.

Mary returned with her pitcherful of water, and they set to work to clean him up. In the daylight, in the open air, Mary seemed to glow with well-being and sensual good health. He reflected bitterly that they did not seem to have spent a disturbed night. Why should he be the victim?

At length, when he felt stronger, he communicated in sign language his wish to leave them and return to mainland Cairo, but they in turn made vigorous signs indicating that he should stay, no, must stay. 'Yoll. Yoll,' they repeated insistently.

Balian replied in English. 'I am sorry, but I am not waiting for him or doing anything else that will involve me in your schemes, whatever they are. I am going back to the caravanserai. Thank you for your hospitality.'

Balian made a half bow to Bulbul – Mary he did not look at directly – and strode off hastily. Mary and Bulbul did not rise but sat there watching until he was out of sight.

Balian felt like crying as he entered the caravanserai later that morning. True, he was thousands of miles away from home, yet here at least there was a tiny enclave of Christian and European values, of figures familiar to him since childhood: the merchant, the friar, the ship's captain, the pilgrim and so forth. As long as he stayed awake inside the caravanserai he was, he felt, staying in a world unbemused by oriental fate and dreams.

This feeling of high exhilaration did not last long. He

became aware that the others in the caravanserai were taking pains to avoid him, whether because of his illness or because he had been seen to go off with Vane he could not guess. The Venetian consul, it was true, shouted to him as he passed, 'Where were you last night? Not out whoring, I trust?' But there was something forced in the consul's jollity. Everything was in a great bustle. The public holiday for the circumcision of the Sultan's son was over, and the government offices re-opened today.

Near the entrance of the caravanserai a party of pilgrims was in the process of organizing itself to visit the Dawadar's office to secure the visas necessary to proceed to St Catherine's. Balian, feeling more confident about such a visit in full consciousness and in the company of his fellow Christians, tagged on to the party. So he set out again for the Citadel. The group was not composed solely of pilgrims, he discovered, for some of the party were Venetians selected by the consul to protest at the arrest of Giancristoforo and to plead for his release.

So a group of twenty or thirty Westerners made their way through the crowded streets to the Citadel. The sky had cleared and the day was brilliant. The irregular skyline of Cairo was picked out sharply against the deep blue of the sky. At points, where it could penetrate into the streets, the sun was blinding. As they approached the Citadel in daylight Balian found that it bore little resemblance to the miasmic fortress of evil of last night. He lowered his eyes and listened to the almost professional chatter of the pilgrims around him: the quality of the hostels in Compostella, the state of the relics market, the rise in Genoese pilgrim tariffs and so on. 'St Catherine's is only six days away.' 'Out in the desert, there one can find peace.'

Balian was almost alone among the pilgrims in being fashionably dressed in the Burgundian style. For the most part they presented a sombre array as they shuffled up the hillside with their broad-brimmed black hats, shaggy beards and light-grey cloaks, the pilgrim's red cross crudely stitched upon them. They were covered in dust from head to toe, and they stank. When silent, their eyes glittered, considering within themselves perhaps the mystery of the rosary or perhaps the efficacy of relics, driven onwards and upwards by inner fires. Balian wished that he was truly one of them.

At the top of the hill there was a long wait outside the first gate while the officers of the guard conferred. The pilgrims squatted on their hunkers. It was the first of many long waits that day. The sweat streamed continuously into Balian's eyes, stinging him with its salt. If one moved rapidly in this heat, one was liable to faint. Much to his surprise, Balian found that he was eventually approached in conversation by Emmanuel, whom he judged to be one of the toughest and most experienced of the pilgrims. Emmanuel had been in Egypt before and had been up the Nile looking for its origin, he said, and he chuckled mysteriously.

'Of course, your friend would know all about that.'

'My friend?'

Emmanuel did not reply directly but pressed his lips together and, putting his hand on Balian's shoulder, drew his attention to the view over Cairo from the gateway of the Citadel. Over the hippodrome, the stables of the Mamlukes, the *suqs*, the palaces of the nobility and the mosques, the eye travelled across the Nile to rest upon the pyramids of Giza, barely solid in the shimmering haze. Emmanuel pointed at them.

'Most of the locals here say that those are Joseph's granaries; he had them built by slaves to store away the produce of the seven years of abundance.' His grip on Balian's shoulder tightened. 'But that is characteristic of their infidelity and coarse worldliness. I have been out there to Giza and I have spent the night out there and slept on top of one of them, with only a rag wrapped round my neck to protect me from cutthroats.' He hawked up some spit.

'Those buildings were never granaries, and no human hand ever built them either. Nothing but magic could have raised them from the earth, and those who go scurrying about in their insides aren't looking for the grain of abundance either.'

He finally spat and a glistening gob of spit landed very close to Balian's feet. Balian's hand went instinctively to his left hip, where his sword would have been if he had been in a Christian country. Emmanuel noticed the reaction, and his tone became more conciliatory when he began to speak again as they moved through the outer gate into the first courtyard.

'I was just trying to let you know what the feeling is among those of us who are true, believing Christians about your friend Vane. Well, it's my belief – no, it's more than a belief: I know – that inside those mighty stone things out there lie thousands of the dead waiting for the Last Days and the Resurrection. They do not know anything of putrefaction and the worm but lie there, changeless, waiting for the Trump and the rolling up of the heavens. They used to embalm the dead in this country, and now the Arabs out at Giza trade in these bodies. Hundreds of years ago those corpses were soaked in an embalming fluid, *mumia* they call it. Vane is one of those who pays a good price for such morbid things. That traffic, like most of the man's enterprises, imperils his immortal soul, and I counsel you as a friend to keep yourself free of him.'

Balian replied that it was advice that he devoutly hoped to be able to follow, and the conversation flowed on to less difficult topics. Emmanuel's vocabulary and manner of delivery still reminded one of his nautical past, and his experiences had been no less extensive and colourful than his vocabulary. While they continued to stand or squat, first in one great white courtyard and then in a second, he discoursed on the Egyptian nobles who had visited Pope Pius, on the phoenix's temple at Heliopolis, on the Prophet's tomb in Medina that hung in the air suspended by great lodestones to bemuse the credulous.

Time passed rapidly as Emmanuel's words ran on about strange seas, flying horses and cities at the end of the World. In the second courtyard they were allowed to look down into Joseph's Well. Here and there were little kiosks, stained white with pigeon droppings; the purpose of the kiosks was mysterious, but Emmanuel said that they were probably spy posts. He went on to give his opinion on what could and could not safely be said of Prester John and the assistance that this great potentate might furnish to a new crusade, and from there he rambled on about how he had journeyed up the Nile, questing for its origin.

Emmanuel had pursued his journey through chasms and gorges, beyond the last cataract, until he entered a desert land where the river ran smoothly between steeply shelving banks and there were few watering places where animals could drink. Therefore, Emmanuel said, the animals mingled at these rare drinking spots, and copulation took place across the species. The closer to the source he got, the more monstrous the creatures became.

At length Emmanuel approached Happy Valley, where the castles of the Laughing Dervishes were situated. 'And there, on the threshold of Happy Valley, I learnt of the worst horrors yet, monstrous designs hatched in their cracked brains. They are an order of men dedicated to ribald hocus-pocus. They initiate with riddles and meditate on puns. They have a Shaykh whose identity is so secret that even he does not know who he is!'

Balian giggled and Emmanuel smiled. 'Well, we laugh, but there is such a thing as dangerous nonsense. In the eastern lands the heat and the idleness breed among the inhabitants leisured and lethal fantasies. But that was not the horror I was about to tell you of. I read in their secret book, *The Galleon* –'

But here the conversation had to break off, for they were now shepherded in small groups into the outermost corridors of the palace, into the shade at last. Once inside they were searched thoroughly for secret weapons.

They were assigned a dragoman to interpret and began the long trail up through sloping arcades to the Audience Hall. Normally the Sultan Qaitbay held court there, but today the Dawadar presided to receive and, if necessary, vet foreign visitors. *Shavushs* in smart uniforms, carrying tipped staves, ran up and down the corridors shouting instructions. Guards clashed their pikes as one small group after another entered the hall. At length heavy drapes were pulled aside and Balian and Emmanuel's group entered the hall itself. It was a massive cavern of marble, striped black and yellow, hung with great festoons of netting, draped from the centre of its vaulting like a mad spider's web. Gyroscopic brass censers spun at random across the floor. The dais in the centre of the hall was deserted; this was reserved for the Sultan on the days when he gave audience. Instead, a little to one side, on a chair of ivory and horn, dwarfed by the distances of the audience hall, sat the Dawadar. He did not, of course, rise to greet the pilgrims as they entered. Beside him stood his squire, who displayed the armorial bearings of the Dawadar, and behind sat an orchestra of lutes, *rebecs* and viols that played harsh music. The drago-man gestured frantically, and the pilgrims kissed the ground. They advanced a few steps forward and kissed the ground again. And again. The floor was very cold and smelt of some sickly incense, patchouli perhaps. Raising his head from the floor a third time, Balian eyed the Dawadar coldly.

The Dawadar was young and negligent. He slumped in the depths of his chair and let his long-nailed hands dangle loosely over its arms. He wore a white jacket, white trousers and a yellow sash. His head was shaved in the normal Mamluke fashion, but his eyelids were painted mauve. He transacted none of the business. This, in fact, was done by his translator and a panel of scribes in a corner of the hall. The Dawadar just looked on, apparently without interest. One by one the pilgrims shuffled off to collect their visas from the panel of scribes, but when it came to Balian's turn the Dawadar motioned with his hand and muttered to the translator.

The translator came forward and said to Balian, 'My master says that unfortunately there is no visa here for you today. He asks you to come back the day after tomorrow.'

Balian knew that it was useless to protest or question. Clearly now the Dawadar was regarding him and struggling to repress a smile. Balian bowed and walked out of the hall, pushing past the Venetian delegation waiting still to raise the matter of Giancristoforo's arrest, conscious as he did so of the Dawadar's eyes following him. Other petitioners moved on forward.

He said aloud to himself, 'I must pray to St Catherine that she will free me from the toils of mystery and delay.'

A leisurely sojourn in Cairo to collect intelligence no longer seemed attractive to him.

He walked at random in the city for hours before he began to take note of his surroundings and realized that he had no idea where he was. Then he began to try to follow a straight path in the hope that it would take him to the Nile or one of the walls of the city, but the roads, forking and curving back upon themselves, would not allow him to do this. He found himself having to sit down frequently and rest; the place was like a furnace, and his sleep in the past few nights had brought him no refreshment. He attempted to ask the way of several groups of small children, but his words brought gestures of non-comprehension.

Darkness came on rapidly. He thought of something Emmanuel had said: 'One street resembles another very closely in Cairo, especially by night, but the perplexed traveller may direct his steps according to the stars. Beware, though, for it is not unknown for the stars to move in their courses with the aim of misleading the unwary.'

This did not seem worth the effort then, for Balian was sure that he would prove to be one of the star-crossed wanderers whose unhappy fortunes had been evoked by Emmanuel.

Time and again he found himself crossing the Place of the Zuweyla Gate, with its lively concourse of entertainers and entertained, but the bear dancers, the storytellers, the performing slaves in cages, the shadow theatre, the music for evening made no appeal to Balian. He wanted to sleep.

Re-entering the square a final time, Balian noticed a little alley he had not been down before and moved off into it, fleeing from the lights and the crowd. The darkness fitted him like a glove. All day it had been hot and dry, yet here the walls ran with damp. He edged himself forwards, feeling his way along the walls, thinking about each step as he made it. A wall ended and he groped his way round a corner. He did so with caution. There was always a faint fear in his mind that his exploring hand might meet something welcoming, something soft and living and unknown. In the dark distances and obstacles were magnified, he knew. It was like feeling a boil in one's mouth with one's tongue.

Noises were reassuringly faint now. Without losing touch with the wall, he sank down to the ground and curled up in the blackness, intending to sleep there in the gutter. Thoughts of insects, dogs and, above all, footpads detained him. He lay at the foot of the wall, shaking and looking sightlessly up. He carried no money with him. He had nothing but the body and clothes he lay down to sleep in. There is nothing they can take save my life, he thought as he arched his neck to meet the imaginary knife of a stealthy robber. No knife met his throat. 'Nobody wants to die, but we all want to sleep,' he pronounced drowsily.

He found it difficult to compose himself for sleep. He twitched and jerked. A light breeze blew over his face, or was it whispers of Arabic? He opened his eyes.

The moon was up and something extraordinary was happening. He walked back into the Place of the Zuweyla Gate to get a better view. A rope had been stretched from the Citadel to one of the tallest of the minarets. High over Cairo a man walked, treading the rope with soft, padding feet, eyes fixed on the towers of the Citadel. The crowd oohed and aahed.

Two dwarfish men stood in front of Balian and he heard one of them say to the other, 'Don't you wish you were him?'

'Don't be silly,' said the other. 'Even he does not know that he is him. Look, he is asleep!'

Balian looked and it was quite true. The funambulist's eyes were closed and he was sleepwalking. When he wakes, he will fall, he thought. Then he became aware of two familiar figures

68

pushing their way through the throng towards him, the one in a grey burnous, the other in a ratskin coat and broad-brimmed felt hat.

His fear gave him stimulus to pull away from the dream. He must have dozed off, he thought groggily. The play had already begun. He was still, in fact, in the Place of the Zuweyla Gate, in the tent of the shadow theatre. The candlelit screen was in front of him and behind it silhouettes of pasteboard and filigree danced on sticks. The play was, as ever, about that one-eyed rogue Karagoz. Karagoz had found employment as a servant in the house of the Emir Fulaan and, grumbling, worked under the supervision of the emir's major-domo, Said Ali Anna.

Karagoz, as well as having only one eye, was hook-nosed, pot-bellied and equipped with an enormous phallus. He longed to stop work and leave the house to spend his hard-earned money, but the ever-watchful Ali Anna kept him at his job. A lady and a doctor, Dr Said, passed by the emir's house and watched Karagoz working.

'He works hard,' said the lady.

'If he did not work hard, he would not be tired enough to sleep,' said the doctor, 'and he likes sleep better than anything else. He is a very lazy fellow really, but he is asking me to commend him to you and to let you know that he hopes he may find a place in your affections.'

'I hadn't noticed him doing anything of the sort,' replied the lady.

'That is because perhaps you are unacquainted with the Language of Flowers? See the yellow gillyflowers and willow branches he is arranging in a vase? A branch of willow signifies a graceful lady. The gillyflower signifies the unsatisfied lover.'

'Well, he has stopped arranging flowers now.'

'Yes, but he is going upstairs. That is the Language of Symbolic Action. It means that he wants to have sex, and now look! He is picking up a broom. That is the emblem of an erect penis.'

'And what does his enormous erect penis signify?'

'It stands for a broom and it means therefore that he wants to get on with his sweeping.'

The silhouettes capered about and the children tittered uneasily.

Balian was unable to enjoy it. Could they find him in here? Why not? This was some sort of dream, wasn't it? He struggled to wake and found himself lying on a bed. He lay there with his eyes closed, listening to scuffling sounds. He did not know how long he had been vaguely aware of those sounds. At some point the scuffling changed to rapid and irregular thumping accompanied by shrill squeaks. Not daring to move from the mattress, he opened his eyes and turned them unwillingly to one side.

A man lay quivering on the bed beside him. He appeared to be sinking into the mattress. As soon as he saw that Balian was awake, he began to cry in a thin voice, 'Help me up, help me up,' and extended an arm to Balian. Balian, now on his knees and peering into the half light, took it with some reluctance and pulled. A sudden jerk and he saw what it was. He released his grip, falling back on the bed. The creature was up, though, and it hopped round the room continuing to squeak. It had to hop. It had one leg, one hand, one eye, half a head and half a torso. Its mad bounds took it round and round the mattress, always keeping its profile towards Balian, a glittering eye, bared teeth and an arm that it repeatedly raised to its forehead and dropped again in an uninterpretable gesture. Its bright eye and pallid skin gave the impression of fevered nervous energy. After a while it left the room, summoned elsewhere, Balian surmised.

He shook himself free from the vision and found himself sitting up in the kiosk, describing the dream to Zuleyka. Zuleyka was sitting cross-legged on the floor, hands together in her bosom. She found no difficulty in giving a name to the apparition and reciting the story.

'That was Shikk al-Insaan, close friend and companion of

70

Saatih ibn Rabia, whom you also met. When they were children their mothers spat in their mouths to give them dream power, but now they are very old and marked by their corrupt practices. Saatih was always thinking and thinking, and he asked men questions that should not be answered, questions whose answers would destroy them. Driven by intellectual curiosity, he denied his bodily instincts to such an extent that his body began to deny him and decay. So he lolls, as you saw him, on his bed of leaves and palm branches, lost in thought. Now the rot is beginning to attack the jaw and soon he will have only the top of his head to live in.

'Shikk is similar. Saatih and Shikk are from the profusion of forms of an uncertain creation. God gave every man a female soul and every woman a male soul, but Shikk denied his soul and is accursed. According to al-Idrisi, he comes from the China Sea or, it is said, from the woods of the Yemen. The latter opinion is more correct, for *yemen* in our tongue signifies the right hand. When pilgrims and spice merchants, coming from the Indies, enter the Arab Sea, then the Yemen is on their right and Africa is on their left. Africa is where his other half lives. The Africans call her Barin Mutum, and she is of the left hand. In Africa everything is different from what you see in the lands of Islam. In Africa the hair growing from the point at the back of a man's head circles round to the left; in the lands of Islam it circles round to the right.

'You were lucky. Shikk is swift and cruel, for he has no heart, and with his half-brain he thinks and talks but he never knows what he thinks or says or does. Barin Mutum is as capricious and cruel as he is. They are never bored but they have no conscience. Shikk is unhappy. His penis is too small and, while he may eat with the right hand, in the lands of the Arabs one may wipe the bum only with the left hand. The laws of etiquette so prescribe it, therefore Shikk is forever looking for men to enslave them in their dreams and make them perform this task for him.

'In the last hundred years Shikk and Saatih have grown greatly in power. Even twenty years ago there were still many

71

of the Invisible College of Sleep Teachers, besides the Father of Cats, residing in Cairo. There was Rabanus who performed conjuring tricks to demonstrate the properties of the human soul; a man called Ancient who invented the dream notation we still use; Haitham the Taleb who recited the whole of the Koran nightly in his sleep, thereby bringing blessings to the creatures of the Alam al-Mithal; Sulami the Master of Black-Bodied meditation; the Sleep Runners; the School of Sabean Interpreters; and many others.

'Even ten years ago a few of these men were still alive, but Shikk and Saatih visited them frequently, brought them to impotence and finally killed them. Some died young. Only the Father of Cats made himself their master and made them his hounds with whom he hunts through the night. One by one he destroyed his colleagues. He is the last of the Invisible College.'

'What does Shikk look like,' asked Balian, 'on the side that does not have the eye and the arm?'

'You will never see that side. It is in Africa.'

'Zuleyka –' he began.

'Yes. Go on. Failure to ask the question is always fatal.'

But a familiar breeze was blowing across his face and he already knew the answer to the question he was going to ask. He awoke in the gutter and the blood started to rise within him and came vomiting out.

5

A Panoramic View of the City

One mosque looks very like another. Slum areas reduplicate themselves in every quarter of the city. The inhabitants are unhelpful or unable to give directions. It is so easy to get lost and so often in wandering round a strange city, without intending it, a man will return to where he started and yet in returning to the place he will fail to recognize it as his starting point, so that when he picks up his steps again, he starts from the same place for the first time. I cannot provide a plan or map. I have never had one. Perhaps an overview of the city might help. Distance might make things clearer . . .

Fearing lest he lose himself again, that day and in the many days that followed, Balian set himself to master the geography of Cairo, a difficult thing to do, for most ways looked alike and twisted and turned under the buildings without any obvious purpose or direction, but he took his bearings from the peripheries of the city and the skyline.

First there was the Citadel, perched on its crag of limestone to the south and visible from almost anywhere in the city, a ramshackle accumulation of fortifications and pleasure houses that had grown together in the last three centuries.

In front of the mount of the Citadel the curious and highly elaborate minarets of the Sultan Hasan mosque were often visible. Further to the south, overlooking both the mosque and the Citadel, were the chalky yellow cliffs of Mount Muqattam.

To the north and east were the domes and cupolas of the City of the Dead, a necropolis of mausolea and cemeteries. Some of the tombs of the greater Mamlukes were palaces of marble and porcelain. By day a place of diversion, by night the area became the haunt of cut-throats and the indigent; nightly violence and starvation swelled the population of the City of the Dead. Beyond the City of the Dead and towering almost as high as Mount Muqattam was a ridge of white hills running from north to south along the eastern edge of the city. These hills were artificially formed by centuries of debris and refuse. When the wind blew from the east, a putrescent stench crept over the chilly and deserted streets of the City of the Dead and fine white dust swept all the way across Cairo, making one choke and one's eyes run. This could last for weeks at a time especially in late summer; the Venetians called it the *tramontana*. Sometimes, often at night, one of these mounds of rubbish would spontaneously ignite, shooting jets of fire and garbage spectacularly into the air.

Due north the city slowly petered out beyond the wall in scrubby clumps of palm. It was here that the livestock markets were and the camel pens.

The north-west, the area between the Nile and the old city, was as yet unwalled. The river boats docked at Bulaq, and from there their cargoes were brought on pack animals into the city proper. The great emirs and the Karimi merchants dwelt in the west. Some way to the south was the Ezbekiyya, the newest of the suburbs to rise out of the swamps formed by the shifting of the Nile's course towards the west. Here was the palace of the Emir Ezbek (now somewhat decayed), his stables and a great artificial lake, bordered by pleasure pavilions, on whose waters the boats were rowed by prostitutes. Further to the south were the Lake of the Elephant and the Island of Roda. Finally Saladin's Aqueduct and the Hill of Zeinhom, another rubbish tip surmounted by windmills, approximately marked the south-western limits of the inhabited city, but on almost all sides the fringes were being surrendered to the plague and the nomads with their flocks.

This year foreign visitors were not allowed to cross the Nile's western bank and visit the pyramids. According to the authorities, the danger from the bedouin was too great. Even on the east bank the bedouin sometimes raided the City of the Dead. As for the Nile itself, even when one could not see it one could trace its course below Roda by following with one's eyes the vultures and kites that hung and swooped over the river, for the Nile bore the carrion of the slaughter houses of Cairo north to the sea.

The core of the city itself was circumscribed by the river and hills of refuse, the castle, the aqueduct and the abandoned slums. Most of the bazaars lay in the densely packed quarters of the north-east, nestling in among, and parasitic upon, the rubble of the old Fatimid palaces, and behind the commercial streets one found small courtyards and large tenements, into which were crowded communities of closely knit creeds and tribes. This was old Cairo, so crowded that often a man and his mules might take a day to press their way across it. The main street, the Qasaba, ran through its heart, down from the Gate of Victory, between the ruined palaces and out through the Zuweyla Gate south to the Citadel. The Jewish, Coptic and Armenian quarters lay within the old walls. The quarters of the Blacks and the Tartars straggled along the Qasaba outside them.

Balian found himself spending a great deal of time in the vicinity of the Zuweyla Gate, where the dancers and entertainers gathered. This was also the place where criminals were brought to be garotted or beheaded; their bodies were then impaled outside the gate on the long poles which bent uneasily under their weight.

If one followed the Qasaba south from the Zuweyla Gate, through the Tartar Ruins, one penetrated the zone of the barracks and the military élite; arms markets, horse markets, stables, exercise yards and finally the Black Hippodrome, where the Mamluke soldiery exercised daily in ritual mock combat. The city was like a disordered mind, an expression of archaic wishes and half submerged memories of vanished dynasties.

Habitually Balian lay down to sleep in an alleyway, close to the Zuweyla Gate. One night Yoll came and squatted down beside him. The monkey clung to Yoll's back, arms tightly wrapped round his neck.

'It's the Englishman! What's wrong with you? You look terribly ill.' Yoll too looked ill, tense and strained, but Balian did not remark on this, fearing to be impolite.

'Those dreams . . . Yoll, have I got the Arabian Nightmare? What is the Arabian Nightmare?'

Yoll winced and settled himself and his load on the ground before beginning. 'The Arabian Nightmare is a disease. It is said to be transmitted from person to person by sleeping close together. It comes out of the mouth at night like smoke. They say that the person who was first to be afflicted with this disease has come to Cairo, all unawares of what he is bringing with him.

'The story goes like this. Some years ago there was a couple living in Damascus who had no children. The husband indeed was impotent and did not seem to desire his wife at all. Whether this was sorcery or one of God's afflictions I cannot say, but the wife decided that their problem might be solved by magic, so after making many inquiries of the wise men in the town, she learnt of a powerful magician and set off to seek his help.

'Now this magician lived in a castle on a sunny hill near Mecca. The way from Damascus was long and dangerous but the magician received her kindly when she arrived and he showed her all but one of the marvels of his castle; he showed her the ape that he kept on a silver chain and whom he had trained to play chess.' Here Yoll winced a second time. 'He showed her his bed of satin, which floated on a pool of quicksilver, and he showed her the eagles which he bred in the towers of the castle and which he used to hunt with.

'Moreover he agreed to sell her a magical aphrodisiac in the form of a cloud of smoke in a bottle. But the vital essence

76

would require many weeks of distillation before it was ready, and the magician had to go away for a few weeks on pressing business. Then, on reflection, a solution occurred to him, though he had to stifle some misgivings. The woman should stay in the castle and, in return for his hospitality, do something for him; this was to look after the last and greatest of all the marvels of his castle. The magician took her into a room that he had not shown her before and revealed to her his son.

'This boy was indeed a marvel of human beauty: his eyelashes were long, his cheeks were fat, his eyebrows were like crescent moons and his mouth like a scarlet bow. The boy showed her that he could understand the speech of birds, and the woman knew that the magician was speaking the truth when he told her that his son would be the Fifth Messiah.'

'The Fifth Messiah?'

'It is a heresy very prevalent in Cairo these days. Its devotees hold that since the Prophet Mohammed prophesied the coming of the Messiah and the End of the World, there have been four Messiahs and four Ends of the World, but the great mass of uninitiated humanity have been too dull to notice, so things have gone on much as before. But the Fifth Messiah, when he comes, will take vengeance on those who failed to recognize the four Invisible Messiahs. It is a shocking heresy. They hold that he will depose the Caliph and the Sultan and set new ones in their place. He will reconcile the Muslim with the Christian and the Jew, and the lion with the lamb. His followers say that he too is in Cairo at this very moment, in disguise and waiting only until the time is right to proclaim himself.

'To return to your original question, the magician with all his arts had studied the ancient prophecies of the birth of the Messiah and the signs that would attend his birth. Then he purchased an Abyssinian slave girl and, with his knowledge of starcraft, had her conceive with his seed at the ordained time.

'So the magician left his treasured and miraculous son with the woman and set out on his journey. But the woman, as one might expect, was suffering from years of sexual frustration and she desired this youth very greatly, while he for his part had not seen a woman, apart from his wet nurse (who was old), since the day he was born, so he was very interested in the woman. So they came together and only a few days had passed before the woman had seduced him. They spent blissful weeks together making love on the bed which floated on a pool of quicksilver.

'Then one day they saw from the battlement that the magician was returning. The woman swore the boy to silence, but the magician, entering the castle, saw from the boy's face in an instant what had happened and how the virtue of the Chosen One had been deflowered, yet he was cunning and said nothing. Instead he continued to make the woman welcome, until at last he said that the aphrodisiac gas that he had promised for her husband was ready and he handed her a brown bottle. The foolish woman thanked him profusely, said her farewells to the magician and his son and hurried back to Damascus, where her husband was waiting for her with some impatience. That night they eagerly unstoppered the bottle and the unfortunate husband inhaled its coloured vapours with enthusiastic snorts. What they then discovered was that the contents of the bottle did nothing for the man's virility; his penis hung as limp as ever. What they never learnt, because of the very nature of the affliction, was that first the husband and then, shortly afterwards, the wife had been smitten with the infinite torments of the Arabian Nightmare. And so this terrible scourge was released upon mankind.'

'What a ridiculous story!'

'It is a fable of the market place.'

'And the Arabian Nightmare, is there no cure for it?'

'None, unless indeed the blemished Messiah may still heal the leper and the cripple and has also the power to lift the curse of his father.'

Balian thought for a while. Then: 'Yoll, why is there a monkey clinging to your back?'

'Ah, yes, there is, isn't there? Well, thereby hangs a tale . . .'

But Balian did not want to listen to any more of Yoll's tales and he pulled away to other visions. Sun and moon whirled

78

over the city, day and night alternated with dizzying rapidity as he moved from one to another. Some women asked him to look down a bottomless well; he refused. The Sphinx, which the Arabs call the Father of Terror, barred him entry to the pickled treasures of the pyramids. He was brought before an image of a lady in a mask, suckling two children. He read, in the book which Giancristoforo had left him, about the brain which is *'of the colour of lampblack or the Nubian'*. Arab voices whispered in his ear. He caught glimpses of Vane and the Father of Cats and avoided them. And so, on and on, until towards the end of the night he re-encountered Zuleyka. Zuleyka, in effect, raped him, teaching him in the process the Abyssinian nutcracker technique and the Dolorous Kiss.

When it was over Balian told her of his meeting with Yoll and asked her, 'If the story of the magician at Mecca was a fable of the market place, why did he tell it to me?'

'Yoll loves telling stories, but no one had heard that one in the market place. It is an allegory aimed at you.'

'What was that monkey doing on Yoll's back?'

'That was no monkey. That was an ape, a different animal altogether. Apes have no tails.'

'Well, what was it doing there?'

'I wish you would rest from these questions. You give more away by asking them than you gain from their answers. The ape is Yoll's genius. Only he will not recognize that. You did well to leave the pair of them. But, if you should see him again, ask him about my Chinese box. He took it without my permission.'

'Zuleyka, do I have the Arabian Nightmare?'

She scowled and bit her nails before replying, 'The Arabian Nightmare cannot be remembered when awake. You are awake now but you can remember the night's dreams. It follows that you are not a victim of the Arabian Nightmare.'

'But I am not awake. Yet.'

*

79

He awoke, bloody, in the gutter. However, he still remembered his dreams. He was beginning to wish he did not. He went back to the Citadel to see the Dawadar, but it seemed that the Dawadar was not giving audiences that day.

He trudged off dizzily to continue his exploration of the city. There was a Cairo of buildings and monuments and another Cairo which knew nothing of them. A second city moved in perpetual motion on bare, calloused feet: cooks, water vendors, axemen, letter writers, tinkers, porters and dairy maids took their trade with them from quarter to quarter and served their customers wherever it suited them.

At night a different city came into being. Many streets and quarters shut themselves off behind strong gates, which barred the way against the riots of disorderly Mamlukes. Other parts of the city, particularly towards the west, along the Nile and in the Ezbekiyya, were brilliantly lit all through till dawn by thousands of naphtha torches.

In the Bayn al-Qasreyn, the only extensive open place in old Cairo, it was the custom for the men and even a few of the women to promenade in the cool twilight. Later, when respectable people had gone back to their homes, the streets were left to the lamplighters, carousing Mamlukes, prostitutes and the sleepers. Balian, of course, was not alone in sleeping in the streets. Most of Cairo, the vast mass of its poor, slept in the open. By day the larger families formed gipsy-like encampments at street corners and in abandoned ruins; by night they were eerie, hunched figures in shapeless huddles of cloth.

Day or night one pressed through seething masses of sweaty cloth and gleaming flesh, a maggoty concourse of crowds and over-ripeness. Yet, though he walked through the streets of Cairo ceaselessly, the city was almost totally unknown to him. The real city was perhaps elsewhere, a world of private interiors, etiquette and familial duties guarded by the huge nailstudded double doors, the porters watching from their benches and the lattices of *meshrabiyya*, thousands of secret beds and gardens. The appeals of the beggars, the cries of street vendors, the military orchestras: these were public voices. Only rarely, late at night and by chance, did he hear a family arguing or a woman quietening her child.

Day and night Balian studied Arabic, both the language of the street corner and the more formal prose of his oneiric teachers. It was not that he mastered the language but rather that it mastered him. He found himself thinking in a language in which nouns shaded imperceptibly into verbs, a language which seemed to discount being in the present, a language with a special verb form for colours and physical deformities, a language of rhythmic syntax and many tiered layers of sense, communicated through hawking stops, gutturals, odd emphases and doublings.

Distorted echoes and vaporous images radiated from short clusters of sound. One such complex, with which he was to become very familiar, revolved around the letter sequence Q, R, D. *Qird* meant ape but it also meant Iblis, the Devil. *Qarada* meant to be worm-eaten, to collect butter and to keep silent. *Qarida* meant to heap up clouds. *Qarrada* meant to take the ticks off a camel, to deceive and to invoke the Devil in cursing. Finally *taqarrada* meant to curl and twine tightly, while *maqrud* meant exhausted.

The Arabic they spoke, he found, did not contain meaning, only hinted at it, like a finger pointing somewhere else. He learned how to notate and interpret their tongue by watching and matching their gestures. The voice might say yes, but the eyes flicking away said no. The extended palm and fingers fanning the air signified temporizing. The index and ring fingers emerged to avert the Evil Eye. A finger scratched the side of the nose in warning. Hand pressed to the heart indicated gratitude. Beneath the babble of tongues spoken in New Babylon, Arabic, Turkish, Mongol, Italian, Armenian, Berber and others, there lay one silent language underpinning them all. Everybody used it, though Bulbul and Yoll used it most flamboyantly of all.

Balian had become one of the international brotherhood of beggars that met in Cairo and one of its humbler members, moreover, for within the homeless, propertyless dregs there was nevertheless an élite – the *harafish* – gangs of beggars and petty criminals organized under the patronage of one or other of the wealthy emirs. It was the job of the *harafish* to demonstrate in favour of their emir if he should be summoned to the Citadel, to collect information and rumour and to combat the activities of the *harafish* of the other emirs.

In return, registered supporters would receive bread daily at the emirs' doors. Daily too the military orchestras played outside the houses of the emirs, so that in the morning, in the area around the Citadel, the air was filled with the sullen rolling thunder of drums and ragged choruses of the *harafish*.

In the summer everyone was dirty and ill-tempered. When the winds blew in the wrong direction, then clouds of dust from the stinking white artificial mountains beyond the walls moved down into the city, and rivers of dirt flowed up the great thoroughfares and across the ceremonial parade grounds. There were fights between rival gangs of *harafish*. Sometimes a foreigner, Copt or Jew was set upon. The harvest had been bad, there were rumours of corruption, and violence simmered.

Balian shunned the caravanserai and his co-religionists. He feared that for them he was tainted by enchantment or the plague. He never stayed long in one place for fear of being traced by the Father of Cats and Vane. Sleeping made him only more tired, so he slept a lot during the daytime too now. It came upon him rapidly, first rolling black waves that clouded his vision and then, usually, a plummeting fall into total unconsciousness. Wakefulness came equally suddenly. With sickening abruptness he would find himself sprawled in the sunshine and the blood. His stomach empty, his head heavy with dreams, he walked through the city half asleep. Yet he no longer needed to find his way from sightings of minarets or dust mounds; the tilt of the ground under his feet or the angle of sunlight on a wall at a particular time of day told him enough.

One day he became conscious that something was following him, a lazy white dog, a bitch with heavy dugs, padded behind him, whining continuously. When Balian sat collapsed in the shadows of the houses, the dog would circle him, breathing heavily and whining, her lips hanging loose in a sly sort of grin. In streets, in deserted ruins and in crowded market places Balian was aware that a flabby white shadow trailed behind him, and at nights, when Balian slept in the open, the dog would lie down too at a distance, panting in the hot night air.

But slowly the conviction grew upon Balian that he was being haunted and that the dog was an illusion seen by him alone. Considering the matter carefully, he came to see how it was that the white bitch faithfully mirrored the inner corruption of his own soul, intellectually and spiritually passive, idle and easily amused. These were aspects of his soul he could no more throw off than he could lose the white bitch. He lay by now a little delirious from fatigue and loss of blood in the shadow of the Tartar Ruins. Facing him in the sun, sitting like a sphinx, was the white bitch, her saliva dribbling into the sand below her chin. Suddenly the bitch staggered to her feet and padded unsteadily towards him. My last hour, he thought. He stretched out an arm to shield his face and found himself touching fur. The bitch was real. She licked his face, between wafts of stale breath smelling of rotten meat, and staggered away to be seen no more.

Still, it is a sign, he thought. He was no longer sure of himself. Other voices, survivors of the night, clamoured all the time for attention.

All night long the man who suffers the Arabian Nightmare moves under the blankets. He sees what is happening. He knows what is happening, but he can do nothing for he forgets. He dreams that his penis is cut in half like a banana, that red-hot pokers pass from ear to ear through his head and that he retches drily on an empty stomach. He dreams of fainting; he dreams he is unconscious and, unconscious, finds that he is powerless to mitigate the pain by thought. The experience is purified and redoubled. He dreams that he dreams in this tortured body. He dreams of his body tossing and writhing on a little bed and his mind prey to horrible illusions. He suspects, no, he is horribly and totally convinced, that the figure tossing in the bed is dreaming of having his penis cut in half like a banana. If the pain were not so awful, if he were not asleep, he could do something about it. If he could only awaken the figure on the bed. If the figure on the bed could only awaken him.

Then it seemed that the two of them were shaking each other awake, shivering with pain in the dawn light. There was a dialogue they half understood. The awful thing was that they knew that this moment was not itself the Arabian Nightmare, though it was imminent again; it grew within them or hung perhaps in the shadows of the room. My brother, my double, he brings the Nightmare with him, they thought of each other. The figure tossing on the bed turns his attention away from them, though only with an effort, for logical space is getting smaller.

The tools he had to work with were very small, almost invisible, like complicated traceries of threads and, like threads, they broke easily. He took a few steps, logical steps it seemed, in a certain direction and found the way shrinking. Then claustrophobia began to close in and he began to fear that what he was doing led to a cul-de-sac anyway. It was becoming more and more difficult to separate mental images from visual images. Both brought pain. There was, though, he dimly remembered, a paradox about two sleepers who dreamed each other. Or was it really about one sleeper who dreamed of two sleepers dreaming each other? It was difficult to be sure. If there had been such a problem, how had he ever escaped it? He had a swift image of a man first treading in a treadmill and then being hurled around within its momentum. That should have been him. He was sure it should be so.

It occurred to him to wonder how it was that he should have reached this rather uncertain conclusion and sought to retrace his steps. Then he knew that he was delirious and that he did not wish to experience again what he already had been through that night.

Then he thought that his suffering was made more acute by being invisible, bloodless and logical, so he lay there trying to visualize the city that he was in. Cairo. Every street was something that had to be traversed, every door a mystery. His bones glowed with pain like red-hot charcoal. It was a painful problem. Somewhere in this city he lay dreaming, or rather, he thought with unusual clarity, in a city very like it. Over in the corner of the market under the Sultan Hasan mosque, he saw two dwarfish men selling sweets, or was it that he made himself see them?

I shall examine these men, he thought, and see how well they can ape reality. I shall ask them something, the answer to which I do not know. He paused and wondered whether he could give true value to such an answer, then drifted across towards the men. They saw him coming and grinned.

'What is my name?'

One of them smiled, gap-toothed. 'My name is Barfi and his is Ladoo.'

'No. What is my name?'

'I am sorry. I did not hear you correctly. Did I hear you ask me to tell you your name?'

'Yes.'

Barfi scratched his head. 'Did you know our names before we told you them?'

'No, I don't think so. I am not sure.' Had he known before they spoke? If he had, then he would surely know what Barfi would say next. He felt a horrid sense of mounting inevitability.

'It is a very strange question.'

It seemed the inevitable thing that he would say, and yet had he known that it was exactly this that Barfi would say? And was this the test of anything anyway? And after all he did not always know himself what he would say next, waking or sleeping. What was it that he hoped to verify? Perhaps Barfi or Ladoo would tell him. He felt confused and bored. One particular pain disengaged itself from the general mesh of pain; he wanted to urinate very badly, but this investigation must be pursued to its end.

This time Ladoo spoke. 'Perhaps you are Yunis, the dealer in rags.'

Barfi looked at Ladoo oddly. 'We have never met Yunis. Are you Yunis, and are you testing us, please?'

Barfi and Ladoo moved closer together. They looked baffled and frightened. He, for his part, felt that fate was offering him some obscure sort of challenge. Something had been begun that had to be gone through.

'Yes.'

No, it was not fate, but some inexorable and unpleasant logic, only now it was clothed with visible menace. He looked desperately around for other people or animals or birds.

'If you are Yunis, you are behaving very oddly.'

It had to be played out to the end. The pressure in his bladder was excruciating. He could not imagine what he could reply, nor how Barfi and Ladoo would respond to his reply, and it seemed for a moment impossible to continue without some image, no matter how vague, of how this adventure might go on. There was no range of possibilities and probabilities within which he could work. Yet somehow he managed to croak, thinking as he did so how odd his voice sounded in the still dawn air, 'I might be Yunis. I have come out into the streets looking for human companionship.' It seemed such an odd thing to have said that he could not even imagine how someone might reply to that in the waking world.

Once again things were off on the wrong foot. He considered fleetingly whether he dared urinate in front of them. He should have avoided all this from the first by asking about their merchandise. But perhaps he was being too self-conscious. They probably saw that he was a little strange and gave the matter no great weight, but he raised his eyes and saw that they did. They were whispering together.

'The nights are hard for me. I beg you to pass the few

hours which remain in talking to me. I really should be most grateful.'

There's no point in trying to catch them out, he thought. I know that I am dreaming them. I must just be grateful for their company.

Ladoo nodded, though they still looked suspicious, and Barfi began to talk. He talked about their trade and the profits to be made by working at night, though on this particular night they had sold nothing. And, of course, there were dangers in working at night too. The Mamlukes liked to keep a protective and profitable interest in such businesses. And then there were these horrible murders. It was said that Fatima the Deathly walked the streets again.

'They say that she cuts men's penises in half like bananas,' interjected Ladoo jovially.

The man passed his hand over his brow. 'Please help me. I think that I have got the Arabian Nightmare.' Then he remembered his appointment with the Ape and knew that the night was only just beginning.

6

From the Dawadar's Garden
to the Arqana

One of the mysteries in my tale is who is the man who suffers the Arabian Nightmare? From the nature of the affliction it is apparent that it could be anyone, even you. But no, I did not wish to suggest that you had the Arabian Nightmare. At the very least that would be an impertinence and I digress inexcusably. No, what I wished to say here is that the tale I have embarked upon is more complex than I had bargained for. Balian, the Italian painter, the mysterious prostitute, the sailor called Emmanuel, the Dawadar, the Father of Cats, Vane, my sister Mary, my good friend Bulbul: so many characters and there are more to come. We still have not met Fatima the Deathly but only heard of her by report. I grow nervous lest after all I may not be able to hold it all in my head and bring their stories to a successful conclusion. It is best now that we pause so that some of the characters may be better known.

The Dawadar was in his garden, reclining on a pile of cushions. On either side of him knelt his two beautiful, moon-faced daughters. As the shadows spread through the garden the birds had begun to sing again. A swan swished through the long grass. It was sick and drugged and regarded them with a myopic eye. The heat, far from diminishing, continued to build up. The Dawadar's thoughts were boiling in his brain. He absently shredded a palm frond between his fingers, so as to leave only its skeleton intact. It was surely too hot to move at all, yet beyond the walls he could hear the city in its usual turmoil. It was too tiring even to visualize it. As always the girls were talking about men and sex.

'Bint Azaz says that in the lands of the Franks it is all very different. They never shave their private parts, and the husband and wife spend the whole night together in the same bed, and when they make love the wife lies on her back. Do you think that it could be better when the husband is uncircumcised?'

The Dawadar groaned inwardly.

Her sister came back at her scornfully, 'Sleep with a Frank! Better sleep with an ape! At least an ape can get it up.'

'And what would you know about it?'

The Dawadar lost his temper. 'Out! Out! Out! Back to the house. Go on, out!'

He relaxed and some lines by Hafiz of Shiraz ran through his mind:

> *O green parrot,*
> *Who discourses eternally of mysteries,*
> *May thy beak never want water.*

The green parrot was, he knew, a figure for opium. He took another handful of the stuff from the bronze dish beside him and swallowed it meditatively. He was considering his daughters' behinds as they moved languorously away from him into the house. The opium had a bitter, nauseous taste and coated his mouth with a dry fur. It was the Dawadar's opinion that opium gave no positive pleasure. It merely eased the pain of being in a body, the congestion of blood in the veins, the scraping of sinew against bone, the shaking of the brain's porridge within the skullcase, all part of our everyday level of pain which was to be noticed only when opium alleviated it. For the Dawadar, pleasure was the absence of pain, while good could be defined only as the absence of evil.

He listened to the shouts and whispers from beyond the wall, the voices of Cairo, whose dangerous tides lapped round the edges of the garden, or sometimes he only imagined them.

'Cairo is worse than Bagdad, full of prostitutes and hashish eaters. I shall be glad to get out of here!'

'A loaf of bread costs two dinars!'

'Foreigners are everywhere in the city. If you believe that they have come here just to trade, you must be mad!'

'Listening to storytellers is a waste of time.'

'These people who go hunting for buried treasure, who are they? In my opinion, they are just trying to escape from their wives.'

'The Laughing Dervishes are on their way from Alexandria. They claim that God has sent them to mock our rulers.'

'He was young, so it was no surprise to us that he was found with his throat cut outside the Bab al-Nasr.'

'I am waiting for permission from the Dawadar. It's been two years since I sent in my petition.'

'Patience is beautiful.'

'Do you know what is to happen next?'

The Dawadar's lids began to droop and then to flutter as he struggled to stay awake. There were certain problems, he thought, that could be considered with safety only in full consciousness; for instance, the Father of Cats and his pursuit of the young Englishman who was having such trouble in leaving the city. Swift or slow, the Dawadar dimly sensed that it was a story that could have only a nasty ending. The Englishman was a natural victim, the Father a master, a tormentor, a manipulator.

The Dawadar spent most of his days dozing on opium. He saw barely enough of life to fuel his dreams: a couple of hundred faces, the view from the Citadel, a handful of incidents, treasured and constantly reused in inner reflection. The world is all made of one substance; it will suffice to examine any portion of it thoroughly.

The Dawadar looked through the garden with slitted eyes. His daughters were still moving away from him down the path and little bits of opium still clung to the teeth. The garden was beautiful, but there was nothing to which he could put a name; it was a mass of spikes and blossoms, in the twilight-black shot with purple, releasing a heavy, blended scent. In his mind he moved among its anonymous branches and looked back from the deep shadow of the trees to see himself sitting in the middle of the garden, a lonely figure in a vulnerable sprawl with the idiot smile of opium cutting across his face like a gash in an over-ripe melon. The opiate fantasy weakened and with a lurch he found himself back in the middle of the garden. He passed his thin hands over clouded eyes and waxen skin, dreaming awake of what might be if things were otherwise. Between twenty years of harsh military asceticism in the barracks of the Citadel and a future that teemed with erotic intrigue and political metaphysics, a drugged arrest was achieved.

He closed his eyes and let himself drift off into reverie. The city was falling apart. Bread supplies could not be assured. It was not safe to walk the streets at night. The end of the Sultanate was prophesied. Curious people had come to Cairo. The doctors of al-Azhar said that a man with the Arabian Nightmare was now in Cairo, but how did they know? The arrival of the Laughing Dervishes was imminent. Then there was this Englishman . . .

The Dawadar was committed to the siesta, or what he thought of as his beauty sleep, in an almost professional sense. He was writing a book on beauty care for soldiers, administrators and other men of action. He had provisionally entitled it *The Key of Embellishment and the Way of Adornment for the Slaves of the Sultan and the Swords of the Faith*. In it he demonstrated the importance of the siesta in relaxing the muscles of the face and smoothing away those worried wrinkles. Whatever crisis raged within, one should strive always to keep the face limpid. In it he also suggested that the sweating fit that accompanied an opiate doze cleansed the pores and produced a nice clear skin.

The range of the book was broad, its depth profound. How could the man in the saddle preserve his skin's natural oils while on campaign? Could tattooing ever be recommended? What sort of make-up should one wear to attract women and what sort to attract other men? The use of resin as a depilatory. Massage. Toupées. Codpieces. Kohl, henna and varnishes. Nor did he neglect the psychological aspects. For instance, in the struggle to look beautiful, just as in armed combat, it was crucially important to feel oneself to be young. It was important too to acquire the élite face, to look like money, for money rouses desire more surely than perfume . . . It was difficult. A pioneer thinker, he did not underestimate the problems of working with those heavy Turkish features, often battle-scarred and lined with the stress of affairs of state.

He awoke, as he always did from his siesta, shaky and cold and with the sense of rising from great depths. The same troubles of the day returned to plague him. The city was falling apart. Bread supplies could not be assured. It was not safe to walk the streets at night. The end of the Sultanate was prophesied. The doctors of al-Azhar said that there was a victim of the Arabian Nightmare even now in Cairo, but how did they know? The arrival of the Laughing Dervishes was imminent. Then there was this mystifying Englishman, and something would have to be done about that Italian . . .

Giancristoforo awoke to find again a dark figure, humped and shrouded, standing almost on his feet, looking down over him. Then it disappeared. This was his only visitor. Even before coming to Cairo, he had been familiar with it and known its name; it was called Azrael, the Angel of Death. Azrael visited everyone, but not everyone saw him. He appeared at the weak points of a man's life. The closer he was to the foot of the bed, the closer the man was to death. When he bent over the man's head, then death was indeed imminent. Azrael pulled the soul out of the body, beginning with the toes; it was very painful. Giancristoforo never awoke without a sense of dreadful anticipation. To open his eyes in an empty room was always a joyous relief. But sometimes the room was not empty. A dozen times now Azrael had stood before Giancristoforo, each time a little closer. Closer, closer and closer, Azrael was the shadow of his life, steadily shortening.

'Millions now living will never die,' he had been told. A bitter intelligence, for he now knew that he would not be one of them. Yet there was comfort of a sort in the knowledge that he was not alone here and that someone watched him while he slept. The blobs of colour which had formed the angel danced momentarily on his pupils and then dispersed, leaving only the faint reflections of a torch in the outer chamber.

He was in the Citadel, in the subterranean area known as al-Jubb; more specifically, he had learnt that he was in that portion of it which was known as Arqana, the Oozer, for obvious reasons. He was sodden wet, yet very hot. The foetid heat crawled over his body like sensual ants. Water glistened on the walls which were very close. Drowsily he ran his hands over his sticky body and then up to feel the closely pressing walls of this unnatural womb. He disgusted himself. He paddled his hands listlessly in the waters around him. He recalled dimly how, years ago, lying on a hillside near Pavia with friends under the sun, he had vowed to himself that, no matter what might happen to him in the future, the intense pleasure of this moment was more than sufficient to compensate him in advance for it. But as he now reflected, God had heard him on that hillside near Pavia so many years ago and accepted his challenge. Now his anguish was so intense that his body, his soul and his life were all scarred for ever by present pain. Nothing balances against anything, he thought. The I that laughs and the I that weeps are two different Is . . . That morning, in the coffee house, Balian must have thought him touched in the head by the heat. He wondered at the impulse that had led him to summon over that rather dreamy and witless young man and to talk so intensely at him. Perhaps he had seen some element in him that was common to them both. In any case it had probably been a mistake. Giancristoforo had not realized at the time how closely he was being watched by the sleep teacher and his men. Presumably suspicion would fall on Balian for having talked to him. They might be looking for that book too; Giancristoforo had abstracted it from Vane's baggage.

The book's title in elegant rhyming Arabic, *The Dream of the Old Pilgrim in Search of the Bezoar Stone of Wisdom, in which the Tongue of Informed Eloquence is Let Loose on the Pastures of Ignorance*, had left him at first uncertain as to whether he had found what he sought. The preface however reassured him.

He said, 'The Old Pilgrim awoke from a long dream and asked, "Tell me in what animal is the Bezoar Stone of Wisdom to be found?"

The figure of Good Counsel appeared and he said, "The Bezoar Stone is a secretion of the Rukh."

"Good, and what is the Rukh?"

"The Rukh is a bird with a name but no body." '

Then Good Counsel advised the Old Pilgrim to inquire no further, but, of course, the interrogation went on. Fleetingly Giancristoforo recalled how the dialogue and attached commentary continued, but he hastily relegated it to the area of his mind in which he tried not to think about his intentions towards God. He tried to think of something else and thought of the real purpose of his mission to Cairo. He hastily tried to think of something else again.

Doubtless that old fool of a consul was making protests about his arrest. The only effect of those protests would be to stimulate the authorities to fetch him from his cell and to try to determine why he was so important, to put him to the question. He did not exactly look forward to the Dawadar and his torturers, but it was the Father and his assistants whom Giancristoforo really feared. But his friends in Cairo were not without resources, and it was far from improbable that his escape could be engineered before he came before the inquisition of the Mamlukes and that he would see blue sky once more before his final meeting with Azrael.

7

Inside the House
of the Father of Cats

*In the beginning I described my tale as a romance, and it is in a sense,
yet of course it is also a true tale. My audience may feel that an air
of unreality is given to my narrative by the fact that the narrator
features in the dreams of the sleeping Englishman. Yet you too may
have featured in the dreams of those who know you. Have you given
thought to how you may appear to them then . . .?*

Vane was recrossing the city, supporting the Father of Cats
on his arm. Birds cruised at the periphery of his vision, raising
their wings like lead and bringing their heavy fans down to
beat the syrupy, gleaming air. Dust stirred upwards around
their feet and hung in the syrupy gleam. The cries of street
vendors came from far away. It was the light of late afternoon
and the colours seemed not to come from our sun. All was
quiet and slow, like a city under water. They were looking
for Balian.

'Rashid thinks that he saw him in a dream last night, but he
cannot be sure where.'

They crossed out of the Ezbekiyya district into the Street
of the Cross-Legged Tailors. Seated at its entrance a man
raised the severed stumps of his arms to them in supplication.
They passed on down the street into the Suq of the Perfumers.
In the *suq* three children with hideously advanced conjuncti-
vitis tried to take them into a certain house; the reason for this
was not clear. A man intervened to shoo them away. As they

thanked him, he turned towards them and revealed that half his face was falling away in rotting red lumps. As they doubled back towards the Citadel, they passed a cat basking in the sun. One of its eyes hung out loosely from its socket, connected only by the ganglion.

'Have you ever noticed,' asked the Father of Cats, 'how on some days one encounters many more crazy men or cripples than on others?'

Vane made no reply. It would have been hard not to notice.

'It is a manifestation of the power of my enemy. On certain days he draws them into the streets from the suburbs and the cellars as a warning, to show us the extent of his kingdom. Now there are more of the leprous and palsied in the city than there are healthy men. One of these days, he will give the signal and they will rise to kill us all.'

Vane shuddered inwardly. He recalled that he had heard talk that the Thieves' Guild was not always satisfied with money. If they found that the victim was carrying too little, they might also take an arm and a nose as well, so initiating the victim into their brotherhood. Christians and Jews were particularly vulnerable, for they were not allowed to wear a sword within the territories of the Sultan.

The Father of Cats found signs of the coming troubles enciphered everywhere. Deep in the Alam al-Mithal, in a remote region where there were more signs than meanings, more causes than events, pressure was building up and flowing over from basin into basin, until it had begun now to trickle into the real world, but the Father knew more than he was prepared to tell Vane about these things.

He was, Vane thought, a shrivelled intellectual toad, sitting at the centre of a web of impersonal relationships . . . a spinning toad. Vane had been with the Father of Cats twelve years now, yet the latter's character and aims remained profoundly enigmatic.

The Father never talked about his past and his own instruction in oneirology and the related sciences. It was a point of pride with him, Vane thought, to discover more about other people than he divulged about himself to them. Cold, cagey and austere, he never seemed to relax with visitors until he had assured himself that he had a hold over them or had indeed recruited them as disciples. The School thrived and the Father was certainly master of all the levels of dreaming as far as Vane knew them, yet he never felt that the School and its mysteries were an all-consuming preoccupation for the Father. He always seemed to have some other project in hand. On some days he would be visited by Mamluke officers, tradesmen and other people whose faces and bearing made it obvious that they were not interested in the inner world. The Father, he surmised, had projects in hand, projects of staggering complexity, projects within projects linked to yet others, schemes the failure of which were essential to the success of other greater designs, and these in turn were covered and insured by feints and bluffs in other directions, all moving towards some overwhelming plan whose objective could not even be guessed at by others and of which the old man himself was, perhaps, only dimly conscious. All this was to be gathered by allusion.

Occasionally the schemes, if indeed they were schemes, appeared not to be going well and the Father sat moodily tense in a corner of his room, seeming not to know Vane's name, seeming hardly to know his own. More often these days, though, he gave the appearance of confidence.

Something was coming into being and it would fall easily into the old man's grasp. Then he was alert and spry. Vane thought that he listened not with his ears but with his hooded eyes, and then the Father issued decisive, often waspish, directives. Elated or moody, there was always something hard about him. He was too lean and sinewy to make a good meal, Vane irreverently judged. It was hard to imagine him asleep, and he did not allow anyone to see him asleep.

Vane recalled their first meeting. The gate of the House of Sleep was masked; around its corner, hunched in a niche, the porter had nodded Vane by. Vane had walked on, noting as he did so the swirl of calligraphy over the gate which read, 'O you who are about to sleep, entrust your soul to God, who never sleeps' (a piece of conventional piety to which the Father, Vane was later to discover, had no commitment whatsoever). A servant had vaguely indicated where the Father was to be found, and Vane walked in unannounced. The Father had been sitting on the floor with his back to him.

'I have been expecting you.'

'How do you know who I am?'

'I dreamt last night that you would come.'

'How extraordinary!'

'Not at all. I have dreamt that dream every night for the last fifteen years.'

That was to be the pattern of the years to come, for the Father customarily employed a blend of flattery and mockery in his education of Vane.

In his youth Vane had commenced the study of theology at Oxford. He was an enthusiastic student, but since he was also poor, he had supported his studies by petty theft, only to be told before the end of his first year that his suspect conduct and notorious morals would forever debar him from receiving his bachelorship. So he had crossed to Europe to serve first as a routier, then to work for himself as a mercenary and jack of all low trades, but times were hard and his enterprises dangerous.

A temporary common interest in grave robbery had brought him together with the Jew, Elias de Medigo, from whose lips he first heard casually muttered reference to the sleep teachers who moved up and down the roads of Europe and Asia like tinkers. These sleep teachers, according to Elias the Cabalist, subsisted by telling fortunes from dreams, but to the initiate they taught the art of conscious mastery and self-fulfilment in dreams. So far Vane's career in crime had not brought him the wealth and women he craved so desperately. He was curiously attracted to the notion of achieving this sort of self-gratification in a secret inner world.

So Vane's travels began, crossing and recrossing the

Danube and the Carpathians in quest of them. His first apprenticeship was to a Turk in Thessalonika; there he learnt all the Turk could teach, including his language. Then he continued eastwards in search of other masters, in Constantinople, Erzincan, Tabriz and Khiva. There was, he discovered, an invisible network of masters, who passed him from hand to hand.

As his studies progressed, he travelled as much by night as by day. The landscapes of his travels began to commingle – fantastic sugar-loaf mountains, underground cities, Tartar pyramids of skulls and smoking lakes. Finally in Bokhara he had word of a great master who taught and practised in Cairo. Melancholically he turned back west towards Cairo, relishing the journey and its perils and dreading the moment when he should be brought face to face with what he told himself he sought – a master. As he journeyed back through the lands of the White Sheep Turks and the Black Sheep Turks, he became aware even then that the Islamic world was stumbling towards crisis, as two great empires, the Ottoman and Mamluke sultanates, found themselves increasingly at cross-purposes in the no-man's-land of Anatolia. In Cairo an atmosphere of apprehensive restlessness was already in evidence.

The Father of Cats, unlike the sleep teachers Vane had previously encountered, practised in the open under the patronage of the Sultan and some of his prominent emirs, though he was not popular in the city as a whole. When times were hard, as now, he was the victim of sermons from the *ulema* and the Dervish shaykhs, but he and his disciples survived and prospered. It was here in the House of Sleep that Vane's serious apprenticeship really started.

The whole place smelt of cat's piss, for those cats which were not being experimented upon roamed the house at will. Those which had been picked for experiments were kept in wicker cages in the cellar. The slaves who fed them wore thick leather gloves, for at this time the Father was using cats to assess the effects of sleep deprivation, and their enforced insomnia made them unpredictable and sometimes savage. The slaves would not talk to Vane; they looked on him with the same awe as they did their master. So in the early days these tormented creatures were Vane's only friends.

The work was hard at first. The day was spent most often in the study of the interpretations and commentaries given in the *Dreambook* of Joseph the Hebrew and in the works of Artemidorus and Ibn Sirin, but the night was when Vane's studies were most intensely pursued. The Father taught him how to recall his dreams, pulling them out from the night as if they were fishes. He taught him how to carry the remembered dream in his head with no diminishment of detail. Then he taught him how to dream lucidly and in full consciousness. As soon as this had been achieved, the Father took to appearing in his dreams and instructing him all through the night.

The first time this happened Vane heard rhythmic whispering in the darkness. 'Dreams are like the sea; they sweep in to cover the brain in little waves and then withdraw, but the waves ripple out from something that is always there, the World of Images, the Alam al-Mithal. Instead of waiting for the waves to cover you in a fixed daily rhythm, you may, if you wish, swim out to explore their deeps.'

As the Father spoke, Vane saw with peculiar clarity, as if he was actually standing on the edges of it, a strange sea, a deep-green sea but viscous, and its waves were tipped with white tendrils that waved slowly and appealingly towards the shore. The old man was standing beside him, genial, crackling with good humour. He rolled up his *gallabiya* and waded in, remarking as he did so, 'The sea of dreams is more than a metaphor. It is an image in the Alam al-Mithal.'

That first time Vane did not dare follow him in.

In the mornings instruction would continue over a breakfast of hunks of bread which were dipped in bowls of honey, and images which had been raised in the night were thrashed over in the daytime. Inside the head is a candle, the inner candle of vision. The candle casts its invisible rays out through the eyes, enabling us to see the world around us, but these rays can be directed to other purposes. For instance, one can put a man in a trance or visit pestilence on people and animals. At night these rays cannot pass through the eye sockets into the outer world, for the whole head is clouded by vapours rising from the stomach. So it is that the Alam al-Mithal secures its illumination. Only the instructed man can be its master.

Vane's instruction continued with the art of detecting drug-induced or poisoned sleep, the art of resting and sleeping within dreams and the art of duplicating the real world exactly in one's head, stage by stage, through a painful disciplining of the visual memory. Then the Father took him further into the pit and Vane learnt that the sleeping mind may descend through many levels. The most superficial was called the Zone of the Dog, a perplexing state barely distinguishable from wakefulness; the Zone of the Elephant was altogether more full-blooded and fantastic; then there was the Zone of the Lizard, which was less colourful and more conceptual; and so on and on. In each zone the space seemed smaller and the colours fewer. Somewhere in the heart of it all, his teacher told him, was a centre, infinitely small and dark, which could be approached only with great dread, the Zone of the Pebble (but even before that Vane learned to fear the Zone of the Ape).

It was months before the Father allowed Vane to assist him practically. Then he commenced to understand why the Father had been so ready to accept him as a disciple. It was not just that Vane's muscular physique gave him the strength to survive the rigours of the teaching or that it was useful for dealing with some of the less satisfied of the Father's customers. Though the Sleep Discipline relied first and above all on mental force, the assistance of drugs was also, on occasion, necessary. Sometimes the Father of Cats had disappeared for months on end, collecting and purchasing such drugs. Vane was now appointed by the Father to accompany him on those trips. The range of drugs and chemicals needed was wide indeed, but the commodity which drew the Father on into the furthest parts of Upper

Egypt was *mumia*, and Vane now came to realize that the skill which the Father valued in Vane before all else was his experience as a tomb robber. (*Mumia* is a morbid compound of bitumen, natron and preserved flesh, black as pitch. The Father, speaking of *mumia*, said 'The flesh is not a dead husk animated by some spirit. It is life itself!') The hunt was dangerous – there were fights with the bedouin and other tomb robbers, the Mamluke governors had to be avoided and sometimes, when they were on the very edge of success, some mechanism within the tomb itself, millennially ancient, would set in motion an ambush against them. Vane enjoyed these adventures, and as the stocks of *mumia* in the House of Sleep rose, so did the spirits of the Father also rise.

The Father relaxed the discipline of the House. He went so far as to lead Vane into a lotus land of subservient odalisques in the dream zone of the Cobra. In waking life the filling of the great urns in the upper storey of the House was celebrated more solemnly. The Father gave a *mumia* feast.

Embalmed fragments, sugared or dissolved in wine, were offered to the Father's young men. The Father told them that, in consuming their ancestors and deriving nourishment from them, they were celebrating the mysteries of death and the resurrection, sleep and reawakening. Appalled, they listened to him and, frightened, they chewed gingerly on the unattractive little morsels.

'What effect will it have?' asked Vane, greatly daring.

'*Mumia* preserves the form of life in death, just as the dream preserves a form of wakefulness in sleep. Therefore *mumia* intensifies the dream. It does this by leading the dream to reproduce itself, so that each dream carries within its womb another dream. It is the interior image of infinity. You are eating eternity.'

He smiled patronizingly. They continued to chew. Once the last fragments had been consumed, however, there was an explosion of talk and a release of tension, and men began to dance and clown. The ritual feast transformed itself into a genuine celebration. Towards the end of the party, drugged and drunken disciples riotously careered through every room in the House of Sleep, displaying a candle at each window and hanging a rug over every sill. Then, when the job was done, Vane and the others staggered out, laughing and shouting, to admire the effect. There were two windows from which no rug hung and in which no candle shone. They regarded the latticed windows soberly and went inside. Vane had not yet learnt about the other inhabitants of the House.

8

Climatic Conditions

Or do I indeed mean climactic conditions? No, not yet I fear . . .

It would not be easy for Vane and the Father of Cats to find Balian. He was somewhere among the hundreds of thousands of Cairo's poor and maimed who whispered and drifted through the city like dead leaves. They were all half alive and barely rational. But all sorts of things with no rational voice moved across Cairo with them, winds, animals, spirits, moods.

There was the *khamsin*, the wind of fifty days which blew from the south-east heavy with dust, and the hot tongue too of the *simoom* coming up from Nubia and licking round the streets, but there was also the northerly *shamal*, worshipped by the blacks and other polytheists as the lifegiver. Clouds of flies moved to invisible commands and packs of wild dogs formed, dissolved and reformed. Then there were the flocks that were brought into Cairo, sheep and goats mostly; vast herds of goats were to be found amid the Tartar Ruins, shepherded by Arabs and picking a living from the garbage. In the rainless summers more garbage lay putrefying in the city than either the goats or the nightsoil men could deal with, and then djinn were released in their poisonous vapours to fly upon the breezes amid the crowds, bringing pestilence with the *khamsin* and the dog winds. Every summer some citizens went mad in the winds, so it was wisest to sally forth into the dusty lanes with a kerchief over one's face.

Hardly to be distinguished from the djinn were the moods, most often turbulent and melancholy, which swept over the town as rapidly and unaccountably as a thunderstorm. Dust devils too were dangerous, seeking, as they flicked about his ankles, to draw the unwary traveller off into unfamiliar paths. It was for this reason that all rejoiced when the rains came, for the rains held the spirits down and the spiders, daughters of the rain, came out and the air, purified of old passions, smelt new again.

By degrees, as Balian wandered about in a steadily weakening condition, he found himself no longer competent to distinguish always between the Cairo of nocturnal fantasy and the real city. The voices of people 'that he heard in the street it did not seem to him that he heard in the street at all but in his head. The voices boomed or whispered in the ventricles of his brain, some close to his ears, others distant but still from within. It was difficult to catch the sense of what they were saying. Only occasionally did a voice, usually a word, explode within the skull, jerking him alert.

And colours. Once, dazed, he spent a whole afternoon staring at the wall of a garden in shadow. Was it brown or grey or blue or slightly orange? What was the colour of the wall, and what was the colour of the shadow? It unsettled him and at the end of the afternoon he decided that he dared ask no more such questions for fear of seeing the colours of his landscape seep away – leaves were green and the sky was blue.

People he looked on with still less confidence for, insubstantial, they became one another. The Mamluke emir he saw exercising in the Black Hippodrome became a cobbler at the other end of the city later in the day. The negro muezzin at the mosque of Ibn Tulun was the same negro Balian saw washing down the steps of a bathhouse in the Armenian Quarter. There were pairs of dwarves everywhere. He dizzily surmised that Cairo was inhabited by perhaps five hundred people who raced up and down the city, exchanging hats, cloaks and beards, always ready to meet him in new guises, to accompany and watch him.

He thought that it ought to be possible then, by going through the wrong door or saying the right word, to pull Cairo apart. The palaces, houses, mosques and gardens might evaporate in sizzling steam and its demons rise screaming in the air. He let the dust trickle through his fingers. Close to, things seemed real enough. There was no door and no demons, only a dirty and diseased foreigner grumbling in the dust.

The fountain flowed on and its waters gurgled as they ran.

It was midday on Friday, the time for the main prayer of the Muslim community in the Sultan Hasan mosque. The Dawadar stood near the front of the congregation, in line with many of his fellow officers. They were open to the sky and the sun's rays raged in the closed courtyard. Around them rose the smell of wet and sweaty linen. The Dawadar surreptitiously sniffed a pomander that dangled from his sleeve. The service was almost over. The *khutba* had been pronounced in the name of the Sultan. Then the Imam had preached from the *minbar* on the Seven in the Cave. Now, descended from the *minbar*, the Imam was leading them in the final *rakats* of the prayer, leading the congregation into the mysterious *suras*. Thousands of bodies rose and fell in unison, heads touched the matting and then bobbed up again.

'Truly, we did not create the world as a sport and a delusion.'

Suddenly there was a giggle, at first almost lost in the massed intonation of the *sura*, but it would not stop, high-pitched and getting louder, despite audible attempts on the part of others to suppress the giggler. It was coming from somewhere near the back. Then someone else was giggling.

The Dawadar turned round to glare and so did the Imam, but the contagion was spreading. Some indeed were no longer able to muffle it but had broken into open laughter. Others were red-cheeked, shaking silently with the effort of controlling it. The laughter was getting wilder. Looking round again, the Dawadar understood and felt a faint twinge of nerves mingled with a dreadful yet delicious sense of anticipation. What he saw scattered here and there amid the congregation were the conical red and yellow caps of the Laughing Dervishes. With even greater impudence than they could usually muster, they were proposing to stage one of their celebrations here in the chief mosque in Cairo during the Friday prayer.

The prayer had broken up entirely. Some hung, grimly shaking, to the columns at the edge of the cloister; most lay upon the ground and sobbed with laughter, their faces contorted with an almost hideous hilarity.

A gust of it caught the Dawadar too and even as he wondered, 'What on earth am I laughing at?' he started giggling and then cackling hysterically. He kept trying to stand up, but the laughing demon that was within him kept throwing him to the floor again. For a moment he felt himself sober, his tearful face pressed to the flagstones, degraded. He found time to ask himself, 'What are we laughing at, unless it is the idea of laughing at nothing?' before a new wave took hold of him and his neighbours. If he had not been possessed himself, the sights and sounds around him would have been truly terrifying, but as it was he rode the wind with the others. Only the dervishes stood erect, laughing at, and in control of, their own joke.

In the end it was the body that gave way under the pressure. One's ribs and stomach ached so much. The laughter deepened and slowed and then died out in various parts of the courtyard, only slowly, for there were repeated swells of giggling as one scarcely sober man looked at another. But it had almost fallen into silence and the ecstasy passed, with its prostrate victims revelling in their newly regained tranquil seriousness, when the revelation came.

A middle-aged man, not a Dervish, raised his head from the ground and, speaking in a painfully husky voice, said, 'I have had my vision. I am chosen to tell you, citizens of Cairo, that the Messiah of the Fifth Seal, the last and final Messiah, is in your city today. He knows the Arabian Nightmare and he has been purified by infinite suffering. Wait for him, for he will lead you into the Citadel.'

He had hardly finished speaking before he was seized by hostile Mamlukes. The Dervishes had apparently been filtering out of the mosque while the man was speaking. Once again they had demonstrated their power.

The Dawadar rose to go. He felt terribly weak. He felt as though someone else had been using his body to perform heavy manual labour. As the Dawadar stumbled on, heading home, it entered his head as an amusing thought that he might be the man with the Arabian Nightmare. He smiled, embarrassed with himself, and let the conceit drop.

The second outrage happened three days later, around sunset. He was taking a siesta at home when there was a hammering and a shouting at his door and the porter let in a pair of excited Mamluke troopers.

'Peace be upon you and your house.' They made formal obeisance.

'Yes. What is it?'

'Your excellency must come with us.'

'Well, what is it? Come with you where?'

'To the lake here, the Ezbekiyya Lake. There is a man on it. Your excellency must give orders for his arrest.'

'But why?'

But here the troopers took him by the sleeves and hurried him down the path to the lake nearby. The side of the lake they came out on was quite crowded. The pool was fronted on this side by the pleasure palaces of some of the great emirs and many of the servants had come to the water's edge to watch the fun. The Dawadar, shading his eyes against the sun, peered across the waters to where the boat which was clearly the centre of attention seemed to drift aimlessly. Then he started back with surprise and swore. There were two men in the boat. A small ferrety-looking man was resting on the oars;

the other was sitting up playing a lute and singing at the top of his voice:

> 'The big bamboo is thick and strong,
> The big bamboo . . .'

He was obviously drunk. Singing drunks were common enough on the pleasure pools of Cairo. What shocked the Dawadar and amused the others was the man's appearance – the white hairs, pinched cheeks, wispy hairs on the chin, the black robes, the ornamental baldric and the black turban and horned crown. The drunk was surely the Sultan? Or his double? An impostor. Other officers besides the Dawadar had been summoned, and some troopers were putting a boat out on the lake to cat-calls from the jeering throng of servants and riff raff. Observing this, the figure in the boat put his lute aside and stood up rather unsteadily to address them,

'This is the proclamation of the splendid, the victorious, the glorious and beloved of God. Sayf al-Din Qaitbay Ibn Abdallah al-Nasiri, al-Mansuri, al-Azizi, al-Qaimai, Sultan of Cairo and Damascus, Lord of Nubia, the Yemen, Cilicia and Barka, Guardian of the Two Holy Shrines, Provider of the Veil of the Tomb, Protector of the Caliph, Commander of the Jihad, Master of the Arabs, the Turks and the Persians, Sustainer of the Poor, may God prolong his reign and confound his enemies, as follows. We denounce and execrate the impostor who sleeps in the Citadel and we promise all our loyal subjects . . .'

But here he broke off and was not allowed to finish, for the Mamluke boat had rowed alongside. His oarsman, seeing that it was all up, dived off and swam to the other side, where he succeeded in making his escape through the thick clumps of baobabs. The 'sultan', however, was clearly too drunk even to attempt this. The Dawadar and some of his fellow officers had him taken to the Arqana for examination and questioning. The resemblance to the real Sultan was indeed startling, even when viewed close to. The Dawadar found the appearance of this double eerie – more than that, profoundly disturbing –

for it had long been a conviction of the Dawadar's that the body was the mirror of the soul, that the body represented in flesh and substance the nature of the soul. We love a beautiful body because we recognize in it the beauty of the soul that so infallibly shapes the body. Physical resemblances, therefore, were not slight tokens. Perhaps some nature was shared in common between this drunken mountebank and the Sultan.

Moreover, there was another disturbing thing. Under his robes the man was discovered to be a leper. He was bastinadoed lightly to make him talk (for a heavy bastinado killed), but the man sobered up quickly and said nothing.

A message was sent to the Sultan asking if it would amuse him to see his double, but a message came back ordering his instant and painful execution. So he was taken on a hurdle to the place of execution outside the Zuweyla Gate and then, to the delight of the assembled populace, Melsemuth was brought out from the royal treasury. Melsemuth was an automaton, a seven-foot-high brass doll powered with springs and coils. The condemned would be strapped to the doll, leg to leg, chest to chest, arm to arm. Then the doll, wound up, would begin its funny clockwork dance. The gestures and kicks would get wilder and wilder. Finally as the coils were running down, Melsemuth would garotte its dancing partner and stop.

Only at the last moment, as the false Qaitbay was being strapped to the automaton, did he break his silence and speak to the people from the platform. 'May God forgive you. You have made a terrible mistake. If you kill me now, my twin will follow close behind. We share one fate.'

A plea of desperation. Melsemuth began its ungainly hopping step. The Dawadar did not stay to see the end of the execution but returned to his duties in the palace in a sombre mood. The image of the Sultan, but ravaged by leprosy and alcohol, seemed to him to signify something more than a fatal prank and foolish demonstration. Perhaps the executed man had embodied the crimes of the state. Perhaps, rather, he was a talisman who warded off the attacks of sin and disease from the person of the Sultan. 'For everything in the universe there was a left hand and a right hand.' Was there also another Dawadar, his genius?

The third outrage began in the Citadel the following day, though the Dawadar did not learn of its outcome until some time later and it was a long time before he was able to make any connection between this occurrence and the other two.

In the depths of the Citadel Giancristoforo was pursuing his disordered meditations, when the sudden blaze of reflected torchlight on the waters of his cell drew him to the grille of his door. A jailer stood on the other side.

'A friend asked me to give you this. He asks that you study it carefully. I shall be leaving you some light out here.'

The jailer disappeared.

A friend. That could surely only be Yoll. Giancristoforo examined Yoll's gift doubtfully, a small wooden box with a piece of paper stuck to one of its sides. He read what was written on the paper. 'Here is your release. It is said that "On the opening of every cunt is written the name of the man who is to enter." This is the Box of Rapture from Cathay. Open it and find your name.'

He hesitated.

'It must be done, Bulbul.' Bulbul looked glumly at Yoll and nodded. Of all those who were attempting the entrancement of *sirr* that day, Bulbul was the only one who had had previous experience of the operation, and so it was Bulbul who looked pale.

'We have been lucky so far,' Yoll continued, 'but if we leave it as much as a day longer, they will come for him and beat him and threaten him with Melsemuth and he will talk. It is a certainty. He does not really know why he is with us and he is a coward. He would talk, and when he talks we are lost.'

A few days ago there had been wild talk of forging passes and a warrant for his release, of using the false Qaitbay or even the tightrope that still stretched between the minaret of

Sultan Hassan and the Citadel to get him out, but, in the end realism prevailed. So Bulbul nodded again but he dreaded what was to come, not so much because of what it did to the victim as because of the effects it had upon the operator. All forms of *sirr* were exhausting; some might be lethal. Bulbul had learnt to dread that sensation of sinking deeper and deeper, through and then away from words and images, the slow and cautious willing of oneself to relinquish, piece by piece, all grip on external reality in order to manipulate the hidden world.

A few houses away in a street in the same quarter a woman had already begun the operation, and elsewhere in the city three lepers sat on a wall, apparently enjoying the sun, meditating.

'Let us commence,' he said.

A boy sprawled in the corner began to pluck at a lute. Bulbul and Yoll had a drawing, a self-portrait of Giancristoforo, to work with; across it was marked the design of calligraphic worms. They sat together at the window focusing first on the face then on the design, then back to the portrait, backwards and forwards. The design and the face drew Bulbul in until his black heart and Giancristoforo's started to beat as one.

Giancristoforo continued to stare at the paper long after he had finished reading it. The whorls of script were intricate yet self-contained; the hand was Bulbul's, not Yoll's. The ink seemed very black and the paper brilliant yellow. As he stared he saw that between the black lay great chasms of yellow that yawned beneath the writing, sandstone gorges in which one stood, lost in their immensity and marvelling at the black letters that raced and danced above.

With an effort he turned his attention from the paper to the box. He looked back briefly at the narrow alleyways formed in the spaces of Bulbul's sworling script. Three white-faced men sat on a sunny wall and beamed at him. His hand hovered over the box. And jerked forward to open it. The worm-like after-image of the script lingered on his eyeballs for an instant, black against the yellow of the torch flame. Then he perceived the box as empty. Only he thought he could hear a scuffling sound, so soft it might have been a dream whispering in his head. Hesitantly he lifted the Chinese box to his ear. Then, from the corner of his eye, he thought he saw a long yellow grub raise itself on its tail and extend itself over the side of the box, a brief squinting image of a mouth made to suck and pierce, a blob of black and yellow, then it was gone. He put the box down to float empty on a pool in the middle of his cell.

Bending over the floating box, he became aware of something squelching and poking in his eardrum. He stuck his finger in his ear. Whatever it was, his finger seemed to have driven it further in. His next thought was of the worm and that thought was devoured by sharp, excruciating pain. The pain spread and ate away at all his thoughts. All that he knew was offered to the worm. It was his thought that it grubbed away in the carrion of his brain-pan and rendered it charnel liquor – and that thought too was swiftly consumed. The pain was behind his left eye now. Something pierced the eyeball and sucked at it like a raw egg. Now the vision of his left eye and his right eye warred with one another. The right eye saw his hand shaking over the box in the empty cell. The left eye saw the worm in the head, saw it swimming in the liquors of the brain towards a box that floated on those waters. The box opened and a second worm which had been nestling in the box heaved itself up over the edge to joint its brother. Now the pain was in both eyes and the inside of Giancristoforo's skull was his cell, the inside of his cell his skull. And there was another box and, when opened, another worm and, inside that box, another cell that was also a skull and another worm, and another. The surface of his thoughts became covered with worms thrusting up and down, black and yellow, like a page of Arab calligraphy. His last knowledge was of the edges of his brain, how it rippled and heaved under the pressure of their maggoty feast.

The strain on the operants outside was enormous, but Bulbul was their guide. The entry had been, as always, difficult. First there was the face with its unyielding profile hovering shakily before him and he slipped unsuccessfully from side to side on the edge of the skull. Then, quite suddenly, the face filled out and acquired dimension, so that Bulbul and the others could pass in. They wriggled like worms into the chambers of Giancristoforo's head, mastering its structure. Then, familiarized with its pattern, they set to their work. In the later and most fascinating stages the operant became aware, albeit always dimly, of something small at the centre of the brain beyond reach of thought or memory, quite beyond conscious seizing – the primal matter of consciousness perhaps. One glimpsed from a great distance an area, brilliantly lit by internal flashes of lightning, in which tiny little men flickered and ran carrying letters, emblems and numbers amid blocks of flashing rods and colours. It was beyond meaning. Bulbul yearned to linger in this territory beyond meaning, but, held by the others, he drew away.

The fascinated guard even came into the cell and sat and watched for a while. Giancristoforo was in continuous spasm. His hands clawed at his face, trying to pull the skin from the skull. The rhythm of the fit slowly and insensibly accelerated. The guard went off for dinner. After dinner the guard reported the matter to his superior officer. The officer reported the sickness, possibly mortal, of the prisoner in the Arqana to the archivist, who was delighted. After Giancristoforo's consignment to the Arqana the record of his whereabouts had been mislaid; over nine hundred prisoners, living or recently deceased, were stored away in the cellars of the Citadel and there was space for more. Every day the Dawadar passed on to the archivist messages from Michael Vane insisting on the urgency of locating and interrogating the Italian spy. A search had been ordered but the head jailer followed instructions at his own pace and in his good time. A happy accident, then, that the Italian's sickness had been reported to the archivist. The following day the archivist sent a message to the Dawadar and later that day the Dawadar descended into the Arqana. By then it was, of course, too late. The torch flares revealed the prisoner to be dead, hunched and knotted in the tight bonds of rigor mortis.

'*Sirr.*'

Later still the Dawadar reported to the Sultan, walking in the quincunx garden, and, as he had feared, the Sultan was angry. Then, after some tranquillizing silence, they agreed that the House of Sleep should be consulted again, before the pursuit, arrest and interrogation of the Englishman, Balian, was ordered.

9
How to Leave Cairo

Sad about the fool in the boat. Qaitbay's double, I mean. Yet at least you have been given an impression of the pleasures of boating on the Ezbekiyya Lake – if you should ever come to Cairo . . .

Balian dreamt he awoke from troubled dreams to find himself staring at a man who floated above him, face down, a couple of feet or so beneath the coffered ceiling. The man was white from head to toe, with hair that fanned out from his head like tongues of white-hot flame.

'Who are you?'

The man replied in a draught of wind, 'My body is of the night.'

'What is your name?'

'My body is of the night.' He circled round the ceiling, then spoke again. 'Rise up and join me.'

'I cannot.' But then to his mild surprise, Balian found himself standing beside the bed.

'You must try, for it is possible if you will. The air is heavier than you think and your spirit lighter.'

'I cannot.'

'Wriggle your ankles and kick your feet very rapidly.'

Balian did so.

'Now spread your arms outwards and bring them in again. And again.'

At first Balian glided along the floor. Then he began to ascend. Slowly he pulled his way up to the ceiling.

'You must not think of yourself as lower than you are,' the whispery voice rustled in his brain.

Balian and the white man floated towards one another. The man pointed out of the window to the city, all spires and domes.

'You are awkward. You must learn to do this better. All that should be yours.'

'Teach me to fly properly. Be my master.'

'I belong to this place. I will not be your master – nor your servant, which is what you mean.'

Balian, who found this all very difficult, replied, 'Why should I fly? I don't like it.' He was angry, but the man smiled.

'Flying is only a figure for something else. If you cannot succeed here at this, then you will fail elsewhere at other things. You must strengthen your will, for you do not need a master. In truth, you have too many masters. It is being said that everyone is your master.'

And with that, the man or spirit flitted out of the window and, with a couple of low swoops, disappeared through the garden. Balian fell back on to the bed into sleep and other dreams.

Later he asked Zuleyka about it. Zuleyka said that the only thing flying could symbolize was flying.

'That man always talks nonsense. He's just a flying instructor, somewhat deranged by conceit about his own very limited skills.' Then she said again that she wished Balian would stop asking so many questions and would concentrate on improving his performance in bed.

He awoke as day was breaking, feeling weaker than ever. The days were becoming hotter and yellower; it was as if the two great spheres of Earth and Sun were being ground together.

It was imperative to make an early start. It was out of the question to go to the Citadel again. Even the attempt to revisit the caravanserai and reclaim his things and *The Dream of the Old Pilgrim* might be dangerous. Since seeing her broken on the wheel, Balian had lost his old enthusiasm for visiting the shrine of St Catherine at Sinai; besides, it could be said that he had already paid her a visit and fulfilled his vow. So he decided to leave Cairo for Alexandria, on foot and begging. He turned north, intending to walk out to Bulaq through the gardens and orchards on the fringes of the Ezbekiyya quarter. It was still pleasant in the long shadows of early morning. What made the light of morning so different from the evening light? Shopkeepers were sprinkling water on the ground before their shops to keep the dust down. He could actually smell the sunlight on the stone and the water on the dust. Balian's heart rose. He passed from shops into narrow, leafy paths hedged in with bamboos and bulrushes, dark and damp. He turned to look at the minaret of Sultan Hasan and the towers of the Citadel, already wavering in the haze. Everything was so quiet. A gang of labourers made way for him on the narrow path.

To be leaving Cairo! It seemed like a dream. Perhaps he should pinch himself to prove it was real. He recalled an observation in *The Dream of the Old Pilgrim* to the effect that there were two things one could not do in a dream, look at the back of one's hands and remember one's own name. He would.

He did not break his pace as he looked down at his hands – or so he thought. But when he opened his eyes he saw that his hands were in the dust and his face was only inches above the dust. Blood trickled from his nose on to the backs of his hands. The sun was now high in the sky and he had not yet left the Ezbekiyya. He picked himself up and grimly set off again north-east towards Bulaq. But this time the roads were hot and dusty and the crowd was on the move and the grit got in his eyes. There was pressure on his chest. His legs were heavy. He should have set off earlier instead of sleeping until midday. The sleep had done him no good. But to leave Cairo! If only he could . . .

He pressed on hopefully and anticipated reaching the groves and orchards he remembered so vividly from his last dream, but his body grew heavier and his eyelids seemed to be as heavy as his legs. His eyes blurred. He sat down at the foot of a fountain and then, finding this an unreasonable effort, lay down. He would look for the strength within him to continue. He felt his body undulate in waves of heat and he imagined his pores opening and closing in fast, irregular rhythms. Awareness dissolved and flowed through the blood stream and hung, shaking, to the thunder of his bones before it finally fell into the web-like complex of sensations and humours. There was no centre of strength within him. Only heavy opiate sleep. He slept.

He awoke and picked up his steps and slept and woke and walked and slept again. It was always like that. Sometimes he thought that he found its futile repetition more comforting than the prospect of escaping Cairo. Sometimes, misled by dust devils, he took the wrong path. A couple of times his path was blocked by the Father of Cats and his disciples casting about for him among the vagabonds who filled the open places of the city. He had seen the Mamlukes too making inquiries about him, but the description they had of him as a young foreigner, elegantly dressed in the Burgundian style so ill accorded with his present state that their chances of identifying him were negligible. Indeed, he was able personally to hinder them in their inquiries.

His attempts to leave became increasingly ridiculous and faint-hearted. The exhortations of the white man came to mind and he decided to fly out of Cairo. He stood behind a wall where he could not be observed, fanned out his arms and fingers and, standing on tiptoe, wriggled his ankles – and pitched forward on to his face. It is all a matter of the will, he told himself, but how can I will myself to have the will I have not got? He tried to visualize himself as a ragged bird hanging, the cynosure of all eyes, over the crowded bazaars, floating on the heavy air and beating his way towards the Citadel, but the vertigo this induced was so strong that he was unable, momentarily, even to rise to his feet.

Once – a momentary triumph, this – he walked or dreamt he walked out through the suburbs of Cairo and into the leafy paths and orchards on the northern edge of the city only to find, as he walked on, that the houses were appearing more frequently again and then more closely packed until indeed he was not far short of a Zuweyla Gate, centre of a second Cairo, the mirror of the first.

'Such cities are like falling drops of water, reflecting one another on their surface.'

He walked on. A boy was flying a kite and running along a ridge of dust heaps to maintain its height. He stopped to watch. The sight was so unusual. Children did not play in Cairo, but, sinister and dwarfish little adults, they gathered on street corners and sold their services in the market as secret messengers, untrustworthy guides. The kite danced and bobbed among the brown storm clouds. The boy, without ceasing to run, turned his face to Balian and bared his teeth in a fierce smile, pointing to his kite as he did so. Then he disappeared over the dust ridge, leaving Balian depressed.

I can no longer imagine a world outside Cairo, he decided calmly, but the apprehension that his imagination might shrink yet further saddened him.

Cairo's Freaks

*Every visitor finds it difficult to leave Cairo. It unfolds itself like a
story that will never end. My audience are foreigners to this place. It
attracts them (if it attracts them at all) precisely by its exotic nature.
I have been at pains to single out and emphasize the exotic elements
in my story. As now with these freaks. I mean no harm by calling
them freaks. Some people would regard me as a freak myself . . .*

The dwarf lay asleep, thinking. At least he thought he was
asleep. He listened to the rhythm of his snoring. Yes, he was
asleep. But wait a moment. Were those his snores? He listened
to their even rhythm more carefully. Surely that was Ladoo's
nasal rasp? Or, now, hang on, did he mean Barfi, he being
Ladoo and too tired to think at this late hour? If I am not
thinking clearly he thought, it is surely because I am asleep.
It is difficult to think properly in one's sleep. No, it is impossible. I am sure I am asleep. First, because I am not thinking.
Secondly, because I am snoring or, if not me, then someone
I cannot distinguish from me is snoring, so it comes to the
same thing. Thirdly, I am motionless. Fourthly, I can see
nothing.

Of course, he thought with a flash of nocturnal brilliance,
this does not rule out the possibility that I am dreaming,
dreaming indeed that I am asleep. It is unusual certainly but
not impossible. Passers-by do well to distrust what a sleeping
man says in his dreams. If I were my companion Ladoo (or

do I mean Barfi?), I certainly should not believe me when a voice issued from my recumbent form saying, 'I am asleep.' I should say to myself that the man to whom the recumbent form belonged was either shamming or deluded and I should give him a good kick to clarify his ideas.

The darkness was filled with snoring. He lay there pondering the pros and cons of being kicked, by a friend perhaps or maybe just by a casual passer-by. There was the physical pain, of course. But against that there was the considerable clarification of mind that would go with it.

He went on to consider in a leisurely fashion which he would mind more, being kicked by Barfi or being kicked by Ladoo? It was perhaps one way of determining which of the pair he was. Perhaps. On balance he thought that he would prefer to be kicked by Barfi. Now, did that mean that he was Barfi and only he, Barfi, was a fit and proper person to correct and clarify his mental processes, or did it mean that he knew that Barfi was his, Ladoo's, best friend?

Those snores! Were they really his? If they were, they were keeping him awake and that was intolerable. It did not seem to him, from what he could recall of the tastes and susceptibilities of the distinctly similar personalities of Barfi and Ladoo, that either of them would put up with this racket for a minute. Unless they were asleep, of course. Unless he and I are asleep, he corrected himself. Even so, the snoring seems terribly loud. Surely it would have awakened one of us?

'Are you awake?' he called out into the darkness.

'Yes. I'm awake all right,' came the comforting answer.

'I didn't wake you, did I?'

'I'm not sure.'

Then quite suddenly he realized that the snoring had stopped, but which of them had ceased snoring in order to participate in this conversation? This would be a tricky matter to approach. For two reasons. First, no man likes to have it hinted that he snores. Second, still less does he like to encounter and converse with individuals who labour under the delusion that they may be he. Both propositions could be construed as insulting.

'It is said that the snoring of a virtuous man is pleasing in the ears of God.'

A long pause, then the reply came. 'It is said also that God never sleeps.'

Another tack would be preferable.

'Do you know, when I woke up just now, I had no idea at all who I was? I just lay there in the darkness without a name or an identity. I even thought I might be you! Such was the extent of my confusion on awakening from my dreams that for a few seconds I could not think of a single characteristic that distinguished me from you.'

'That was certainly most distressing. I should certainly have been most cast down had that ever happened to me. Tell me, I beg you, what in the end allowed you to make the crucial distinction between our two natures?'

This was difficult. Then he remembered that there was now a third person sharing their room. On this night, as on other nights recently, the man with the Arabian Nightmare had accompanied them back from their sweet stall near the Zuweyla Gate.

The man with the Arabian Nightmare huddles, shaking, in a corner of their room. To him their nightly dialogue is only an extension of his nightmare, their words and thoughts only echoes of his delirium. For, in his nightmare, he too cannot distinguish Barfi from Ladoo or the nonsense they talk when awake from the nonsense they mumble in their sleep. Such thin creations of the vapours of the Alam al-Mithal scarcely exist. The pain muddles his thoughts, but a thin megrimous drivel continues to whisper and whistle in his skull.

'Yet to be Barfi means not to be Ladoo. To be alive as Barfi means to be dead as Ladoo. To be alive as a man means to be dead as a horse. To be dead. Not to know that one was dead. Not to be, not even to be the thing that was ignorant of its own death.'

It was the certainty that one day he would be dead and,

when dead, not even disturbed by that awful state that so disturbed him now. Better to lie for centuries in the dark than to be truly dead.

'Yet asleep here, now, I don't know whether I am a sultan or a beggar. I might as well be dead.'

The man with the Arabian Nightmare stirs and whimpers.

The staring eyes and bulbous noses of Barfi and Ladoo loom over his face. He sees that the dwarves have turned on him. They have decided that it was he who was snoring and they are now trying to shake him awake. He struggles to resist, but his struggles only bring him closer to awakening and his thoughts begin to turn themselves into images.

He dreams that he awakens men who are dreaming of shaking dreaming men awake – all like a stumbling column of blind men, each man with his hand upon his predecessor's shoulder. He hears the worm crying for its brothers and the worm's brothers crying for their putrid feast.

The Ape rattles its chains. He has looked into *The Dream of the Old Pilgrim* and read there that he ought not to have looked into it. In waking life he is being sought and, if he is identified and his nightmare brought out into the daylight, then he will learn to anticipate his sleep with dread. The night is slipping away from him.

The hunt for Balian was only desultorily pursued by the Father and Vane, for the Father now had other schemes in hand and Vane had not yet been told clearly why they were looking for him at all. The Father's schemes seemed to be very close to fruition and he stood beside Vane, relaxed and reminiscing, almost as if, Vane reflected, his career was due to end imminently.

They stood in front of the cage of the somnambulist, not far from the Zuweyla Gate.

'I created him while you were in Constantinople,' the Father said, almost purring with pride, before sharply looking into Vane's face to see if his cleverness was appreciated and to assure himself that Vane was not smiling privately at an old man's vanity. Vane, however, had learnt never to smile unless he knew that the Father required it, so the Father continued, 'One of the *ulema* at al-Azhar had declared that men have their dreams only in the instant before awakening, the development of action and the sense of duration being both delusions formed retrospectively upon awakening. I determined to give a public demonstration that he was wrong. I purchased this specimen as a slave – his real name is Habash, by the way – and issued invitations to the doctors at al-Azhar to come to the House of Sleep one night in Muharram and see me demonstrate the true nature of dreaming. The demonstration took place in the cellars. I had the slave drugged into insensibility and Hussein strapped him to the floor. I had his head shaved over the middle of the skull.

'My aim was to cut out the gland which enables a man to distinguish sleep from wakefulness. I therefore made an incision as near to the top of the skull as I could judge in the unsteady torchlight. Although I had performed a trepanation before, it was much harder than I remembered, first to penetrate the skull and then to remove the bone, but fortunately the gland is close to the surface of the skull and I was scarcely off my mark at all. I removed the gland and the patient continued to breathe heavily as he had done throughout the whole operation.

'Nothing happened for a long time. We had some tea and the doctors talked drivel about the location of the spirit within the body. Then one of my servants drew our attention to the fact that, while we had been talking, Habash's eyes had opened. I should say distended rather, for they were open to their fullest possible extent, so that the white was visible all the way around the pupils. The pupils, though, moved ceaselessly from side to side and Habash's whole body twitched and quivered under his bonds. I gave orders for him to be unstrapped and set upon his feet. This was done, though he did not seem to be conscious of it at all. He stood in the middle of the cellar, staring intently into a corner where no one was. What he said could not be understood. He stood there talking and smiling at that dark corner with such conviction that my slaves thrust their torches into it to prove to themselves that there was no one and nothing there.

'It was also clear to us all, though nobody dared remark upon it, that he had an erection. The doctors from al-Azhar were in a panic. So were some of my slaves. They thought he was talking to a djinn.' The Father smiled. 'One does not talk to a djinn with a smile and an erection. I stood up and explained how with my knife I had cut out the inhibitor which prevents us from using our bodies as well as our minds in dreaming. Some say that the theatre of dreaming is the head alone, but my negro was in every sense dreaming in my cellar. I think the doctors were too shocked to listen properly to what I had to say and one of them raised the objection that he was drugged, not sleeping. We watched him make his approach to his invisible lady, his rebuff and his apparently successful attempt subsequently to rape her. Then he collapsed.

'The doctors departed, professing themselves disgusted, but there proved to be a market for such a sight and Habash has fetched a good price here at the Zuweyla Gate.'

'An interesting experiment,' Vane murmured politely.

'A demonstration, not an experiment. I knew what its outcome would be before I started.'

Vane looked on. Habash's cage was the centre piece of a group of other attractions: snake charmers, iron eaters, yogis and such like. Habash the somnambulist slept (for it was late) on his feet and in motion, dancing, howling and waggling his fingers at the sky. Occasionally his rapid and uncontrolled movements brought him crashing against the bars of the cage, and he would stand hanging on to the bars, briefly awake, before relapsing, whimpering, into sleep. Some of the audience jeered; some sat open-mouthed. Vane felt faintly nauseated. It was not the cruelty but the vulgar pride of his – certainly learned and cunning – master that nauseated him.

'He was the first of the channels through which the Alam al-Mithal could break into reality.' The Father gestured expansively, then fell sombre. 'It is better that they keep him caged. His keeper tells me that of late he has begun to dream of murder.'

The Father was pointed out to the audience by the proprietor. The crowd around them looked at him and Vane with a mixture of respect and dislike. Vane surmised that, to them, the Father was in no way different from those surgeons who mutilated the children of beggars to give them a living.

Embarrassed, they moved away from the Zuweyla Gate.

'The reverse case is equally interesting and has been treated by me. It is the case of a channel being used by the Dunya, the real world, to flow into the Alam al-Mithal. A very ordinary man was honoured by becoming this channel, but he was a patient of mine, a grocer called Abu'l-Mejid. He dreams that he is lying on his mattress asleep. When he dreams that it is raining outside, it is raining outside and when he dreams that someone has come into the room, someone has come into the room. All his dreams are like that – very boring. He is a strange, dull man and his dreams are strangely dull, but one can see quite easily, I think, that they are dreams. Abu'l Mejid dreams with his eyes shut. If someone comes into his room and he dreams that he sees someone come into his room, then he is deluded, for his eyes are closed.

'The logical problem is easy to solve, but the grocer did not come to me for lessons in logic. He came because his life is being eaten away by monstrous boredom. I am still treating him. With the right foods, I have hopes of giving him nightmares.'

He paused.

'It is still true, however, that many of the disorders we have been treating are logical disorders. One needs only to point out to the patient the ground on which his error is founded and he is cured, as if by a miracle; the mysterious depression disperses. You know them – Ahmed the cobbler dreams that he is Hasan the prince, who dreams that he is Ahmed the cobbler. They profess not to be able to distinguish life from dream and they tell you that they are dying of paradoxes.

'One cannot doubt that such sicknesses arise from the inappropriateness of the images they use to think with. They visualize life and dream as containers, and they think either that the dream is locked within the casket of waking life or that waking life is locked inside the dream. But, as we know, dream and life are not boxes and their relationships to one another must be seen in quite a different way. That is why your training in lucid dreaming was so important.'

'Was?'

'Was. Soon these skills will be irrelevant. Things are on the move. Things are due to change.'

'No. Nothing ever happens in this place. Things are always being supposed to be just about to happen.'

Vane had hoped to draw him on this, but the Father only looked at him hard and whistled tunelessly through his remaining teeth. Then, 'By the way, I never asked. Did you have any luck with your little quest?' Another indecipherable stare.

'No, you never did. No.'

'Well, well. Today's quest too seems fruitless. I propose that we leave the hunt for Balian to the Mamlukes. Besides, there will be others looking for him soon. I have other business in the city, but I expect to see you at dinner.'

And with that they separated.

Vane walked on, enjoying the coolness of late afternoon. Crossing the open spaces of the city was like moving across a chess board, chill and dark in the shadows, still brilliantly warm in the places the sun could reach. He was crossing a dark square now near the Bab al-Luq, where the rich merchants' houses were, when he saw a face, high up in the dark shadows of an upper-storey casement, staring down at him. It was a woman's face, round and plump and shining silver as if it was the moon. Vane stopped. His heart throbbed and ached, as if an invisible hand was squeezing and shaking it. Fatima, Fatima, it must be, but she is so pale! Mutely the woman at the window pointed to the door in the street below.

An old Mooress sat beside the door, drinking beer. She watched him curiously as he came towards her and she shook her head vigorously as he went in. It was dark inside but Vane could just make out the broad stone staircase in front of him and he began to climb. He had climbed about a dozen steps when he became aware that somebody was quietly climbing up behind him, matching him step for step, but making an odd sort of flapping noise as he or she did so. Vane turned, braced for trouble, his fists clenched and ready, if necessary, to launch himself on his invisible attendant, but the figure behind him also stopped and coughed loudly. Then, in throaty Arabic, 'Go right up. She awaits you.'

Vane threw a few coins down and, turning as he did so, raced up to the door and into the room.

'Enter Michael Vane, false knight who never yet was dubbed!'

The door swung back behind him.

'Hail to the Knight of Dreams!'

'Welcome to the undertaker's assistant!'

'You have come to us.'

'You have found your whore.'

'Welcome. We would have words with you.'

'If you have never had dreams of us before, you will have dreams of us now.'

'Be at peace. Your life is not in danger.' Laughter.

A candle in the middle of the floor. Glints of silver and of white. Fluttering white draperies. Two spotted hands gripping a sword hilt. A pestiferous smell.

Vane's eyes accustomed themselves to the darkness. Eight knights in full armour, save for their helms, stood in a semicircle round the room, resting on their double-handed swords, rocking almost imperceptibly backwards and forwards. One of them, in the centre of the circle, spoke. 'I am Jean Cornu, Grand Master of the Knights of the Order of St Lazarus of Jerusalem.'

'So who are you and what is that?'

But Vane knew who he was and what they were. He had seen the Knights of Lazarus before, years ago, on the island of Rhodes, where their headquarters sheltered under the protection of the far greater Order of the Knights Hospitaller of Rhodes. The Order of Lazarus was a small brotherhood of fighting monks, less than a hundred knights certainly, and many of these knights very old. Yet they were, Vane discovered subsequently, an object of special fear to the infidel, for these were the Leper Knights who were reputed, falsely no doubt, to feel no pain in battle. Looking closely at Jean Cornu's face, he saw now the gleaming white spots set in the skin like teeth.

'Today we are assembled here to meet you, though only briefly, for we have other work to do about the city. We have something to offer you.'

Vane kept quiet.

'Fatima,' pursued Jean Cornu smoothly, 'and we hope that you may be able to do something for us in return.'

'It is possible. Tell me, first, what has Fatima to do with you, and where is she?'

Cornu's eyebrows rose and he spread out his arms expressively. 'To whom should she come, if not to the Brothers of St Lazarus? You forgot her quickly enough, but the Brotherhood has been kinder.'

The smell and closeness of the air were making him giddy. 'That's not true. She left without my knowledge. I did not know, I swear it. Where is she?'

'You know and we know that your oaths are valueless. She is in the next room. Our message will come through her.'

A leprous knight moved to usher him into that room. As the door swept open, a foetid blast so thick that it seemed to make the air shimmer hit Vane in the face. He recoiled, then entered nevertheless. He had to stoop for the ceiling was very low. Fatima stood pressed against the far wall as if her flesh had been caked on its ruptured stucco.

Vane spoke. 'You wanted to see me?'

'No, the other way around.' Her mouth moved painfully. 'I am an image, not an imaginer. You know I cannot see, for I exist only in the eyes of others.'

'For God's sake then, Fatima, what is it that you want? Speak.'

'No. I want nothing. I cannot have desires. My sister, yes, nothing but desires, but not I. I am only a brainchild. If I were real, I would wish the death of the Father of Cats, but I am only a brainchild and how can a brainchild wish the death of its creator?'

'If you are a brainchild, then you are a child of a very beautiful thought,' said Vane, moving closer towards that pale and passionless face. 'Let me embrace you.'

'No, you would not enjoy the experience.' Then she lowered her eyes and with her left hand she tugged at her right forefinger. 'But you may have this as a keepsake perhaps until I come again.'

The finger came off and she pressed it into Vane's hand. He fainted and lay delirious under nasty dreams for what seemed a long time. When he recovered he found himself outside again, staring at the Mooress with her jug of beer. His hand was empty. He stood up rather unsteadily and walked back into the house. The flapping figure came up behind him on the stairs.

'They've all gone, sir. You won't find anyone here any more.'

It was true. Vane walked back to the House of Sleep in the dark.

There was another visitor to the House of Sleep that night . . .

11

The Government of Cairo

I promised my audience that they should meet Fatima the Deathly and now they have. I at least have not cheated them. I am known throughout all Cairo as an honest craftsman and a sure guide to the wonders of the place. Of course, I have my failings – I must just stop for a moment to get an insect out of my ear. No, it's just wax. See! Where, I wonder, does the stuff come from? There is certainly some admixture of dust from the streets, but the waxy stuff itself never came from the streets. It must come from inside the head, possibly from the brain. Interesting if it were from the brain . . . But I am rambling. As I was saying, I have my failings.

When I was taught my trade as a storyteller I was taught never to play games with my audience. Winks and suggestive gestures were unethical. The Qasasyoon, the Masters of the Guild of Storytellers, were strict. Starting out as apprentices in the art we lived in constant terror as we fumblingly told our stories, for it was an occasional practice among the Qasasyoon to insert themselves, heavily muffled and incognito, among the audiences of beginners, and if they judged that the luckless apprentice in question was tormenting the audience with his own cleverness or, worse, drawing attention to his own person in order to seduce, then the Qasasyoon would rise from the audience and, throwing off their burnouses, beat it out of the youth with sticks.

I never agreed with them on that. If my audience is dumb I will call out to them. I like to break off to talk to individuals in my audience, whereas my fellow Qasasyoon will point out that this is not only an error of style but it irritates the audience. People in the audience hate to be singled out in this way. They prefer to imagine themselves as invisible to the narrator. Now, the Qasasyoon were prepared to indulge them in that, but I have no patience with the fantasies of the audience. I am always acutely aware of my audience, and even at the risk of alienating them I will call out to them to bring them back to everyday reality – and me, Dirty Yoll.

The Qasasyoon and I agreed on very little and I had a hard training. I started out in the Tartar Ruins. I had no rebec player then, no boy to pass round coffee and collect the money, no throne to talk from – just a circle drawn in the dust. When the Ape was there I used him to attract an audience and, as I told my stories, I kept a sharp eye out for the Qasasyoon. I could usually spot them, even in their shrouds, from the way they tried to keep their eyes looking dopey and uncritical. Even so I was beaten many times in my youth as I struggled to refine the art of interpolation.

But enough of me. In the section which now follows I do not appear at all . . .

Qaitbay, the Sultan of Egypt, had a fear of falling asleep. Watched over by his *khassakiya* guards and his physician, he would lie there with his eyes closed, willing himself to go to sleep, determined not to move a muscle, but sick with fear inside.

Often on such nights he would rise from his couch of horror and, flinging on a *jallaba* for concealment, he would sally out from the Citadel, attended only by his poison taster and the black eunuch, Masrur. This was such a night. He emerged from the postern gate, sniffed the air and decided that he wished to visit the Father of Cats, and so the trio purposed northwards towards the older Fatimid part of the city. The Sultan eagerly drank in the squalor and the turmoil. Just outside the postern gate, their ways crossed with a leper carrying a sword. A little further on in the Tartar Ruins the Sultan and his attendants passed a young beggar sleeping on a wall and they noted that his mouth was rimmed with blood. Just outside the old part of the city at the Place of the Zuweyla Gate, they paused to watch a negro dancing in his cage.

Here near the Zuweyla Gate, it was crowded all through the night. The Sultan scrutinized the faces of the crowd quite closely, for he remembered that the Dawadar had told him the other day that he believed that for every face that it was possible to imagine God had created an individual to fit it. 'Yes,' the Sultan muttered to himself under his hood, 'there had to be someone with that sort of face.' The Dawadar's observation had impressed him; he found it oddly comforting.

Thinking upon this and similar lines, Qaitbay came to the House of Sleep, knocked and entered, unaware as he did so, that he was watched, as everyone in Cairo was, by some diseased old beggars.

The porter made deep obeisance to the Sultan as he and his companions swept through the gates of the House of Sleep. Then those gates swung shut behind them, for the Father of Cats would receive no more visitors that night. The Father came up from the cellars to receive them. He attempted to kiss the Sultan's foot, but the Sultan drew it under his robe and raised him up. The Sultan was ushered over to the colonnade on the far side of the courtyard where cushions were spread out for them, but the Sultan's attendants settled on mats near the gateway where they would spend the rest of the night quietly gossiping. Lit not for heat but for light, a brazier was brought out and placed in the centre of the courtyard. The night was breathlessly hot and the Sultan's companions sweated gently into their robes. The Father of Cats and the Sultan eased themselves down and silently regarded one another for a few moments. They were curiously similar – two lean and scraggy white-bearded old men, each accustomed to the exercise of absolute power.

'Peace be upon you, O Sultan.'

'And upon you, O Father of Cats.'

'Peace be upon your house.'

'And upon yours also.'

'How is your health?'

'Good. It is good, praise be to God.'

'Thanks be to God.'

'And how is your health?'

'Good, very good, praise be to God.'

'Thanks be to God.'

'And your house also?'

'All is well in my house, praise be to God.'

'Praises and thanks be to God.'

'And your house? How is it with your house?'

'Good as you can see. You honour it by your presence, praise be to God.'

'Thanks be to God. It is said, and truly said, that the hospitality offered in your house is so lavish and unstinting that the guest of the house forgets indeed that he is its guest and not its owner.'

'The Sultan is pleased to jest. The hospitality of my house, such as it is, is only the palest of the reflections of the reflections of the reflections of the hospitality and generosity of the Sultan, whose reputation in these respects extends to the limits of the known world and whose munificence is talked of even among the animals and djinn.'

'God has blessed me with many things, not least a reputation I have done all too little to deserve, but surely the greatest of all the blessings that he has showered upon me is the friendship of the Father of Cats?'

'I fear that the excellence of the Sultan's character is such that he will never acquire the companions that his countless merits deserve.'

'Such words of praise, from one so learned and wise, are already more than I deserve.'

'It is the times that make men wise. Under your benevolent rule, O Sultan, God has blessed Egypt and all men may become wise or rich as they choose.'

'It is said that the wise and the rich are the pillars of the virtuous state.'

'And it is said that a thorough knowledge of sound maxims is nine-tenths of wisdom.'

'Thanks be to God.'

'Thanks be to God.'

A couple of sighs and an uneasy silence.

'The hospitality of my house is yours. Would the Sultan be agreeable to my preparing for him that same drink that he has sampled here on previous visits?'

Another pause. A pair of cats came forward to be stroked. The Sultan knew that the Father was referring to the opiate sleeping draught that he always took when he came to stay the night at the Father's house.

'I should he delighted to receive some of your excellent hospitality.'

The Father clapped his hands and gave orders for the preparation of the compound before the Sultan's eyes. While this was going on, the Sultan gave a little cough and said, 'All things are well with me and my house, thanks to the blessings and protection of God, the most merciful and all wise.' He hesitated. 'Yet of late, I must confess, some trivial things, which at another time I should certainly have found amusing, are irritating me ever so slightly.'

'Ah.'

'There is the arrival in my town of the Laughing Dervishes, from whose childish tricks no man is immune. Where do these foolish men come from?'

'Ah.'

'Then some days ago my officers told me that they had arrested a man who was in all respects my double, with my face, my eyes and even my clothes.'

'Your double? They found your double? Be at peace my Sultan. Every human personality exists in two parts. I too have my double. There is the part of me that is sitting here talking with you and there is the part which I am not and of which you know nothing. It is very rare for one to become aware of the other, yet in a sense your life is only half a life without your double. I wonder if you know or have heard of Shikk?'

136

'The name is certainly familiar, but I cannot recall his having been presented to me.'

'Shikk is a half man. He has one eye, one ear, one arm and one leg.'

'I should like to meet this prodigy.'

'Alas. He is not one of your subjects. He and his fellow Saatih inhabit the Alam al-Mithal. But perhaps you will meet him. The Alam al-Mithal has come very close to earth. Shikk's case is extreme, yet even so it can be said that the man who is shadow-free has little to keep him on this earth.'

The Sultan did not conceal his mystification. 'But this man who looked like me, are you saying that I should not have had him executed for his impudent impersonation?'

'Oh, you had him executed!' (The Sultan did not perceive that the wicked old man was laughing in his beard at him.) 'As you know, the affairs of waking life are not my concern. I am not your Vizier or Dawadar. I am not the man to hold the power of life and death over your subjects. I am only a humble inquirer into life's mysteries.'

The drink was now ready and was brought in a brass beaker to the Sultan. Some cakes arrived on a dish. The Sultan snapped his fingers and the poison taster came from across the courtyard, tasted a couple of the cakes, then sipped from the cup. He made a face and passed it to the Sultan. The Sultan drank it, grimacing all the time. The stuff tasted foul. The poison taster returned to his place.

'Then there is likely to be trouble over our grazing rights on the Anatolian frontier. The Ottomans will dispute . . .'

The Father rudely cut him off. 'I tell you, I am not interested in all this. I am your sleep teacher. Tell me about your sleep and your dreams.'

Qaitbay sank back on one elbow. He was beginning to feel a little more relaxed.

'Father, I have been afraid to sleep for fear that I have the Arabian Nightmare.'

'You don't have it.'

'I don't?' The Sultan's voice was suspicious.

'I can tell. There is a look about its victim. The suffering it brings hollows a man out. Rest in peace. The Arabian Nightmare has not touched you yet.'

'There is something else in my dreams.'

'Ah.'

'It does not concern me directly save as your friend. I dreamt that I saw you from a great distance, coming out of the House of Sleep. You had seen me too and you were approaching to greet me. But another man came out of the House of Sleep and came creeping on behind you until there was only a handspan between him and you. I saw that he had a knife clenched in his fists, but I stood paralysed and powerless to save you as the man closed in to bury his knife in your back. So I counsel you, dear friend, take care. You have many enemies and I may not always be able to protect you . . .'

The Father stopped him there. He was furious. 'The poor old man! Why did you not save him? Why didn't you warn him? You can't afford to let friends die like that. What did you think you were doing?'

Qaitbay was offended. 'I told you. I was paralysed and, besides, it was a dream, an omen from the spirit that watches over us.'

'Tcha! What nonsense! In any case dreams are not omens. They do not predict events.'

But inwardly the Father was disturbed, for he knew that while dreams could not predict events, they could and did generate them. (Vane, listening concealed in the shadows, was also disturbed by the Sultan's dream.) The Father allowed no uneasiness to show, made an angry gesture and went on. 'But that dream was not about what you thought it was about. The old man you saw murdered was you, not me.'

'Me?'

'Yes. You. You only ever dream about yourself, however you disguise yourself. I stand for you in your dreams. I have that honour.'

'So I dreamed my own assassination?'

'No. You were dreaming about what you want. You only

ever dream about what you want, however disguised. In this case death stands for sleep, death's elder brother, deep dreamless sleep. It is your desire for this that has brought you here tonight. Nothing signifies what it seems to signify; everything points to something else. However, if you can remember dreams like that, you cannot possibly have the Arabian Nightmare, for happy oblivion invariably follows its tortures. What is more . . .'

'There is more?' The Sultan's eyes were beginning to fog over though he still sat erect.

'Of course there is more! To what purpose has my teaching been, if in your dreams you sit there, paralysed, watching your friends murdered, your wives raped and your palaces fall down? No. You must intervene, my lord, and intervene successfully. We shall try again tonight.'

Qaitbay had slumped right back on the cushions. He was too tired to respond to his teacher's fury. He wondered if it wasn't the truth that the Father was offended at being murdered in someone else's dream.

'You have not entirely resolved my doubts, O Father of Cats, concerning the Arabian Nightmare. Of course, when I am awake I know that God would never suffer the Protector of the Faithful to become its victim. It is only in my dreams that I have this fear, and in my dreams I am so confused that I can never quite succeed in demonstrating to myself that I have not got it.'

'It is only in your dreams that you are afraid that you have the Arabian Nightmare?' The Father looked pleased. 'That at last is a sign of progress. It is a sign that you are beginning to attain some faint degree of lucidity in your dreams. Now relax, close your eyes and remember, awake or asleep, you are the Sultan.'

Qaitbay did not close his eyes immediately and for a while the stars swung crazily above him, before drug-laden clouds blotted them from sight and the Father of Cats knelt beside him, whispering in his ear.

Towards morning, a little before the *fajr* prayer, the Father came down to the courtyard and, checking that the Sultan's companions were not looking, gave him a kick in the ribs. Then he recited to the still very groggy Sultan the old Arab proverb, 'He that sleeps one-third of the night has done as well as he that sleeps half the night, and he that sleeps all night will awaken an idiot.'

Pulling their woollen robes around them and shivering, the Sultan and his companions went out into the grey and misty streets of Cairo. Again they did not leave unobserved.

Later that day, while he was engaged in a difficult and ultimately unsuccessful dissection of a cat's brain, the Father paused wearily and wiped his instruments clean. He looked at the bloody cat. 'Each man kills the thing he loves.' Then he stared at Vane mockingly.

Vane wondered who was supposed to be loving and killing whom, but he scowled and said nothing.

The Father however was not to be deflected. 'Have you ever killed anyone, Vane?'

Vane, panicked into a patent lie, shook his head vigorously.

The Father's eyebrows shot up and he smiled slowly. 'You should! Kill a man, Vane. It is good to kill a man. He who has killed a man sleeps easily.'

Vane replied woodenly that he had always understood that murderers, having a bad conscience, slept very badly indeed. The Father denied that there was any truth in that fable of the market place and maintained that there were five things that a man had to do before he was fully a man: smoke opium, sleep with someone else's wife, learn a craft, go on pilgrimage to Mecca – and kill a man.

When the Father left the house that evening Vane, inspired by a sense of fun or by murderous impulses – it was not clear to him which – followed. The Father was walking slowly and apparently thinking deeply. Vane tiptoed behind him, bringing his knife out of his belt as he did so. And so they proceeded through street after street, an old man on his way to an unknown destination in the western part of the city, with Vane's knife constantly hovering an inch or two from his backbone. Vane had resolved that if the Father turned, he would thrust the knife in. Indeed, he would have no alternative. Then suddenly they were in the crowded open space in front of the Zuweyla Gate. The Father walked on into the crowds and Vane perforce slipped the knife back into his belt.

Then he doubled back towards the Ezbekiyya quarter, intending to spend the evening, as he had spent several previous evenings, in the almost certainly futile quest for the kiosk where Balian had said that he found Zuleyka, but some way short of the Ezbekiyya, to his delighted surprise, he saw or thought he saw the yellow robes and familiar form of Zuleyka.

'Zuleyka?'

But the smell of decay told him the answer before she spoke, revealing her face as she did so. 'No. A prostitute and a pearl are alike; both will deceive you in the dark. Will you walk with me?'

Vane matched his pace to Fatima's teetering steps. 'Let me touch you.'

'No. I am falling apart.'

'It is leprosy?'

'No. Would that it were . . .'

'I thought you had left Cairo. I went abroad in search of you.'

'No. I can never leave Cairo.'

'What do you do here? Consort with your sister?'

'No. We separated after our escape.'

'But Cornu and his brethren look after you. They are your friends?'

'No. I thought so at first but we are only temporary allies. I make my killings and they shelter me when I am pursued.'

'You kill at random?'

'No. I am surprised at you, Michael. I should have thought that you or your master would have made the connection by now. Emirs or beggars, openly or in secret, they were all my father's customers.'

141

'Grandfather, you mean.'

'No. His ideas and her body were my parents.'

'You were not always like this, so oracular.'

'No. Things are changing. My sister's mind continues to deteriorate and my body with it.'

'So will you kill the Father of Cats?'

'No. He is too strong for me. I dare not approach him. You must do it for me. If you ever loved me, kill him. Kill him and take over the House of Sleep. Kill him before worse befalls you all. If you ever loved me, do it. Ease the old man into his grave.'

It was on the tip of Vane's tongue to say that he still loved her, but he thought of those reports of murders done nightly in Cairo and the revolting details that were circulated about them. The shy girl he had once known had been replaced by an implacable ghoul. They walked on in silence for a while. Vane thought about his walk behind the Father earlier that evening. He had no fondness for his teacher and he did not deceive himself into thinking that his teacher had any fondness for him, but the thought of killing the Father revolted him. He was so lean and stringy, the skin all dry and leathery and the sharp bits of the bones almost poking through. He would have preferred to kill him in the dark while the old man slept, but he never seemed to sleep. Vane visualized him extended on the floor, eyes open and unwinking, glaring at the ceiling.

They were approaching the teeming thoroughfare of Bayn al-Qasreyn. She turned and raised her hand apparently in farewell. Vane was desperate. 'Come with me. I'll find you a place where we can stay.'

'No. I told you, I'm falling apart. I'm losing strength and colour rapidly.'

'Shall we meet again?'

'No. Look for my sister. You should have loved her. She lusts after you and says yes to all men.'

'Will I find your sister here?'

'No, not any more, but you will often find her in the City

of the Dead towards the end of the day.' And with that the murderess raised her hand again and slipped into the crowd.

Vane went back to the House of Sleep and that night set himself to dream again that he was once more in the hidden room. Zuleyka turned to him and asked if her invisible playmate might appear. He nodded and she turned to the wall, singing as she concentrated. Slowly some of the cracks detached themselves from the wall and hovered in the air like tendrils of smoke. Then slowly too these tendrils of smoke assumed form and filled with colour and Fatima, pale and shaking, stood before them, moulding herself and coagulating in the air. They tested her with riddles. Zuleyka teased the spirit and amused herself, but Vane, fascinated by Fatima's impassive round face and unfaltering answers, was drawn on by deeper feelings. Zuleyka ran her hands over him incessantly, feverishly, but he sat there not noticing, staring and staring at her imaginary playmate.

He dreamt also of the somnambulist at the Zuweyla Gate. Knife in hand, the somnambulist emerged from his cage. The street was unsteady under the huge negro's feet, and light and shadow swept through the enclosed space in irregular diagonals. Once the somnambulist's face turned and the torchlight showed the distended whites of his eyes and a tracery of silver sweat.

12

An Impression of a City Garden

Why, I ask myself, do I dislike Balian so much? Now that's odd! I might have expected to find ear wax in my fingernails but why earth? I start again. Why, I ask myself, do I dislike Balian so much? He is perfect material for my story, malleable and dreamy. I suppose that his virtues as material for a story must be considered as vices in a person. I judge him to be spineless and passive. He just lies there waiting to be entertained or, alternatively, unpleasantly surprised. I therefore have great pleasure in relating what happened to him next. Lie back on your couches, relax and listen! Hear what happened to him next . . .

Balian was in the Bayn al-Qasreyn, scavenging in the market for rotten fruit and vegetables – with little success, for the Arab boys were there too and they were more practised than he, diving on the decayed morsels like birds of prey. Then Balian became aware that someone, a woman, was looking at him and trying indeed to catch his eyes in hers. He raised his head to find a young woman, only lightly veiled, caressingly eyeing him over. The eyelids fluttered; she turned away and, with a barely perceptible movement of her hand, she motioned him to follow.

Soon they left the broad highway of the Bayn al-Qasreyn and moved up through stepped and cobbled alleyways that became progressively narrower and darker. In this part of Cairo it was as if one walked in perpetual night. Only the occasional ruin allowed light and space. The woman hurried on, never looking back, until at length they found themselves in a small courtyard. She knocked at a door set deep in the wall and cried out to those behind it. A Nubian of enormous proportions opened the door and she, stepping in, turned to beckon him to do likewise. Balian followed her into a garden. A beautifully tended walk between cypresses stretched before him, at the end of which was a summer house. Seated on the steps of the summer house sat a young lady, a girl almost, unveiled but heavily swathed in silks and embroidered brocades. A golden eye hung over her forehead and her hands were covered with jewelled rings. One hand supported her pensive head, while with the other she dangled a peacock feather fan.

She did not stir as Balian entered the garden but stared moodily into the distance. Although Balian's guide had disappeared, they were not alone in the garden, for an old man in a dirty white turban sat sunning himself in front of the summer house and the porter stood close behind Balian. He started towards the lady, but after some paces the porter's hand fell on his shoulder.

'Watch and listen,' said the Nubian.

An ape appeared from the shadows of the summer house. It wore a golden collar and chain and it stood erect and scratched itself. It bowed to the lady and then turned to Balian, displaying perfect rows of teeth. 'You are a Frank?' it said.

Balian's jaw hung loose with astonishment, and the lady tittered.

'Watch this,' said the ape and, turning to the lady, he began to address her or to recite rather, for Balian, listening carefully, determined that the ape was reciting poetry in Persian. It sounded very sonorous and grand. Then the ape approached the lady and stroked her hand with his paw, and, putting an arm around her shoulder, he whispered what were presumably endearments to the lady. She appeared amused at first, then bored and finally she offhanded him. Rolling his eyes at Balian, the ape said, 'Approach. My mistress wishes to know who makes a better lover, an ape or a Frank. Let us see if you can do as well as I.'

Balian felt the Nubian's grip on his shoulder relax and he advanced. He was dizzy with hunger and astonishment. The lady shifted her position. She looked at him encouragingly, but he found it difficult to speak. He had the sensation that he had done this before, had stood in this same garden and found difficulty in speaking to this same lady. Not necessarily very long before. Perhaps only a few seconds ago? Or was it not rather that one day in the distant future he would find himself in the same situation again? Or it might be that he had expected something exactly like this to happen. It was impossible to tell. The feeling was both vague and powerful.

'Lady,' he began at last. 'I am honoured to be your guest and gladly would I talk with you and perform whatsoever you wish, but first I beg you to give me something to eat and drink, for I have not eaten for many days and I am faint from hunger.'

Now the old man in the turban sat upright and spoke. 'The lady wishes you to seduce her with fine words and gestures. She offers herself to you, if you will but persuade her, and she is easy to be persuaded. Hurry up. She only offers herself once.'

Yet Balian had the sensation that she would offer herself again – or was it that she had already done so? He wished to argue. 'Gladly . . .'

'Surely you can do better than an ape?'

'Lady, I do not know what you want of me, but for the love of God give me food.'

'He is no good,' said the ape, sitting beside her, and he began to gibber triumphantly.

Balian tried to rush at them, but he saw from the corner of his eye the porter moving. He turned and the porter's fist smote him between the eyes.

When he came to he was not in the beautiful garden, but dumped beside a fountain on a public way in another part of

146

Cairo altogether. His head ached abominably and he was still hungry. Shall I ever find that door and see that lady again? he asked himself. He fell to pondering the performance of the amazing ape. What did it mean? He had read that the philosopher, the blessed Niko of Cologne, maintained that apes and men were closely related. In his *De senectute naturae* Niko argued that apes were descended from men, that apes were the barbarous and degenerate offspring of men, just as men were the barbarous and degenerate descendants of the perfect Adam in the Garden. Some vestigial ability to speak, Niko claimed, had been reported by travellers who had observed certain tribes of apes in the heart of Africa . . .

This chain of thought was interrupted by a funeral procession. A band of *mashaliyat* – scavengers and washers of the dead – were coming down the road towards him. Their shoulders supported a plank. A cotton-shrouded corpse was precariously balanced on the plank. Hoping to beg a crust of bread from them, Balian rose dizzily to his feet. Since he blocked their way, they stopped and set down their load.

'It is an act of charity we perform.' Their leader jerked his thumb behind him as he addressed Balian. 'We bury those we find dumped outside the Citadel, the scourings from the Arqana – still there are pickings to be had.' And, so saying, he reached into the voluminous folds of one of his sleeves and produced a small box of intricate oriental construction. 'Two dinars to you. A nice piece of work. I can see you have an eye for it.'

'Do I look like the owner of two dinars?'

Their leader shrugged. 'In this city few people are as they appear.'

'A crust of bread, I beg you, or is your charity only for the dead?'

They all shook their heads. 'We have no food to give. Yet follow us. We are going to the City of the Dead. You will surely find food aplenty there.'

Somewhat mystified, Balian followed them. By the time they reached the City of the Dead it was late afternoon and the sun of late afternoon warmed Balian's bones while the rising breeze cooled his skin. The view into the City of the Dead was extraordinary. Scores of families and couples picnicked among the mausolea. The *mashaliyat*, with Balian following, threaded their way between the jolly families and the tombs. They were trying to sell the box and he was begging for food, both without success. Suddenly they heard a voice, above their heads and to the left. They were being called back. Something yellow was indistinctly glimpsed in the shadow of a marble pavilion. Only when he too moved into shadow was Balian able to recognize that it was Zuleyka sitting cross-legged on the stone platform of the pavilion.

'To me! To me, scavengers! To me, you night-soil men!'

The *mashaliyat* hastily dropped their load, letting the corpse roll off the plank into the sand, and they hurried over to her. Balian had thought that she was wanting the *mashaliyat* to bring him to her, but as he staggered on behind them he became aware that she had eyes only for the box.

'The box! My Chinese box! It's come back to me!'

There was a conference at the edge of the platform. She shook coins from her yellow robes into the outstretched palms of the *mashaliyat* and the box was passed up to her. They then returned to their corpse and, hoisting it up once more, proceeded to the burying ground.

At last Zuleyka turned to Balian. 'This is my box, you know. It was stolen from me.'

Balian looked up at it. 'Is there something to eat in the box?' he asked hopelessly.

'Something to eat in the box?' She echoed him cryptically, then reached down her arm to him. 'You too have come back to me. You haunt me like a ghost.'

'A hungry ghost.'

Then he found himself sitting with her on the platform. Zuleyka had a basket of sugared zellabies with her. She called to one of the keepers of the tombs and paid him to bring them some coffee. Balian reached over for the zellabies, but her hand caught his wrist. 'No. You shall not eat until you tell me all that has been happening to you.'

He protested, but he was forced to tell her, though he related the adventure as briefly as possible. Only then was his hand free to lunge towards the food.

'I don't know. Sex with apes is very fashionable in certain circles.'

He paused in his chewing to protest, 'But the ape talked!'

'True . . . perhaps it was an enchantment.'

'So the ape really was a man and the lady a sorceress?'

'Perhaps. It is more likely that the ape was a sorcerer and the lady his mate disguised in human form. Knowledge of magic is not unknown among the animals.'

'So I almost made love to an ape!' Balian shuddered.

'Who but an ape would desire you in your present ragged state? But as usual you lost your opportunity by asking for too much.'

It grew cold. The picnickers were beginning to leave the City of the Dead and the beggars and the birds moved in behind them, foraging for their crumbs. Gorged on the last of the sweetmeats, Balian let himself fall back and closed his eyes.

'You believe the whole adventure was a dream, don't you?' Even as he asked he was drifting, but he thought that he heard her reply.

'Of course. That was the Ape.'

'What is the Ape?'

This time he heard no reply. It was necessary to find sleep, even if only in nightmare.

He was roused briefly by shouting. Zuleyka was gone. Instead the pavilion was surrounded by Venetians and others from the caravanserai. Balian's nose started to spurt blood once more, and he closed his eyes again so that he might not see it. Drowsily he heard the Italians arguing over him. They had come to the City of the Dead that afternoon after hearing rumours that one of their number, having mysteriously vanished, was dead and was being buried here. Some wanted to go on looking for him. Others, though, thought that Balian looked close to death and wished to carry him back to the safety of the caravanserai. Balian was only vaguely interested. The wrangle continued for a while. Then he felt strong arms lift him.

An obscure *pietà*, a scarred Italian sailor bearing a nightmare-ridden youth, stood briefly silhouetted against the mortuary tombs. Then the sailor moved off, carrying his charge towards the caravanserai.

13

From the Zuweyla Gate
to Mount Muqattam

One can break off here as well as anywhere. I have heard stories from the West told and I have listened to them with amazement, scarcely able to grasp that they were stories, so fast was their passage as they sped towards their determined ends like flights of arrows. In the leisurely, sleeping East it is different. Consider the story you are hearing rather as a set of beds loosely strung together – I am sorry, I meant to say beads, of course – a set of beads loosely strung together, just like those rosaries which we have seen bored old men sit fingering outside cafés. No, rosary is not quite right. Better to see it as a string figure – one of those things children play with, plucking at the loops with their fingers to create transitory shapes. I have heard them called cat's cradles. Cat's cradles, rosaries, beds and arrows, what on earth am I talking about? The point is that you can break off here as well as anywhere. You have heard enough tonight. For God's sake, stop! Take some rest. Sleep. What follows is hard . . .

One orange goes up. Another descends. The movements of the jugglers are so very slow. An acrobat spins with almost infinite leisure over his bar. It is very late and the crowds are beginning to thin outside the Zuweyla Gate. The Father of Cats passes from booth to booth. Here is the man who does the rope trick. Here is the gnostic escapologist who wriggles free from any body he may be trapped in. Here is the fire walker who curiously rejoices not because he does not feel pain but because he feels it only in his feet. Here is the mentalist

– a boy who sits on a small wooden stool and achieves orgasms in public by the sheer unaided power of thought. Here is a man in a dirty white turban with an ape on a chair: what they do is not clear. Here is the bear dancer. Here is the fakir who inflicts more pain upon the spectators than he does upon himself as he skewers his cheeks and lips with heavy weighted needles.

And there is more – Bash Chalek, the giant in chains, the shadow theatre, the man who eats pebbles, the bottle imp, the tight-rope walker, the hermaphrodite. This is the Circus of Ordeals. The performers are mostly Mongols or Indians. Nightly they celebrate their shaman's mysteries of death, resurrection and fertility. The girl is bisected, the boy dismembered, the rabbit clubbed to death in its bag – to emerge with the clash of cymbals, living and whole again. Nightly these professional heroes prove themselves against water, fire and steel and demonstrate man's ability to thrive upon pain. Their audience know they are being fooled. That is what they are paying for.

At length the Father of Cats reached the cage of Habash. The lettering over the bars reads: 'See and question Habash, the slave who walks and talks in his sleep. Deaths predicted. Loved ones found.' As he reached the cage the Father of Cats thrust a cup through the bars. Habash did not move. He looked exhausted and was covered in welts and bruises, injuries sustained while crashing against the bars in his sleep. For a long time they contemplated each other silently.

Finally the Father of Cats appeared to lose his patience. 'Well?'

'The cup does not say "Drink me".' Habash folded his arms.

The old man flared up. 'I say drink it.' His eyes bore down on Habash's. 'Drink it and listen to what I have to say.'

Habash sipped at the liquid reluctantly.

'I have lost a book . . .'

'I did not take it.' Though frightened, Habash was still bent on goading the Father of Cats, but the Father, satisfied that

Habash recognized his mastery, had reverted to his customary serenity.

'I did not say that you did. As a matter of fact, the book was stolen from Vane by an Italian spy, Giancristoforo Doria, on the way from Alexandria to Cairo. The book he stole contains within it the source of all stories and the revelation of the mystery of the Arabian Nightmare. Doubtless the Italian intended to sell it to the storyteller known as Dirty Yoll, or to Yoll's patrons, but he was arrested by the Mamlukes before he could do so. The book, however, fell into the hands of a young Englishman. The Englishman's baggage at the Ezbekiyya caravanserai has been thoroughly searched, but both he and the book have disappeared. Now, that book must not fall into the hands of my enemies. You must find it for me.'

Still the negro did not reply, but regarded him quietly. Sullenness was giving way to placidity.

The Father of Cats pressed on. 'Only you can help me for you dream upon your feet. The cup you drank from contained a powerful sleeping draught. You will sleep for a night and a day and perhaps another night and in that time you will search through Cairo in your dreams and surely bring my book back to me. You are already feeling very sleepy.'

Habash did not really agree, but somehow it was easier and pleasanter not to dispute it. He allowed his eyelids to droop comfortably.

The Father seeing that Habash, despite his will, was indeed drifting off, accelerated his speech. 'As soon as I see that you have entered the dream state, I shall open the cage. To find the book is a simple affair. It is a matter of imposing the will on the dream. The Alam al-Mithal wishes to fulfil all men's wishes. Just as I have imposed my will upon yours, so you must impose your will on the Alam al-Mithal. You must bring the book to me here.'

Suddenly Habash slumped. He was sleeping. The Father waited patiently. While he waited, he drained the dregs of the sherbet, for he had sent Habash off to sleep on sugared water and suggestions. Habash's eyeballs rolled. He was beginning to dream. As if drawn up by invisible threads, he rose from the floor of the cage. The Father turned the key, opened the door and gently guided the somnambulist out.

Habash shambled out of the fairground, the Father following. As he reached the Bayn al-Qasreyn he broke into a run, or perhaps he broke into an imitation of a man running, for his fists and arms thrust backwards and forwards, his knees were raised high and his breath was sharply exhaled, but he moved oh so slowly. Always the same houses. There was infinite time to contemplate those houses with their crazy façades, at once makeshift and overwrought, kite-shaped doors and pell-mell roofs and those alleyways and arcades, deceitful perspectives and zigguratic staircases. The moon washed the walls in a dreadful white which showed up the dirt and cracks like plague spots.

Habash looked back and gave a luminous, moonlit smile, for he knew that he was being pursued and he knew that, in the end, there was something reassuring about being pursued. Someone, somewhere, wanted him. The Father of Cats, running behind, caught the smile. The Father had intended to follow Habash running in his dreams, but he observed now how light and dark daubed themselves on to the buildings in thick, jagged, emotional strokes, how the town cracked and bent under pressure, how space and houses warped and buckled and formed themselves around the running figure of the black man, and he realized the force of the terrible energy that he had released and which now discharged itself uncontrollably into the streets of the city, and he knew that he dared follow the runner no further. He stopped and returned to the House of Sleep.

Balian dreamt of tilting streets and falling towers. He continued to sleep that night and most of the following day. His sleeps grew ever longer. When he awoke the pilgrims crowded round.

'Do you want a doctor? We'll find you one in the Coptic Quarter.'

'I want a priest.'

They nodded approvingly and one of the friars thrust his way forward – that same one that Balian had heard preach on the day of his arrival on the dangers of tattooing. They withdrew into a corner of the caravanserai. The pilgrims assumed that Balian wished to be shriven lest he die, yet Balian did not really expect to die; he lived on fevered energies, and the heart pounded with heavy hammer strokes within his ghostly body. He hoped rather to be absolved from his vow to go to St Catherine's in Sinai. Also he wished to challenge the friar.

'Bless me, Father, for I have sinned.'

'Bless you my child. When did you last go to confession and attend mass?'

'The time has passed and I have been sick; I cannot tell. Not since we embarked at Venice.'

'And what sins have you committed since then?'

'None save venial ones, but it is not for my sins that I need your counsel and the Church's protection –'

'You presume too much. I must be acquainted with the nature and frequency of sinning before we can agree whether it was venial or not.'

'Perhaps, but I am threatened with great dangers, dangers not of my seeking nor my making. I am a pilgrim, vowed to Christian endeavour and good devotions this six months. But the Devil visits me with evil dreams and I have come close to the sin of despairing in God many times since I arrived in Egypt.'

'What dreams are these?'

Balian tried to see the friar's face properly before he spoke again but, having failed: 'I dream of entering a city that looks like Cairo, yet is utterly false. I dream of leaving it or trying to, but I am impeded by two agents of Satan called the Father of Cats and Michael Vane. I dream I am awake and I am not and I dream of a temptress, a woman called Zuleyka, who seduces me from chastity, and when I awake from these dreams my face courses with blood.'

'So you dream of fornicating with Zuleyka . . . and is there any emission of semen during or after these dreams?'

'No. I don't think so.'

'I see. And have you nothing more of gravity that weighs on your conscience?'

'No.'

'Well that is good.' A long silence, then, 'St Augustine has it that the possible origin of a dream is threefold. First, there are dreams that come from God and are sent to guide us; second, dreams which come from the Devil with which that wily Prince seeks to seduce us, though he never can succeed in tempting even the soul of a man that is asleep, unless there be in that man's soul a predisposition to corruption; third, dreams that are called natural, which come from the vapours of the inner fantasy and which are swayed by where a man lies and what he has eaten and many things besides, and they signify nothing at all.'

'So God is tormenting me, or I am predisposed to corruption, or I have been eating the wrong foods. Which is it?' Balian could not keep the irritation from his voice.

A sigh. 'You must know, my son, that none of the fathers and doctors of the Church condemns the dream in itself. We are taught that when at night the temperature falls, then man's animal spirit retires into the innermost part of the body, to the seat of fantasy whence arise dreams. Such a dream therefore is a thing of nature and cannot be condemned in itself. Yet, being natural, it is not perfect. Close study of the Scripture teaches us, I believe, that Jesus, who was Perfect Man as well as God, never dreamt.

'There are several grounds for believing this. First, Jesus never slept, and how can a man who never sleeps have dreams? That Jesus never slept we may adduce from the fact that while the Gospels give us frequent reports of the sleep of his disciples, he is never mentioned sleeping. And did not Jesus commune with Moses and Elias on Mount Tabor while Peter,

James and John slept? And, secondly, on the question as to whether Our Lord ever dreamt, must we not suppose that his Divine Nature and Perfect Virtue made him proof against the discomforts and agues of the body and the poisons of bad food? And how should he who came to bring the Truth that shall set us free himself fall prey to dreaming, which is delusion, even supposing that he ever slept, when the best opinion is that he did not? Moreover, whereas as *Proverbs* has it, 'Drowsiness shall clothe a man in rags,' did he not come to bring us the wealth of the Eternal Kingdom?'

Balian muttered that, yes, he supposed it was so.

'Now, to return to your case, I must tell you two problems present themselves: first, whether your dreams are natural or diabolic in origin; secondly, having determined them to be the one or the other, if they are diabolic in origin we must ask why you have been elected by Satan for the visits of his ministers, whereas if they are natural in origin we must still determine whether you have not in these dreams (though it is admitted that on the moral plane they are meaningless in themselves), whether you have not yielded to some temptations that have presented themselves, not by design but *per accidens*, and then, if this were not the case and if the dreams were not shown to be diabolic in origin, then I might shrive you, assuming all the other appropriate conditions to be fulfilled. But if by any chance –'

Balian groaned and then started hastily coughing. 'Father, there is another matter I wish to raise with you also. I wish to be absolved of my vow to go to St Catherine's in Sinai.'

'On what grounds?'

'On the grounds that I have already visited her in my dreams.' Then Balian described to the friar the nightmare he had had about the martyrdom of St Catherine. 'Well, Father, is that not sufficient?' It was impudent but worth trying. The friar hesitated, then raised his hand with the fingers fanned out.

'No. For five reasons. First, because it is more correct to say that she visited you than that you visited her. Second, because we have not been guaranteed that this was a veridical dream, and demons may impersonate saints as easily as serpents. Third, even granted that it was St Catherine who visited you, you were asleep when she came knocking and this showed a lack of respect towards her; all the more reason that you should fulfil your vow properly. Fourth, if one grants that the merits of good works may be earned in dreams, so also then may the wages of sin, and you tell me that since then you have fornicated in your dreams, so cleanse yourself in pilgrimage. Fifth, I do not have the authority to absolve you of your vow; only his Holiness the Pope has that.'

'The last reason alone would have been sufficient,' murmured Balian faintly.

'Not so. Every moral act requires four effective causes and a fifth cause which is teleological, just as the Bible may be read in its entirety on four levels; tropological, anagogical –'

But here Balian cut in. 'Well, Father, you cannot absolve me from my pilgrimage but, tell me, am I guilty of any sin, awake or asleep?'

'It is good of you, my son, to bring me back to the matter in hand. The extent to which concupiscence and its guilt can be imputed to a man who has taken pleasure in vice, asleep or even awake in his mind's eye, as it were, is a vexed one.'

'If I am to be judged guilty of every sin I have committed in my bed, then I am damned indeed.' A wave of melancholy swept over Balian.

The learned friar continued. 'Certainly I should not say that your chastity was weakened by your being seduced, while you slept, by a phantasm of Zuleyka, and the fact that you experienced no emission of semen is probably also a point in your favour, although I can conceive it might be argued that the discharges of blood you mention might be characterized as another type of nocturnal emission (medical evidence of the passion of *ira* rather than of *voluptas*), yet this, I imagine, would be difficult to sustain, for, as Galen teaches us, while blood is numbered as one of the fluids of life, yet it does not contain within it the seeds of life themselves.'

'So I am free of sin?'

'Ah, I did not say that. I suggested that there might be grounds for arguing that you have not sinned in your sleep, but you yourself are eaten up by sin. We have noted that since you were brought back to the caravanserai you have slept a day, a night and half a day. We have noted also, with regret, your desire to discontinue your pilgrimage. Sloth has you in his hellish grip, and sloth is the deadliest of all the sins, for, I remind you, Christ set us all an example by never sleeping. Did he not say, 'The fox has his lair, the birds have their nests, but the Son of Man has nowhere to lay his head'? Now, to return to the question of repetition and the related one of the multiplicity of causes, why is it that an account of the same incident in Our Lord's ministry may be given two, three, even four times in the narrative of the Gospels? It is because sufficient cause –'

'Father, please. I am afraid. Have you ever heard of the Arabian Nightmare?'

A look of dislike crossed the friar's face. 'Everybody talks about that now in Cairo. It has become in their mouths just another of the Egyptian fairytales.'

'It is a fairytale?'

'No, well, perhaps not. I have heard some priests talk of the Arabian Nightmare in different and Christian terms. According to some of these, it is the ordained punishment for the Unforgivable Sin against the Holy Ghost.'

'Father, I have never understood what the Unforgivable Sin against the Holy Ghost was. Surely no man knows?'

'Yes, and no man knows for sure what the Arabian Nightmare is. There is a certain symmetry in the arrangement,' said the friar wrily.

'But you do not accept this view?'

'I do not. In any event it is nothing for a Christian to be afraid of. It is only pain. There is nothing in infinite suffering that hinders the practice of a devout Christian life.'

'But what is the Arabian Nightmare?'

'A truer story relates its origins to Lazarus. You are familiar with the history of the Knights of Lazarus?'

'I have never even heard of them.'

'All that a good Christian needs to know is that they are a holy order of knights who, though grievously stricken with leprosy, war for our Faith against Mahometanism. What we learn from this is that their example –'

'What should a bad or an indifferent Christian know about them?'

'My son, take an example from their devotion and forget your little aches and pains. The example –'

'What have they to do with the Nightmare?'

'The Nightmare is infinite. According to Niko –'

'What has the order to do with Lazarus?'

'He founded the order of leper knights. If I may return to Niko –'

'What is Lazarus to the Arabian Nightmare?'

'Lazarus lay ten days and nights in the grave before our Lord Jesus Christ raised him from it. By this we must understand that Jesus . . . No, I see you have no ear to hear about Our Lord. Understand, then, that when Lazarus rose from the grave and walked among men again, he carried with him an insect which had lain with him ten days and nights. This insect was one that haunted, for preference, graves and cemeteries. All dead men have their thoughts devoured by this creature; it eats through the brain and makes its home in the imaginative faculty, though the corpse, being dead, is not aware of its hungry appetite. Need I add that this insect is not to be understood literally? According to the blessed Niko, it is but a metaphor, signifying the fears of a Christian soul that it may stray into error through ignorance.'

'Thank you, friar. That is what I wanted to know. It is just a Christian parable then.'

'Just a parable! Just a parable! Christian parables are truer than the truth. Suffer no illusion, my son. There are leper knights in Cairo now. The Arabian Nightmare is here in Cairo now. It may be that even at this moment, by the curse of

Lazarus, the torments of death are being laid upon the couches of the living. In the midst of life we are –'

Balian had lost interest. Something had been dimly worrying him, something about the way in which the friar had earlier pronounced the name of Zuleyka. The confidence with which the friar had pronounced the name fanned his suspicions.

'Do you know the woman Zuleyka whom I spoke of earlier?'

'Er – I know her? Why, what man can truly say that he knows another man or indeed woman? To know oneself according to the ancient –'

'It sometimes seems to me that anyone of any importance in this city knows everybody else of importance – importance, that is to say, in my history.'

'Your history! What is your history that you pride yourself on it?'

'Father, I told you, I think, that my dreams seem real to me. That is because my whole life has come to seem like a dream to me, shadow theatre, a mystery played by puppets, a card game in which I am the trump.'

'A game? A play about you? Arrogance as well as sloth!'

'Perhaps, but it's what I feel. The puppeteer pulls my strings; those who know how to play my card play it – the Father of Cats, Yoll, probably you yourself. Only I, it seems, am not a player.'

'This may be an indication of excessive humility rather than of arrogance . . . We shall see. What is this charade which you believe we are all playing at?'

'Not a charade exactly, but the principles that divide men here are unreal. Vane says that he works for Christendom and takes money from the Sultan of Egypt; Yoll also says that he works for Christendom, yet he works to thwart the Father of Cats and Vane. Everybody, whomever he serves, seems to conspire to prevent me leaving Cairo. Everybody plays games with me. I think that you are one of the players. You are playing a game with me now.'

The friar sighed and said, 'Follow me.'

Thinking that the friar was taking him to the altar at the far end of the caravanserai, Balian did so; but, pausing only at the gate to allow the friar to slip a coin into the extended hand of an Arab boy and whisper what was doubtless a blessing in his ear, they went out south through the streets of the city, heading in the direction of the Citadel. When, however, they drew near to its outer walls and began to climb, the friar led him a little to the east along the edge of the walls, and then they were scrambling up the slopes of Mount Muqattam towards its summit, which loomed over the highest walls of the Citadel. As they ascended, the scrubby sycamores and palmettos to be found on the lower slopes thinned and then disappeared. Little showers of stones and sand were dislodged with every step. The friar climbed without ceasing until just short of the summit, and Balian followed, dizzy and breathless. The sun had set, though some clouds high in the west were still fired by its rays. The city was already plunged in twilight. They stood looking down upon it.

It seemed that the friar must speak, that the friar himself must confess and admit that there was no struggle between good and evil in the World, that there were not two parties to the struggle but only one, that party being of those who knew, and that those who did not know were their playthings. It seemed to Balian that this confident and erudite friar must admit him to the secret doctrine.

At last the friar did speak. 'Do you see the city below us? Do you see it? In the evening's dimness does it not seem to you like a child's toy or a gaming board and the people thronging its streets like tiny dolls or even insects? Up here do not their struggles and their ideals and their passions seem ridiculous?'

Balian nodded.

'So I thought it would. My son, in entertaining such thoughts you are playing with temptations as great and as damnable as those which Lucifer showed to Our Lord when he showed him all the kingdoms of the World in a moment of time. Think now, though, that whereas the Devil offered

Our Lord the reality of temporal lordship over all those kingdoms, he is offering you only an illusory feeling of superiority over them. The illusion is one of distance. You should see a city of souls, not a gaming board; you should see men, not insects. You are young and your delusions are youthful arrogance. You think other men's souls do not matter because you cannot believe in your own. Things are real and important whether you think they are or not. The time for games and mysteries is over. You have work to do. You made a vow to go on pilgrimage. I am privileged to know that you also gave an undertaking to the King of France; you must fulfil that too, for the King must have information on the strength of the infidel regiments. So go back down there and do the work you have undertaken. Idleness is your curse; it is not by chance that you have been afflicted in your sleeping.'

'Ah, but how do I know that I am not sleeping now, and how do I know that you are not the Devil tempting me in my sleep?'

The friar got down on his knees. Balian thought that he was going to kiss his feet, but the friar did no such thing. Instead he began to beat his head rhythmically on the ground, crying as he did so, 'This is real! This is no dream! This is real!' When at length he raised his head thin trickles of blood were coming down from the crown.

'Yes, I see now,' said Balian, embarrassed and frightened. Balian left him sitting on the slope and climbed wearily down towards the town.

14
A Tour of the Streets Ending
in an Underground Chapel

*In my youth I visited the Circus of Ordeals almost every day. It was
a favourite haunt of mine – it still is. How I envied those jugglers
able to keep so many balls in the air at once! How I wished to be an
acrobat! An acrobat or a clown. How pleasant to have called it to
remembrance now! But I became a storyteller instead and I
digress . . .*

Now the dark was coming on fast. The air broke up into an
infinity of pearls of greyness. He was in a sombre mood as he
came down the mount. All of a sudden, at the bottom of the
slope, he was aware of a hand resting gently on his shoulder.
He spun round and had time to catch the vision of two white-
faced men standing to either side of him before he started to
run. They too came running behind in pursuit. Balian was
heading north towards the area of the Tartar Ruins and aiming
beyond them for the crowded and lively parts of the city,
where he hoped his pursuers would be obliged to call off the
chase.

Juices of fear jetted round his heart, yet he was conscious
also of a strange elation. Now that the hunt was on, he felt
freer than at any time since he had entered the city.

How many times had he not been hunted in this way in his
dreams? Hunts that invariably ended with his waking with a
full bladder – or more recently with a bleeding nose. He would
have laughed if he had had the breath for it. Sand rose up in

clouds about his heels. It seemed to him that he moved with terrifying speed; the truth was that he was weak from many days' loss of blood and his run was scarcely more than a lope. The curious thing was that his pursuers' pace was no faster as they struggled on behind him, their white robes fluttering in the air.

As Balian passed through the Tartar Ruins, a crowd of children ran alongside him for a while, laughing and shouting and making it utterly impossible that Balian should give his pursuers the slip. After a while the children, unable to draw a response from Balian, dropped away, but when he looked behind him he discovered that the number of his pursuers had increased to four. He was now moving across vast empty spaces of rubble and thornbush. All along the edge of the horizon the barking and yelping of packs of wild dogs could be heard. He knew that they could not possibly be hunting him, yet their noise gave Balian the feeling that, however strong his exhilaration, however fast and cunning his movements, the night could end only with his capture.

He was coming into an inhabited area now, a quarter where many of the wealthy merchants resided, an area of wide streets and tall, monolithic façades which hung over him in the dying light like mountain faces. Balian moved through these architectural chasms, breathing with difficulty.

If only he could find a patrol of the watch. At one point he would have swerved off to the left, down a street which would have taken him back to the caravanserai, but there his way was blocked by two more of the ragged huntsmen. Once he imagined that he saw one standing signalling from a rooftop, directing the hunt. The streets were getting narrower; often they were alleyways broad enough only for one man with comfort. Ways off were often blocked. He had forgotten that large parts of the city, the market places and bazaars would be barricaded at night and locked against thieves. His choices were diminishing. He was entering a part of the city which was unfamiliar to him. Finally there were no choices at all, as he found himself running down a cul-de-sac.

He crashed to a stop against a studded door set in the wall and hammered on it. 'Let me in. Help! Help!' To his amazement the door was opened almost immediately and he fell inside, retching drily. The door swung closed behind him.

For a few moments he lay on the ground with his eyes shut, willing his panicky heart to slow down. Then he rolled over, opened his eyes and looked up to see, shadowed against the sky, a young man standing over him. In the dimness he saw that he was in a garden, a rich man's garden with rows of tamarinds, fig trees and carobs and decoratively plastered walls. His heart slowed eventually. He could hear nothing of his pursuers, but only voices, coming presumably from the women's quarters, and the whine of mosquitoes. It was very quiet.

'Who is the man who bangs at my gate at this hour? Who asks hospitality of Ismail ibn Umail? Was the watch after you?'

'I am Balian of Norwich, a poor Christian pilgrim. I was –'

'Oh, a Christian!'

'I do not know who is after me. They must be outside your door now. They are not the watch and truly I should be very grateful if you would summon the watch for my protection.'

'My walls and my servants are protection enough if need be. But what do they want from you?'

'I don't know.'

'You must have done something.'

'I was coming down from Muqattam, where I had been talking to one of our priests, when two men, but there are more now, tried to detain me. However, I escaped their grasp and ran, and fate and my running brought me here.'

'And they chased you all the way from Muqattam to here! How intriguing . . . Yusuf! Ibrahim! Come here. Ibrahim, bring this man a drink. You sit here and drink this. Get your breath back.' The young man patted Balian on the back sympathetically. 'I'll tell you what we are going to do. You rest a little while. Then we are going to have some sport. We'll let you out of one of the side gates and give you a start. Then Yusuf, Ibrahim and I are coming after you. Then we'll see who catches you first, us or your friends from Mount Muqattam. What fun we shall have!'

'Bastard!'

Balian continued to swear at him hysterically, but after only a little while his host clapped his hands excitedly and said, 'Come, the hunt is up!' and Balian was carried, squirming and kicking, to one of the side gates and cast out into the street. He could only run one way down it. At the other end a group of ragged men were casting about, stooping slightly and raising their faces to the sky, as if they were trying to sniff him out. When they saw him they gave chase. The passageways between the gardens of the rich were very narrow and unevenly cobbled. This second time Balian found it difficult to run at all. His rest, short as it had been, had stiffened his limbs. Once he thought he saw Ismail coming up behind him but only once, otherwise it was always the men in white who were moving up to take him. At every corner a choice, slipping and dodging in the darkness under the walls; each choice was more difficult and made the next choice more difficult yet.

He was too tired to hide, too tired to take decisions. His legs were wobbling under him now and could not support him. He threw himself against a door lintel and clung to it. He shouted for it to open but this time it did not. They crowded round him and prised his grip apart. Somebody dragged a big stone over and brought it down upon his head. He was hit twice before he lost consciousness.

Consciousness recovered, his lids were being pulled back, a wall of fire burned before his eyes and two strange eyes peered into his. 'He is alive!' The torches withdrew a little and, looking up, he could see that a pattern of brick vaulting swirled in an architectural vortex over his head and that he was in a chapel. Since there were no windows, he supposed that it might be underground. Half a dozen men sat around him, among them Yoll and Bulbul, but the leading figure had to introduce himself.

'I am Jean Cornu, Grand Master of the Poor Knights of St

Lazarus, chosen emissary of his Holiness the Pope in Egypt. The others here need no introduction, some because you have met them already, others because they do not wish your memory to be burdened with their names.' The men in white lowered their faces. Balian made no response and Cornu resumed. 'We have taken the opportunity of your loss of consciousness to examine you. For a while we thought we were examining a dead man . . . fatigue, loss of blood, that mark on your head. I imagine you were glad to be caught.' Cornu stood up and started to pace about the chapel around the others with measured steps. 'Here let me say that it pains me that my men beat you. I had not intended that, but then we had not expected that you would run from us like that. We came looking for you as friends and fellow Christians. I had thought that I was the Good Shepherd fetching in a stray from his flock.' His smile was without humour. 'As you must have guessed, the friar took you up on the mount for us; we did not want to come for you in the caravanserai.'

Balian waited until Cornu reached the end of the chapel and turned again. 'What do you want with me?'

'A good question! The answer is nothing. A better question would be, "What did we want with you?" and the answer to that would have been that we wished to examine you to determine if you were the expected Messiah or if you had the Arabian Nightmare or, if neither of these things was so, why the Father of Cats has taken such an interest in you.'

'And what have you discovered?'

Now the friar entered the room. Like Balian's, his forehead was still covered in blood. Cornu ignored both the friar's arrival and Balian's question.

'It is God's work that we do here. Among our duties are the protection of Christendom, by force of arms if necessary, and the succour of the sick. Our present task in Cairo involves both of these.' He turned again. His pacing, Balian observed, made everyone uneasy. Only Bulbul, who had withdrawn to a corner to write, was able to ignore it.

'I am told that you came to Cairo with a mission given to

you by the French to spy out the strength and deployment of the Sultan's legions and the quality of their equipment.'

Balian nodded.

'What have you done to fulfil your mission?'

There could be no answer to this. Cornu's lip curled unmistakably.

'Well, it is not important. There are bigger affairs afoot now. It is true also that you have tried several times to leave Cairo and failed?'

Balian nodded. Cornu was behind him now.

'Why was that?'

Balian croaked in his nervousness, 'The Dawadar refused me a visa to leave. Nevertheless I tried to leave without the permission of the authorities, but things went wrong. I fell ill. Even so I made many efforts to walk out of the city, but I was alone and I lost my way. Sometimes enemies barred my path and I was unaided. Sick, I was shunned by my fellow Christians, yet I pray nightly to St Catherine and all the saints that they will assist me to leave this place. Many times I have set off, hungry and destitute as I was, on the road out of Cairo, yet it seems to me that all the roads turn inwards.'

Yoll, who had hitherto been rocking backwards and forwards, broke in here, clawing the air in his excitement. 'Perhaps all the roads in Cairo do turn inwards! There is a story of a city that became trapped in a bead of sweat from the brow of a –'

Cornu cut him short impatiently. 'We have heard also that you were offered treatment by the Father of Cats for an illness, the precise nature of which is not clear. You shed blood when you wake in the mornings?'

'Yes.'

Yoll banged his forehead against his palm. His ape, startled, leapt off his master's shoulder and vanished into the darkness. He said, 'It is a stigma. Perhaps he is the Fifth Messiah that we all expect.'

'The Messiah will come when we least expect him,' the friar cut in coldly.

'Therefore he will come when we are expecting him, since that will be when we are least expecting him,' Yoll retorted.

'Therefore he will not.'

'Enough!' The friar and Yoll regarded one another, scowling, while Cornu resumed, visibly irritated. 'Of course the Messiah is coming; the only question is whose will he be? His or ours? If it is the Messiah of the Father of Cats, then we have nothing to look forward to, and if this dim, ragged, helpless youth were the Messiah, then nobody would care whether he had come or not.'

Then Balian spoke, fumbling for the words. 'I am certainly not the Fifth Messiah, whatever that is. I am Balian, a gentleman of Norwich, and I require of you to tell me what you want of me and why you brought me here. Then, after satisfying my curiosity, I hope you will let me leave.'

'Of course you are not the Messiah. You are only a poor pilgrim, yet after arriving in Cairo you met Giancristoforo Doria, who was also, let us admit it, a spy like yourself who worked for us and then vanished into the Citadel. You yourself were taken into the House of Sleep, allegedly to have your illness treated. Then, at about the same time, you are seduced by Zuleyka, the bitch of Hell, you encounter Yoll on a street corner and you meet Emmanuel on the hill up to the Citadel. Now, friends or enemies, all these people are known to us.'

The friar stared at Balian, impassive. The measured tread continued. Balian wanted to break down and confess, but he had nothing to confess. 'So? What of it? I did not seek them out. It was chance.'

'Chance! Chance! Too many chances! Well – have you heard of the Arabian Nightmare?'

'Yes, but I still don't understand what it is.'

'The story goes,' began Yoll, 'that, long ago in Arabia, the Nightmare was sealed in a bottle –'

But here Cornu cut him short. 'That is a story and nothing more.'

Yoll started again. 'It is said by others that Lazurus –'

But again Cornu cut him short. 'I know that story too and

it comes from the same source.' He resumed his rhetorical interrogation of Balian. 'All over the city men talk of the Arabian Nightmare and what is it?'

'I don't know.'

'Neither does Yoll, neither does anyone in this room save me, and I know because I have seen it with my own unclouded eyes come creeping out of the House of Sleep like a miasma. The Father of Cats breathes it out. He sits in that diabolic synagogue of his arranging things – meetings, mysterious miracles, repetitions, spreading his monstrous web over the city. Not long ago the men here talked about their work and their wives and tended their animals and baked their bread. They lived on the surface of their skins, where they could always feel the sun and the air. Now they forage around inside their unwashed bodies looking for hidden treasures and their talk is always of dreams and visions.

'What is at stake between the Father of Cats and me is not a struggle between Islam and Christianity – I imagine that the Father of Cats has as much contempt for Islam as he has for our faith – but a struggle between the poisonous infections of the life turned inwards upon itself and the Truth that shall set us free. I have come to fight the Eastern Dream. Dreams are nothing marvellous. Any idiot can dream while the Father of Cats and his creatures, the Laughing Dervishes, make monkeys of us all. The regiments of the Alam al-Mithal march through the streets with the Father of Cats at their head and men do nothing, engaged in a stuporous nightmare of self-exploration which takes them through dream within dream into ever smaller circles looking for the man who is looking for the man. That mad heresiarch has arrogated to himself God's prerogative of infinity, but, for myself, I know that Christ was crucified on a hill called Golgotha; He was not crucified within our skulls. Redemption cannot be found in dreams. Each dream and its interpretation, and every dream that dreams about its interpretation, puts us one stage further away from salvation. The Laughing Dervishes have put it about that in the Armenian Quarter there is a barber who shaves everyone in the quarter who does not shave himself and they beg everyone to go and see this prodigy. But what single useful thing can this man tell us about shaving or anything else? The Cairenes have reverted to infancy.

'The man shaves everyone in the quarter who does not shave himself. He shaves himself then he doesn't, then he does. Now you see him, now you don't. Peekaboo! Then there is the little box that yellow whore Zuleyka circulates, doubtless on the instructions of her father.'

'Her father is who?'

'The Father of Cats.'

It was hard to say who was the more astonished, Balian, the lepers or the friar.

'You did not know? One could even say that he has two daughters.' Then, seeing the questions starting on Balian's lips, Cornu motioned to Yoll. 'Yoll, tell the story.'

Yoll gulped and bent and unbent and waved and began. 'The story is as follows. The Father of Cats did and does indeed have a daughter, known as Zuleyka. After the death of Zuleyka's mother, the Father of Cats became fearful for his daughter's safety, for he knew that the schemes which he was even then hatching would attract the attention of dangerous and powerful enemies to his household. Therefore he had his daughter immured in a secret room high up in the House of Sleep and her name was thenceforth never spoken in public. Only he and a trusted mute servant ever saw her. So secret was her existence that Michael Vane spent many months in the house before he even suspected it. She was rarely visited by her father or the servant, and as she was a lonely girl and also her father's daughter, she devised a strange and ultimately dangerous way of entertaining herself.

'She created an *eidolon*, a thought-form in her own image, a little girl. She called the *eidolon* Fatima and Fatima became her playmate and the confidante of her solitude. Many children have invisible playmates, but Zuleyka was no ordinary child and, as she concentrated daily, Fatima gained in shape and tangibility until she was there in the room whether

172

Zuleyka wanted to play with her or not. Even the Father of Cats and his servant could see her, and Fatima developed a personality of her own. While Zuleyka was impetuous and frivolous, Fatima was moody and stubbornly silent. Often the *eidolon* refused to play with Zuleyka and just sat there brooding and watching her speculatively. Now that she found herself sharing a room with a playmate who would not or could not communicate with her, Zuleyka's loneliness was redoubled, and she began to take refuge within herself in a fanciful inner life fuelled by solitude and repressed passion. Any man but her father would have known that she was going slowly mad.

'So things remained until Michael Vane arrived. Even after he had realized the existence of a secret room and located it within the house, he was still unable to discover the correct way in. It was therefore down a wind tower that he made his descent into the room, to astonish and delight the two girls. Once he had made their acquaintance, Vane became a regular and secret visitor; they played games together, flirted with one another, talked endlessly. Zuleyka, who had despaired of meeting any men other than her father and his mute, began to look on that ruffian Vane with amorous eyes.

'Alas! Vane had eyes only for her quieter and more withdrawn "sister" and, as Zuleyka recognized this, the growth of madness within her accelerated. She longed to find other men to comfort her and she begged Vane to find them a way out of the room. Fatima, who had been born in the room and could not even imagine what it was like outside, did likewise. Eventually Vane, who dreamt of surreptitious excursions with the two girls, or young ladies as they were fast becoming, taught them one evening how to climb the wind tower. The following night, without telling him, they were gone. Zuleyka fell into bad company and wandered around the town with marabouts and masturbated them for the blessings of their seed. Fatima was not seen again – until recently.'

'And what of the Father of Cats?'

'The Father of Cats will have nothing to do with Zuleyka

or her *eidolon*. Vane's role in their escape he has apparently not suspected. It was disingenuous of Zuleyka not to tell you any of this, but now you know the story,' Yoll concluded. 'But we would like to hear what has been happening to you recently.'

Balian told them, concealing nothing. The tale he told, of his allurement in the market place and the lady who led him on to the garden where he met another lady and her talking ape and where he then received a beating, attracted Yoll's interest particularly.

'I learnt of a series of incidents curiously similar to the ones you have described,' he said. 'It happened some months ago. Walking along the banks of the Nile, I was drawn by shouts and laughter into a coffee house . . .'

15

An Interlude – the Tale
of the Talking Ape

*I sense that we are fatigued and a little lost. We must pause and rest
and, while we rest, I shall tell a story to divert you, a short story for
diversion and no other purpose. But first I must observe that what
we really need in order to get our bearings is a clear distinction between
dreaming and wakefulness and between one level of dreaming and
another. If guidance was to be had on this, all would be clear and the
tale would achieve an easy solution. As it happens, if there is one
person in the city who can do the job, it is Dirty Yoll. An interlude
first, then when the interlude is concluded I shall, with all due
humility, present Dirty Yoll's Great Touchstone, which distin-
guishes not only dream from reality but also sleep from death. (No,
it's not pinching yourself. You can as easily dream of pinching yourself and feeling pain from it as of anything else. And if you were
dead, you would not even be able to think of pinching yourself.) An
interlude first then, while I collect my thoughts on the subject. More
ear wax! Urghh! But first, before beginning the interlude, a word
about my name, Dirty Yoll. The dirt's not really mine but the Ape's.
The Ape does not often appear when others are present, but he has
been with me a long time and amuses me in my melancholy. It is the
Ape who keeps me dirty. He has never been properly trained and he
spits morsels of food which he finds indigestible on to my hair and
shoulders. So dirty I may be, but I guard the Great Touchstone.
Now, on with the interlude . . .*

'The hall was huge and yet it was packed with men all looking up at the ceiling. There in the rafters sat an ape with a brass chain around its neck. It shitted on its audience and then picked its teeth carefully before beginning . . .'

C

I will tell you a story concerning one of my ancestors. In days gone by, in the city of Bagdad in the reign of the Caliph Haroun al-Rashid, there lived a poor man called Mansour who made a living of sorts from portering, but he longed to be other than he was. Then one day in the market place he saw a young lady beckon to him. Greatly curious, he followed her and she took him to a part of Bagdad where he had never been before and into a garden where another lady awaited him. Seated beside her was an ape on a chain.

As Mansour approached, the ape greeted him civilly in the human tongue and Mansour was amazed at this. The lady mocked his astonishment and told him to watch while the ape fondled and caressed her. Mansour disliked this very much but fear held him back and he sat and watched while the ape and the lady had intercourse. Then the lady told Mansour, the poor porter, to do the same as or better than the ape and, seeing that he hesitated, added, 'If you do not, I shall give instructions to my servants to have you killed.'

'Mistress,' said the porter, 'that is all very well, but first I must tell you something,' and, having said this, he went up to her and whispered for a long time in her ear. When he had finished, the lady looked very troubled and, motioning to her servants to attend upon Mansour and serve him food and drink, she disappeared into the house, saying that she would return shortly. As soon as she was gone the ape approached and asked Mansour what it was he had whispered in her ear.

'I will tell you,' said Mansour, 'if you will tell me your story first.'

The ape nodded and began. 'I was once a prince, handsome, clever and amorous. Now, for many months I had been having an affair with a lady of the Barmakee house. For a long time I visited her secretly and I frequently begged

176

her to become my wife, but she became melancholy and always refused me. She was beautiful and clever, but at length the lady and my unsuccessful pursuit of her began to weary me. So, politely, I told the lady this and told her that I should return no more to our place of assignation in the Garden of the Barmakees. At first the lady was very sad and begged me to change my mind. I suggested that she find other lovers, but she said that she had never known, nor ever would know, a lover as skilled as I. Then, seeing that I was obdurate, she became wrathful and threatened to make my form fit my spirit and to turn me into an ape. I laughed and turned away, but I did not know that the lady was in truth skilled in the art of sorcery and, as soon as my back was turned, she cast the net of her magic art upon me and turned me into an ape, albeit one with human speech and intelligence.

'She made me her pet and required me to make love to her in that same garden where we had dallied when I was a prince. More than this, the cruel lady devised a curious contest, the manner of which I shall now tell you. Every afternoon she would send her maid into the streets of Bagdad to lure sturdy young men into the garden. There they would be challenged to match their amorous prowess with that of myself, who crouched and gibbered on a chain to egg them on. The young men were usually too astounded to do anything. If they refused the challenge, they were beaten unconscious and cast out of the garden. If, lured on by the great beauty of the lady, they accepted the challenge and failed (as they all did, for I who was once a prince and now an ape was indeed a skilled lover, having few other amusements with which to pass the time), then they were killed and their bodies cast into the Euphrates. So things have been and so they are still, but you are the first man whom she has not had beaten up instantly upon refusal to perform. What was it you whispered in the ear of the lady? Tell me your secret and tell me also how I may regain my original form.'

177

'I will tell you all,' replied the porter, 'but first I must tell you –'

℃

'Here, I am afraid, I interrupted,' said Yoll, 'for while the rest of the audience listened agawp and thunderstruck into silence, I could restrain my fears and curiosity no longer. After all, my reputation as the best storyteller in all Cairo and perhaps even my livelihood were being put in peril by this ingenious talking monkey.

'So I shouted up at the rafters, "Rather than proceed any further with this story of yours, tell us instead who you are." There were murmurs from many in the crowd, who did not wish the story to be interrupted, but I persisted. "Are you not perhaps one of the djinn? An imp of Satan sent to tempt us? Or a product perhaps of powerful sorcery? Explain yourself."

'Now there were some shouts of agreement; many in the crowd clearly shared the feeling that there was something ungodly going on here, and there was very nearly a fight in the audience between those who wanted to take the ape for questioning to the Chief Qadi and those who wanted to hear this apparently miraculous monkey continue the story. But then an old man in a dirty white turban, who had been standing in the corner of the room, intervened.

' "Sirs," he said, "there is no sorcery here but only skill, and the skill is mine and not the ape's; though together we have perhaps been guilty of deceiving you, yet we wished only to entertain. This monkey is my creature and there is nothing supernatural about him. I, not he, am the one who has been telling the story. I am a practitioner of one of the secret, though natural, crafts of the ancient Chaldees; that is to say, I am a ventriloquist, the last ventriloquist left in all Egypt. The ape's lips moved, true, but when he seemed to speak, it was in reality only my voice projected up to the roof."

'The secret of true ventriloquism, he hastened to add, for he was obviously afraid of being accused by some in the coffee

178

house of being a sorcerer, lay in manipulating the muscles of the stomach. If one's stomach muscles were strong and fully under the control of the head, then by slowly expelling the air from one's stomach one could send one's voice this way and that, wherever one pleased.

'At the end of this explanation the man shrugged and smiled, but in fact nobody in the room, least of all myself, was convinced by the disreputable-looking old man's explanation. The ape had clearly been seen and heard to speak. Some of the audience were indeed objecting, when suddenly it was noticed that the ape was no longer sitting up on the roof. It had vanished. At this, the man in the turban was apparently greatly upset and, saying that he was going to pursue and recover his ape, he ran out of the hall into the streets and also disappeared from view.

'There was uproar in the hall. Then people standing around me turned on me and said that, since I was responsible for interrupting the ape's story, I must continue and finish it in a suitable fashion, and they added encouragingly that they would beat me up if I did not. They said that they wanted to know what the porter had whispered in the ear of the lady. So I picked up the story where the ape had left off . . .

℃

'Well,' said Mansour the porter, 'It's like this, you see. I was prepared for just such an encounter as this, so when I had an opportunity, I whispered in her ear, "If die I must, then I must die, but first, lady, answer me this:

> *I ask thee for the seven already named.*
> *They err not, cannot be forgotten, are both old and new.*
> *Whoever walks in them walks in both life and death.*

I think that you will not kill me till you have answered me that."

'And indeed,' said the porter, 'she did not know the answer.'

'And neither do I,' said the ape who was also a prince, scratching his head. 'Tell me the answer. Your secret is safe

179

with me. And tell me too why the lady must have the answer before she can harm you.'

But just then the lady returned. Saluting the porter humbly, she promised that he should have his answer within the year, asked him to be patient and, after ascertaining where he could be found, had him escorted out of the garden.

Three years passed and the porter was hurrying down a street to the Friday prayer when a man tapped him on the shoulder.

'Hey there, Mansour, you don't recognize me, do you? I was the ape in the garden of the murderous lady, but I am restored to my natural form and I am a prince again.'

The porter was astonished. 'How can this be?'

'I will tell you,' said the prince. 'But first you must tell me how it was that you asked the lady that riddle, and you must tell me also if she ever returned to you with the answer.'

'I have not seen her so far,' said the porter, smiling happily. 'As to the other matter, I shall enlighten you, but you must tell me first how you regained your proper form and station.'

'So I shall. Simply, it was very sudden and mysterious. One afternoon the lady and I lay in the garden pavilion. She was embracing me and running her fingers through my fur when, on an instant, we looked up to see a man standing over us, shimmering a little in the hot air, his fists raised over his head in fury. A strange-looking man he was too. He was young but long white hair fell down to his shoulders. He wore a blue and silver cloak and he was a Christian, for he wore a great silver cross around his neck. He cursed the lady in many languages, kicked me away and then kicked her. When he had finished with his cursing and kicking, he turned to me again and examined me more closely. It seems that he saw my true form in my eyes, for he muttered some words and made a pass and I found myself a prince again. He took me by the arm to the door of the garden and told me to thank my God that I had been freed from the witch's spell. He also admonished me, on pain of death or worse, that I should never return to the garden. Perceiving that he was a powerful magician, I saluted him and agreed to do as he said, and so I have done. Then I returned to my rejoicing, if somewhat puzzled, family.'

'Ah,' said the porter.

'It is a somewhat inconclusive story,' said the prince.

'Perhaps what I have to tell you may go some way to concluding it,' said the porter. 'You see, I think that I was not the first to ask the lady that riddle. One evening, four or five years ago, at the end of a long and exhausting day, I had gone down to a house where secret drinking took place in defiance of the law to spend my hard-earned dinars in drinking and forgetting how I had earned them. I like to talk when I drink and I fell to talking with a Christian there – yes, he had long white hair and he wore a cross around his neck. He teased me about my drinking, though he was even drunker than I became. Eventually, in whispers, he revealed to me that he was a great magician. I did not believe him and became angry and then he became angry too. I said that if he was a great magician, he should live in a wonderful palace and have beautiful women to minister to his every need instead of furtively drinking with me in this low-class hovel. At this, to my relief, the Christian passed from being fighting drunk to being melancholy drunk. His story was so sad, he said, that he could not bear to tell it to me, but he would find somebody who would. To my astonishment he thereupon put his head under the table and called out in a loud voice, "Washo! Washo!"

'In a moment Washo appeared. He was a talking ape – as you were once, my friend,' said the porter, slapping the prince on the shoulder (who winced slightly). 'Well, Washo seated himself on the table and, with the Christian's permission, helped himself to some nuts and began, "My master is indeed a powerful magician. I am myself a creation of his sorcery –" '

℃

'Hold hard, Yoll,' said Cornu, who had not ceased to walk around them like a hungry but undecided beast of prey, 'I hope this preposterous farrago of yours is going somewhere.'

'All will be unfolded in time,' said Yoll.

'I doubt if I have the time,' said Cornu. 'The more I listen to your tales, the more I am filled with doubt about their merits. It seems to me that you have waı.dered away from the great tradition of storytelling in favour of strolling aimlessly through unreal cities where the fruits of man's labour are always uncertain for magic sets everything at naught, whose inhabitants are ever seeming to promise hidden treasures but never moral guidance, and where man's very sex is threatened and destroyed by devouring females.'

'But it is certainly true that the women of Cairo are ogresses, every one of them,' interposed the friar.

Cornu ignored this. 'There is something worse too. Within the city lies the quarter; inside the quarter there is a street; in the street there is a house; in the house there is a room; in the room a box; in the box there is a . . . Who knows what is within the box? No man, but all men know that at the end of such a narrative there is certainly something of infinite evil. The way you frame your stories disturbs me, Yoll. The Ape is taking over and the Ape wishes always to hear stories about himself.'

Yoll did not reply to any of this but looked nervous. He longed to continue but dared not.

'I'm going to bed,' said Cornu.

As he walked away Balian leant over to the friar to speak to him. 'When I asked you in the caravanserai if there were not some strange conspiracy arɔund me, you took me up on Mount Muqattam and told me there was not and beat your head against the rock, but now the Grand Master has said that there is.'

'I always lie,' said the friar and then put his finger to his lips, for Cornu was returning.

'I suggest that you all get some sleep too,' he said, 'for the coming days and nights will be hard.'

The lepers all obediently followed him. Balian, Bulbul,

the friar and Yoll remained behind. Yoll was shaking. The friar begged him to continue the story, for they were all keen to hear the answer to the riddle.

16

The Interlude Concluded

To have told the story in that cold dark cellar once was bad enough. To now describe in full how I told that story then is almost unendurable. If only I could find a short cut . . . Poor Yoll.

As he began to talk, Yoll relaxed. 'You will recall that I was in a coffee house surrounded by a hostile audience and that I was engaged in completing the story begun by the ape in the rafters and I was telling you what I told them about what the porter told the prince that he had been told by Washo, the ape of the white-haired Christian. Well . . .

℃

' "My master is indeed a powerful magician," Washo began, spitting out the husks of some nuts as he did so. "I am myself a creation of his sorcery – so too is his glorious palace which he has erected some miles out from the city and furnished with the best that magic can conjure. However, he will not live in it until he has attained his heart's desire.

"Now I will tell you wherein lies his heart's desire. Some years ago my master, lost in thought, was passing down a street on one side of which ran the wall of a rich man's garden. Suddenly a ball bounced before his feet and from the other side of the wall came a childish wailing. A girl's voice promised everything and anything if only some kind passer-by would throw her ball back over the wall. My master did not throw the ball back but, using a spell, passed through the wall, taking the ball with him. They were both struck dumb with amazement, she at his magic, he at her beauty, for though she was only a little girl and not yet mature, it was already obvious that one day she would be the most beautiful in the land. He resolved to make her his bride when that day should come. He told her this and boasted of his wealth and told her the story of how he had gained his magical powers, but she replied that although she was glad to have got her ball back, she was reluctant to marry him, for he was somewhat older than her and his hair, prematurely white, made him look much older. Then he promised to teach her how to practise powerful magic if only she would come away with him in seven years' time, yet she still demurred. So then my master proposed to teach her all the best tricks of his art and to ask a riddle: if she was able to answer the riddle at the end of seven years, then they would be quits; if not, then she was bound to be his bride. After some thought she agreed and he asked her his riddle, which was as follows:

> *I ask thee for the seven already named.*
> *They err not, cannot be forgotten, are both old and new.*
> *Whoever walks in them walks in both life and death.*

"The little girl was a rich man's daughter and closely guarded, but nothing can be guarded from my master's magic, so he came each day for a week thereafter to teach her his spells and incantations – how to charm snakes, how to tell fortunes in ink spots, how to fly in the air, how to make gold and . . . how to turn men into apes. Then he left her, telling her to enjoy herself and her new-found powers and warning her to wait faithfully for him for seven years, after which he would return to find if she had solved the riddle and take her away if she had not. The reason I am telling you this story," said Washo, "is that the seven years' waiting are almost over and my master drinks to calm his fears that the girl may have solved the riddle. However, the riddle is difficult. I do not know the answer and I have been thinking about it for seven years."

'And with that he and his master vanished. Pouf! Quite suddenly, like smoke blowing away! Of course,' said the porter, 'when, as it happened by chance, I was brought to the garden by the lady's maid, I recognized who she must be and whispered that riddle in her ear, hoping to save myself by frightening her. The seven years were almost over and she still did not know the answer.'

'But I do,' said the prince. 'Was it –?'

ℂ

'Wait, Yoll,' said Balian. 'You said a little while ago that the Christian explained to the girl in the garden how it was that he gained his magic powers. I should like to hear that story.'

'Ah, yes,' said Yoll. 'It does not do to hurry these things. I must tell you that story.'

Then, to everyone's surprise, Bulbul, who had been sitting in a corner quietly scratching with his pen, suddenly spoke. 'Be advised, Yoll, and do not tell that story. Think what may happen if Cornu awakens and comes back and finds you still telling stories. Beware!'

Yoll wrestled with himself. 'Well, I will tell it as briefly as possible. The story the Christian told the girl in the garden was this . . .'

ℂ

Years ago a Christian who was studying to become a learned and holy monk (our Christian, in fact) went out into the desert near Damascus to fast and to meditate. Then Iblis – who is also known as Shaitan or the Ape of God – perceiving that this man had become weak through fasting and solitude, went out to tempt him early one morning in the wilderness. The simplest wiles, were, he knew, often the most effective, so he did not trouble to diguise either himself or his aims in visiting the hermit. Instead he came straight to the point and offered the Christian three wishes, whatever he wanted, if only he would renounce the worship and obedience he owed to the One True God and would worship Iblis instead. The Christian sat thinking and thinking for a long time before finally he spoke.

186

'O Iblis, you offer me anything I could desire in three wishes, but, as even simple men know, wishes often have a way of rebounding adversely on their wisher. Things are not always so simple as they seem.'

Iblis shrugged his shoulders (which were covered with horrid scales). 'True, Christian, so it has often fallen out, but perhaps you are so clever or so virtuous that you will find a way round the problem.'

The Christian thought again. 'So let it be.'

Iblis grinned to himself (a horrid grin for his lips were thick and blubbery and his teeth were black), but it was Iblis who did not understand. Then the Christian renounced the One True God in a loud voice and made formal obeisance to Iblis. Iblis was well pleased and told the Christian to wish away.

'For my first wish,' said the Christian, 'I wish you to bring me a pebble.'

Greatly mystified, Iblis cast around in the wilderness and found a pebble near his foot and handed it to him.

'Next I wish for a lizard.'

Even more mystified, Iblis rapidly found a lizard, which had in fact been sheltering under the pebble just dislodged, and handed it to him. The Christian did not trouble to look at the pebble or the lizard but clutched them tightly in his hands and wished for the third time.

'Finally, O Iblis, I wish that you render to God that same service and obedience which I have just renounced.'

Iblis was appalled. He pointed out to the Christian that there was, by tradition, a convention which restricted the scope of what could be wished for and granted.

The Christian replied that, as a simple hermit in the desert with little experience of intercourse with djinn, he could hardly be expected to know about such conventions. Besides he had been at great pains in his first two wishes to give Iblis as little trouble as possible. Moreover, in his third wish he had really only wished in the best interests of Iblis's soul and spiritual well-being. So he thought that he ought to insist that Iblis grant him what he asked.

Iblis was horrified and saw that he was neatly trapped. Desperately he offered the Christian three more wishes if only he would release him from the last dreadful obligation. Having gained assurances from Iblis that, apart from wishing Iblis to become God-fearing, there would be no restrictions on his wishes, with simulated reluctance the Christian agreed.

In the first of his new set of wishes, he wished that he might be freed from his oath of apostasy and from his service to Iblis. Iblis did not like this but he was forced to assent. Secondly he wished before God that his good friend Iblis might always remain in good health. Iblis was enormously pleased by this, and, rubbing his horny hands, told the Christian so.

'That is the least of what I am going to do for you,' replied the Christian, 'for I wish you to have my third wish for yourself.'

Quick as a flash before the Christian could unsay it, Iblis, flapping his scaly wings for joy, hastily unwished everything that had been wished for before, but of course he spoke too hastily, for no sooner were the words out of his mouth than he found that he was no longer in good health. Indeed, he was sickening so rapidly that he thought that he was dying. More desperate than ever, he offered the Christian three more wishes if only he might take back for himself that last wish which he had given to him. The Christian smiled and agreed.

Then the Christian wished that Christianity might be true. Now there are some who hold that up to this time Islam had been the true religion, but from that moment on Christianity replaced it. There are others who hold that Iblis had no power to grant this wish, for all his power came from God and God cannot allow himself to be wished into existence. A minority faction reply to this that though God cannot wish himself to exist or not, he can delegate that power to another creature. The majority opinion, however, is that it is only a story.

Be that as it may, the Christian still found himself with three more wishes (do not forget that Iblis had given one back to him), but because the sun was now so high in the sky and because he was beginning to weary a little of teasing Iblis (for teasing was all that it was), he wished that Iblis might tell him a story to pass the time. So Iblis told the hermit a story and it was as follows –

℃

'Yoll!' This was Bulbul, warning.

Yoll looked flustered. 'Very well then, since time presses I will omit the story that Iblis told the hermit, though it is a good one and is called "The Tale of the Two Dwarves Who Went Looking for Treasure".'

℃

When the story was over, the Christian felt sufficiently rested to wish again.

('He would have done,' said Bulbul, 'for "The Tale of the Two Dwarves" is a very long one.')

Then the Christian, with the second of his four wishes, asked that he become Iblis and Iblis become him. This immediately happened, but as they thereby acquired not only one another's outward appearance but also each other's mind, soul and memories, there was not a great deal of difference to the eye of the uninstructed man.

With his third wish the Christian (or should I rather call him Iblis?) wished for three more wishes. Iblis might again have protested that this was cheating and refused this wish, but he was not a trifle confused as to which of them he was, and he reflected that a new set of wishes might bring results favourable to him, so Iblis (whichever he was – but no, let him be Iblis) made no protest. The Christian then made a secret wish (which I shall reveal at a later time). Next he wished to become a sorcerer with almost unlimited powers. Then, deferring his next wish until a later date, he left the desert and returned to the cities of men to exercise his new-found powers for his own profit.

Iblis watched him leave the wilderness and hugged his hairy

body with delight. According to the storytellers, the reason for Iblis's pleasure was as follows. The Christian who went out into the desert had indeed been a clever and virtuous man, and the very first three of his wishes showed his unselfishness clearly, but, as the later wishes showed, he had progressively succumbed to the cleverness of his intellect and his arrogance had led him astray. So it seemed to Iblis, and God was indeed angry with the Christian.

This was why, though the Christian now had unlimited wealth and almost unlimited powers of sorcery at his disposal, God made him lonely and drove him from city to city, weary and restless. This was the situation of the accursed man when he came to the garden of the rich man's daughter. There he thought that he had found a companion and a mate.

Now, to return to the encounter of the prince and the porter.

'I know the answer to the riddle,' said the –

℃

'Stop a moment,' interrupted the friar. 'What about the remaining wishes?'

'We shall return to them,' replied Yoll. 'Now –'

'Another thing,' interrupted Balian. 'You told us at the beginning of the story that it took place in old Bagdad, but later you said that the porter told the prince that his encounter with Washo, the talking ape, took place in a coffee house on the banks of the Nile!'

'A slip of the tongue,' replied Yoll, 'I meant the Tigris. Now if I may be allowed to continue . . .'

℃

'I know the answer to the riddle,' said the prince. 'Was it all just chance, everything that has happened to us? I will tell you something too strange for chance. I must tell you that when I lived in the guise of an ape I learnt the tongue of the monkeys, and I remember it still. Well, some weeks ago I was walking through one of the public gardens in the city when I heard some monkeys up a banana tree idly amusing themselves by asking each other riddles. The one which gave the monkeys most amusement was the one which you have just repeated to me. To the disappointment of the monkey who had posed the puzzle, it was easily solved by the other two. The answer they gave was the seven days of the week. If only I had known . . . Fate is indeed strange. Though the lady treated me cruelly, I now feel pity for her.'

'Perhaps, though, the adventure is not finished yet,' said the porter, seizing the prince's arm. 'Let us make haste. Perhaps we shall be in time to save the lady from the enchanter.'

But though the porter and the prince ran through the town, when they got to where they remembered the lady, the garden and the house should have been, they had all vanished. The enchanter had been there before them. For years afterwards the prince would not admit this but walked through the streets of the town looking for the garden and lady within it, and he mourned the passing of the years of his captive bestiality.

ℂ

'That is the end of the story?'

'Certainly not,' replied Yoll. 'As for the Christian enchanter and the lady, after the Christian had chastised the lady and asked her the riddle to which she was unable to supply the answer, to her surprise he left her and vanished out of the garden. And (to make a long story short), tired, disillusioned and cursed by God, he returned to the wilderness and wished first for the annihilation of the lady who had so disappointed him and of her house and garden. Then he solemnly wished for his return through the years, for all his wishes save the last to be undone, for him never to have met Iblis and for himself to have no memory of all that had taken place. All his wishes were granted. As far as the Christian was concerned, nothing had happened or, if it had, it took place in less than the blink of an eyelid. He meditated in the wilderness for another forty months before returning to Damascus and going to work in a monastery garden.

'So, to conclude, I told my story and my audience were well content to let me go. I never saw again any sign of the ventriloquist and his ape.'

'Was it the same story that the ape in the coffee house would have told if you had let him continue?' asked Balian.

'I don't know. I suppose not.'

'In many ways it closely resembles my own adventure.'

'I told it to you to show how nature apes art,' replied Yoll.

'I don't understand the purpose of these stories within stories.'

Yoll affected to look surprised and replied, 'But surely a story within a story is the model of your situation, for what is a conspiracy but a story within a story? And what is a spy but a man who seeks to penetrate to that inner plot, the hidden truth? I simply thought, therefore, that stories within stories would appeal to your temperament.'

'My temperament?'

'Oh, yes.' Yoll fumbled and scratched himself in excitement as he spoke. 'You were a spy by temperament long before the French picked you out as one. You do nothing but wander about, solitary, suspicious and uncertain, and people talk to you. You seem to do nothing, but those big dreamy eyes take in everything. Long before you came to spy on the Mamlukes you were spying on life. Your face is like a mask; it therefore advertises your profession – conspiracy hunter. But conspiracies are only the fantasies of simple men looking for simple explanations for events that are in truth very intricate in their causes and purposes. You will not find any one key to unlock events in this city.'

Balian could make nothing of this. 'To return to the story, where did you learn it, or did you make it –?'

17

The Interlude Concluded Continued

Oh, to be telling quite a different tale – the tale of the Caliph Wathiq, for example! This one is longer than I remembered. However, I shall rush like the arrow towards its determined end. There shall be no more diversions, for there are still many things in this city which I wish to show you: Cairo's famous poultry farm, for instance. The eggs are hatched on warm bricks. Every foreign visitor to our city comments on it. The scale of the enterprise is astonishing. One enters any one of a score of great sheds and immediately upon entering the eye is drawn down a vista of coops in serried lines, piled high on shelves. The din the chickens make is deafening and there are hundreds of chickens in regimented lines all laying eggs and there are thousands of eggs heating and hatching on the warm bricks. I do not believe that you can have anything like that in the West! You will see! You will be amazed!

First, to finish the story. It may amuse you, even if I can no longer take pleasure in it. It is cold and dark down here. I sweat and salivate uncontrollably, I see dark spots, my stomach curdles, my throat is tight as if a man's fingers pressed upon it, but we shall not pause to chart the melancholy of my anatomy. On with the entertainment . . .

But here the friar cut in hastily. 'Yes, to return to the story, how was it that a pair of monkeys were able to solve the riddle that had defeated the lady, the prince and the porter?'

Bulbul groaned, but Yoll replied, 'Ah, how could I have forgotten the most important part of the whole story!' He smote his forehead and continued . . .

☾

When the adventure was over – that is, when the prince and the porter had discovered that the lady and the garden had vanished – they retraced their steps and fell to talking.

'You seem like an intelligent fellow,' said the prince. 'How comes it that you are only a humble porter in this city of ours, where all doors are open to the intelligent citizen?'

'As to that, O Prince, I now live in hopes that you will advance my fortunes,' replied the porter. 'But in answer to your question, let me tell you a story.'

('This is, as it happens, a teaching story of the Laughing Dervishes,' added Yoll, by way of interpolation.)

The porter began. 'A long time ago, a long way away, in far off Rucnabad, on a particular day, the Sultan of those lands went hunting in his forests. The hunting was poor until, towards the end of the day, the Sultan and his huntsmen cornered and killed a she-wolf near her lair. Suspecting that he might find her cubs, one of the bolder of the huntsmen searched her lair. He found no cubs. What he did find was a small boy, dirty, stunted and sharp-nailed. It seemed that the she-wolf had been rearing him. The Sultan and his courtiers marvelled, and the Sultan gave orders that the wolf child be brought back to the palace and reared with his own children.

'The boy was brought back to the palace, but it proved impossible to educate him with the sons and daughters of the Sultan, for he was dirty, ill-behaved and conscienceless. He wept frequently and would not speak. Men continued to marvel at his mystery, but in the end he was kept locked up in the Sultan's stables. Some years passed and the wolf-boy, living on scraps thrown to him by the Sultan's grooms, was all but forgotten.

'Then one night the Sultan and his court were at dinner in the great hall of the palace when the butler drew the attention of his master and the guests to a crack in the marble floor. As the Sultan stared, the crack widened and then, as soon as it was wide enough, with much puffing and heaving a djinn pulled himself up through it and hunched uncomfortably in the centre of the dining hall. Even there his head scraped against the roof. Without waiting to be asked, the djinn began to speak.

' "O Sultan, you have a mystery in your palace. I speak of the boy reared by the she-wolf. No man knows his origin. He must discover it for himself. The truth is for him alone. If the boy would know the secret of his birth, he must set out on a quest. Within a month he should come out to find me. I live in a toothed cave in the mountains on the northern edge of your lands. I shall wait for him there."

'The Sultan exclaimed, but the djinn did not wait to hear what the Sultan said. He descended back into the depths of the earth, closing the crack carefully behind him.

'All was consternation in the wake of the frightful apparition's departure. The boy was fetched from the stables and told what the djinn had said. He gave no signs of understanding it, but the Sultan's servants prodded and then kicked the obstinate and seemingly moronic boy out of the palace and pointed him towards the mountains north of Rucnabad. The boy did indeed dimly understand what the servants were telling him, only he was reluctant to leave the comfort of the stables.

'However, he set off through the forests of Rucnabad, moving through the trees on all fours, since he found that he travelled faster that way. The paths in the forest bifurcated and trifurcated, ramifying and rejoining. The boy suspected that, though he travelled fast with his wolf's lope, he might be travelling in the wrong direction. But there was no one he could ask, until one evening a maiden stepped out from the darkness of the trees and stood in his way. The boy could not find the words to ask her where the djinn's cave was to be found, so he drew a picture of a toothed cave on the ground. The maiden looked at it and then, misunderstanding his meaning, pulled up her skirts and drew him into her secret cave. The following morning he left the maiden sleeping and continued on his way no wiser than before.

'Later that same day, though, he met a she-wolf and he found that by conversing in snarls and grunts he was able to make himself understood by her and that she was willing and able to conduct him to the cave of the djinn, high in the thin air of the mountains beyond the forest. And so she did.

'The djinn's cave was indeed toothed, for its mouth was ringed with stalactites and stalagmites. Stepping carefully between their fangs, the boy entered and confronted the djinn who lay in a great mound of bedclothes, which smouldered and smoked because of the enormous heat given out by the djinn's body.

'The djinn looked pleased to see him and produced from under the blankets a slightly scorched letter, saying, "Now you should know that there are all sorts of djinn, good and bad, learned and unlearned. Some djinn even know the Koran by heart. I am not one of those. I cannot even read. But I have here in my talons a letter which contains the truth about you and your paternity. Take it down into the village below and have it read to you. All I ask in return for the favour of handing it over to you is that you come back to me directly and tell me what it says, for your story may be interesting and there is nothing I like more than a good story."

'Then the djinn turned over painfully in his bed and the boy, after growling ruminatively to himself for a while, set off down towards the village. A night and the greater part of a day passed before the wolf-boy returned and stood before the djinn again. He was bloody and covered with bruises.

' "Well, what happened?" asked the djinn, raising himself from his steaming bed. The boy grunted and gesticulated furiously. The djinn did not hide his amusement. "Ah! I had forgotten that you are incapable of speech. How frustrating! You are suffering from what we djinn call aphasia. It is an illness in which the sufferer is unable to put his thoughts and experiences into words. How should you speak, when language is something that is learnt from one's parents? You cannot speak. Therefore you cannot solve the riddle of your paternity. On the other hand, the riddle has not yet been solved. Therefore you cannot speak. Here is a knot indeed! How shall we unravel it? Well, the truth is that you are afraid to discover your origins. The knot is within you. You are silent, and have been silent all these years, lest you should discover the whereabouts of your father and re-encounter the man who you believe left you as a baby to the mercy of the forest and the wolves. But your silence is superfluous. I can now tell you that your father is dead."

'The djinn waited to see what effect his words would have. The boy swallowed and swallowed. He seemed to be almost choking. Then the words came tumbling out. For a long time they were nothing but curses. Finally he cooled down sufficiently to tell the djinn his story and even to find some pleasure in its phrasing.

' "I set off to the village as you told me. The day was hot, so I felt increasingly thirsty as I descended the mountain. I had almost reached the village when, at a crossroads, I met an old man with one eye. He had also, I noticed, a water flask strapped to his belt. I gestured that he should give me some water. He understood my meaning and replied in words, 'Why should I?'

' "I showed him my parched tongue and acted out my distress. 'What is that to me? Still there is something about you. I will give you the water, but first you must answer me this riddle:

> *I ask thee for the seven already named.*
> *They err not, cannot be forgotten, are both old and new.*
> *Whoever walks in them walks in both life and death.'* "

'The djinn snorted. "I imagine that even with his one eye he saw that you have the appearance of an idiot, and he must have calculated that even if, by some extraordinary chance, you knew the answer, you would not be able to utter it. Go on. What happened next?"

'The boy scowled before continuing. "I stared at him in despair. Then it occurred to me that even if I could not get him to give me some water, he still might save me a walk into the village. So I thrust the letter you gave me into his hands and looked at him hopefully. He scanned the letter and returned it to me. He was furious. 'You have answered the riddle,' he said. Then he looked crafty. 'I promised you the water, but I did not promise you the cup.' And with that he poured the water on to the ground before my feet, where it trickled away into the dust. Enraged, I flew at him and tried to tear his throat out with my teeth. Then, discovering that my teeth were neither long enough nor sharp enough, I strangled him instead.

' "I looked, appalled, on the first man I had ever killed. Then I went over his body to discover if there was anything of any value on it. There was nothing but a letter. Taking that and my own letter, which I had shown him, I proceeded to the village.

' "There I made it understood that I wanted to be taken to a man who could read what I had in my hand. I was taken to the professional letter writer who wrote and read all letters in the village. 'Show me,' he said. Then, after he had been reading silently a while, he said, 'This is very interesting.' Then he went away and gathered half the village around him. Then when he was satisfied that he had a large enough audience, he began to read to us all." '

Mektoub. It is written. This is a tale about destiny and its strangeness . . . I never knew my parents. I was a foundling and, as far as my earliest memories stretch, I was raised among the apes of the forest. Then one day, while still a small child, I was discovered sitting on the edge of the forest by humans and I was taken by them to a nearby town. There was a school teacher in the town, attached to the service of the great mosque, and I was entrusted to his care. Insofar as it was within my limited abilities, I learnt from this man the manners and speech of humankind. Eventually the time came for me to be apprenticed to a craft or profession. However it proved difficult to find a master to take me, for my mysterious ancestry weighed against me and I was in truth surly and apparently slow in my wits. But one day my teacher and I were walking in the bazaar in search of a suitable master, when we were approached by a man who said that he was looking for crew for his ship, which he proposed to sail to trade with the islands east of Sumatra.

The school teacher and he readily agreed that I, who stood there sullenly, should be enrolled amongst its crew. The contract was signed and the captain paid the teacher some money. My new master conducted me to the docks. If only I had known then what I was to learn later, I should have turned and fled back to the forests, there to live in savage contentment on nuts and fruits, but I was young, I thought that my wearisome education was over and I welcomed the prospect of adventure! I followed the captain onto the ship. The captain was fairly pleased with the bargain he had struck with the school teacher. Since it was clear that the captain was not rich and it was suspected that his obscure enterprise was dangerous, he had found it difficult to raise a crew. The crew that he had succeeded in collecting consisted, for the most part, of the criminal, the maimed and (like myself) the slow witted.

The captain was an old man, grim and embittered. He was possessed, as I was subsequently to learn, by a consciousness of past sin and a present purpose, though both alike were hidden from me then. The crew served him reluctantly. It was notorious among the crew and indeed widely noised in the town that the captain had no interest in trade with the islands east of Sumatra or anywhere else. Instead, it was rumoured, he proposed to sail the ship to the end of the Earth in pursuit of a secret purpose of his own.

He told us as much on the day we weighed anchor. He addressed us from the poop deck. 'I am on a quest,' he said.

Oaf that I was, I did not know the word (I certainly know its meaning now), so I asked, 'What is a quest?'

'A quest is to ask a question while in motion, that is all,' he replied.

'What questions are you asking?' asked another of the crew, but he became angry and would reveal no more to us deckhands. The only man he really confided in was the ship's mate.

We weighed anchor. What a voyage that was! For me it passed like a dream. I was appointed to watch from the crow's nest and I would sit there day after day looking rapturously out or down. Outwards I looked on pure and limitless blue. There was no horizon. The air in those equatorial parts was warm and jelled. It had a natural tendency to congeal and form images, just as the earth forms stones in the ground through its natural generative powers; so at least my master at the mosque had taught me. Education is a won-

199

derful thing. So I saw mirages – trains of camels and castles in the air, floating islands, ships sailing upside down on the underside of the sky, looming chromatic haloes and distended leviathans. Once in the distance I thought I saw our own ship, labouring in the winds, sailing back towards our port of departure. Doubtless it was my expectancy anticipating the reality. It was difficult to see clearly.

Downwards, I would let my eye play following the complexity of the rigging with its tangles and drapes descending to the deck where the poor crew of bestial half men toiled under the eye of the captain. Marked out by my simian agility to live among the spars and ropes, I could look down on them and contemplate wider vistas. Those labouring animals below, could they and I be ennobled by our captain's mysterious purpose?

Only once were my solitary meditations made to pause. One day we put in at a port on the Baluchi coast to avoid storms. It was there that I attained the summit of my happiness and there too, though I did not realize it at the time, that the seed of my present troubles was sown. On shore leave in the port, I was accosted by a Baluchi girl.

'Your face is like an ape's,' she said. 'Do not mistake me. Your eyes are large. Your cheeks swell and glow with health. The whole face has an animal innocence. Your face is indeed beautiful. Do not mistake me again; I am not a whore. I am a respectable girl of a good family in these parts, but . . .'

' "And here," said the wolf-boy to the djinn, "the professional letter writer refused to read on. He maintained that as there were women and children in the audience, it would not be proper. There was heated debate amongst the audience about his prudery. It ended with the letter writer turning several pages and picking up the story at this point." '

The following morning we reaffirmed those promises and I re-embarked to sail on further east. If only I had known what my captain's purpose was or in what circumstances I should return! As we left the Baluchi coast –

℃

'Hold on a moment, Yoll,' said Balian. 'Just because the letter writer was not prepared to reveal what went on between the ape-boy and the Baluchi girl, it doesn't mean that you can't tell us.'

'Tradition does not relate,' said Yoll. Then, after a very long pause, 'Though intelligence may surmise. To return to the narrative of the ape man as it was read by the letter writer to the wolf-boy and retold by him to the djinn . . .'

℃

As we left the Baluchi coast and the birds that had been scavenging for the ship's refuse dropped away, men's minds turned to speculation on our unknown destination, east of Sumatra. There are many traditions among sea-faring men about what lies at the edge of the world, and every one of these traditions had at least one supporter among the crew. Some said that the world was encircled with a wall of bronze. Some said that we should sail on until we encountered a mirror world of our own and that we should meet ourselves coming the other way. Some believed that at the edge of the world was a primal darkness from which all forms are created. Others said that there was simply a smelly sea without a shore.

Finally the opinion of the Chief Mate was sought. (Though clearly the close confidant of our taciturn and demented captain, he had nevertheless contrived to acquire a remarkable ascendancy over the rest of the crew.) He gave his opinion reluctantly.

'Such questions are bootless. To ask what it is like at the edge of the world is like asking what will you feel like after you are dead. It is like trying to feel the edge of your dream with your hand.'

The captain kept his silence. I was content. There seemed no reason to me for our voyage ever to end. Would that it never had! Nevertheless, of course, it was I who signalled our journey's end, though when I first saw it from my lofty vantage point, the island seemed small and ordinary enough. The captain directed that we anchor off the island and, in a fever of excitement, issued the instructions to land. As we drew nearer it was clear that the island was all rocks and soil. Only a solitary withered tree, rising from the bare soil, stood out against the sky like a spreading crack in the blue.

So we set foot on the bathetic little island.

'This is the island at the end of the World,' said the mate.

The captain only nodded. The crew surged around him and I among them. After the long voyage and all our hardships, was this all? For a moment it seemed as if we were about to lynch him there and then. Little enough difference it would have made, as it turned out.

But here the mate intervened and answered our still unspoken thought.

'Yes, this is all. And it is more than enough. This is journey's end and its reward. Do you see that tree over there?' (How could we not? It was the only thing on the island.) 'That is the tree of incubation. A Hidden Master inhabits the island. He is all-wise but he is also invisible. That tree over there is, as it were, the door that admits one to his presence. The hero who quests after forbidden knowledge may rest in its shade. Once he is asleep and dreaming, he may approach the Hidden Master and ask any question he wishes, here under this tree and at no other place in the world.'

Here the captain strode forward and took his place under the tree. He was nervous, yet determined. He composed himself to sleep there and then, though it was hours before he actually suceeded in falling asleep. We none of us slept, but we watched him sleeping and we wondered. He awoke late the following morning. We crowded round him excitedly. He was still drowsy. He told us his story in a relaxed manner and it seemed to me also that he now spoke to us with the authority of one who has found fulfilment.

'It seemed to me that I slept and that, as I slept, this withered tree shot out leaves, and a forest of similar trees grew up around it, and a mountain rose up over the forest. I looked and a pathway presented itself, leading gently up the mountain. I resolved to climb the mountain and set off in high spirits, for the walk was cool and shady and paradisal birds sang out from the trees. Later the sun's heat bore down upon me. The ascent steepened. I heard the sounds of heavy animals crashing through the foliage and several times I thought of turning back. Successively I confronted a wild cat, a cobra and some singing thing that was not quite a human and tried to lure me off the path, but I pressed on, determined to reach the summit, and they all turned and fled in the end. To cut a long story short' (indeed, we had never heard our captain so voluble before) 'at length, just short of the summit, I arrived at a cave and there at its entrance sat a venerable sage, naked and unadorned save for a crown of dancing lights.

'He had seen me coming from afar. "O quester after knowledge, speak! Ask what you will. Ask any question, no matter how obscure, obscene or difficult. Speak!"

' "Venerable sage, where is my son? Shall I ever find him again?" '

Here the captain fell silent. We waited. Finally one of us asked, 'Well, what did he say?'

'Oh, it never occurred to me that he was supposed to say anything! I'd asked my question, so I just turned and came back down the mountain again and, when I had found my original tree, I woke up.'

It was too much. To have come so far, to have sailed to an island at the end of the world, to have braved so many dangers at the behest of a man who, now he had spoken, had proved himself the biggest idiot of us all! In our fury we beat him to death with stones (and I confess that my stone was at least as heavy as any man's).

'What a waste,' said the mate, looking down regretfully on the captain's corpse.

'What, I wonder, was this man's story?'

'Who was this son of his?'

'Now we shall never know.'

The cries rose from all sides. The mate stilled the clamour. 'Perhaps not, but I should tell you that I have observed that he kept a book locked up in a brass-banded box in his cabin. Perhaps there is a clue there. The key is in his pocket.'

We found the key, hurried back to the ship and opened the box. The mate snatched at the book and began to read. He read it easily enough. It seemed to me then that he was already familiar with its contents. What he read from was no log book, which was what we had been expecting, but the story of the captain's past life. It was as follows.

' "Now I should say," said the wolf-boy, "that the letter writer had been reading slowly and that there had been many pauses for discussion of the wonders of the story. It was now therefore late, and the letter writer said that he was exhausted. He would retire and read the rest of the story in private, and tomorrow morning, when we were all refreshed, he would retell it to us. With that his audience had to be content and the crowd broke up. I was given a meal (my first ever of cooked meat, as it happens) and went promptly to sleep.

' "The following morning, as soon as I awoke, I hurried to the house of the professional letter writer. This time the whole village was assembled there. The scribe had been talking to them, and there were angry looks in my direction. The letter writer, whom I had previously taken to be an amiable fellow, threw the two letters at my feet, saying, 'These letters are yours by right and the story is yours, but I am not prepared to read any more of it to you.' Then, at his signal, stones began to fly. The whole village pursued me with stones and I was lucky to escape with my life. So here I am with all my wounds and bruises and an unfinished story." The wolf-boy looked expectantly at the djinn.

' "Give me the letter," said the djinn, and he began to read in the longer of the two letters where the scribe had left off, but before he had got more than a few words into the story of the dead captain, the wolf-boy stopped him.

' "Wait! Something is wrong here. You told me, before I left the cave with the letter you gave me, that you could not read!"

' "Ah, yes. So I did," replied the djinn. "Well, while you have been away, I have been teaching myself to read. I discovered that my inability to do so was really a nervous disorder. Impatience and apprehension warred within me when confronted with such a document as this. I suffered then from an inability to get the elements in the right order. I was unable to follow the letters, words, sentences and sections on the page in their proper sequence. However, I think that I am mastering the trick now."

'The wolf-boy did not look convinced, but the djinn picked up the story again and proceeded to read with surprising competence.'

What he read from was no log book, which was what we had been expecting, but the story of the captain's past life. It was as follows.

'As I pen this narrative we are, I calculate, within a week's journey of the island and I look back on the strange chain of events that has led me towards it, and I try also, as I sit here in my cabin, to picture in my mind's eye who will read my story and in what circumstances. But perhaps it is pointless to speculate. To begin. The tale I have to tell is a tale of mountain fastnesses, of gipsy girls, of men more savage than any carnivore of the jungle. It is a tale of hidden paradise and wasted youth. It is a tale of – but why go on? You shall judge for yourself.'

(As I listened to the mate reading out the story of our late captain it struck me what a fine literary style our captain had written in, and I resolved, there and then, if I should ever write a similar narrative, to imitate that style, in so far as it lay within my limited abilities.)

But to return to the book that the mate was reading.

'It is in my paternity that the mystery of my life lies and in the unravelling of that mystery that my story is to be found. I knew neither a father nor a mother; at least I could not remember them. I was a foundling in the wilderness and I was raised among bears. I cannot complain of my foster parents; they were as kind as, no kinder than, any humans I have since met. The day came, however, when I learnt to walk upright and to ask a man's questions. How was I born, and why was I different from the other cubs? Who were my natural parents?

'At last the bears told me that I had outgrown their guardianship and that, if I wanted to know the answers, I should go ask the black bear who haunted a certain pool on the edge of the wilderness.

'I saw no bear when I arrived there, only a man fishing in the deep pool. "You have come to ask me questions."

' "I have come to ask the bear."

' "I am he. Actually I am a djinn. I appear to bears as a bear and to men as a man."

' "So I am a man?"

' "Of course you are. Is that all you wanted to know?"

' "Who were my parents?"

' "Does it really matter? Man's infancy is always animal however he is reared. The answer lies within you anyway. When you were born, your mother was certainly there. Your father probably was as well. You have simply repressed your memory of them."

' "How can it be my memory if I can't remember it?"

' "If the memory won't come to you, I shall take you to it."

'With that the djinn picked me up in a whirlwind and set me down some distance from a squat colonnaded temple sitting in the sun and pointed to it. "That is the Memory Theatre. It is not a playhouse but a building adapted to intellectual exercise and demonstration. It will be ideal for pursuing your genealogical researches. I must warn you of two things, however. First, whatever you do, don't let yourself be seduced by the woman at the door. Secondly, inside the theatre you may eat, but do not drink."

'Then the djinn left me. He had not warned me that the lady at the door would be naked, and she smiled at me so sweetly that I found I preferred to enter her before entering the theatre.

'At length I entered the Memory Theatre. Here, inscribed in hieroglyphs on concentric stacked tiers of wood, were the archetypes of all the planets, animals, ships, engines, stones, movements of the body, rhetorical tropes and topoi, classified and cross-classified. I made a nervous circuit of the hall. Then I passed through another door and entered the Chamber of Involuntary Memory. Ah, what horrors! What monstrous images were racked from me there – the Club-footed Ogre, the Ratman, the Vulture, the Sphinx and the Horned Prophet. It was there, however, that I heard the truth about my origins, for amid the clamour of ancestral voices I heard my father speaking to me. "Listen carefully, my son, for the story I am about to tell is long and difficult . . ."

'I advanced to a table in the centre of the chamber where food and drink had been laid out, and I ate and drank as I listened. The voice continued rustling in my head.

' "Indeed, I am perplexed as to where I should begin. Perhaps I should start in the middle? Yes, that seems best. Listen carefully then . . . The night was dark and stormy and I had almost given up hope when I saw a distant light. I struggled up the exposed mountain side to find two dark and hairy men squatting by a fire in a cave. I asked if I might shelter with them. They assented and even offered me food, as their laws of hospitality obliged them to. As we ate, I trembled inwardly lest the story of my childhood among the leopards be known here too. Then one of them belched and, turning to me, said, 'Tell –' " '

The mate who, you will remember, was reading this narrative of the dead captain to the crew, including myself, on the island, turned the page and stared at it with exasperation. Then he turned another and another, until he had passed through most of the book in silence. We stood around him expectantly. Then he swore. 'Now, by the Seal of Solomon and the Seven Sleepers in the Cave, this tale goes on for ever! I cannot and will not read all this. I propose to omit most of it and come to the conclusion.'

'Here the wolf-boy interrupted the djinn's reading. "The

story cannot literally have gone on for ever, for God's creation is finite."

' "True, but Man has since invented infinity," replied the djinn and returned with impatience to the story.

We all protested but the mate insisted and resumed his reading on the last page.

'When I came out, the woman closed the door behind me. I did not recognize her at first and then stared at her with astonishment. She had aged, her belly sagged and there were deep lines in her face. "Yes, I am the same woman. Memory plays funny tricks. You have been in the Theatre for fourteen years. While you were in there, did you eat and drink?"

'I nodded. She laughed for a long time until it was painful for her to laugh any more. I waited for her to finish. "You have been chewing on the biscuit of memory and swigging from the flask of nepenthe," she wheezed, "or, to speak more plainly, you have been remembering the past and forgetting the time."

'I stared at her aghast, but she continued, "Oh yes, and, while you were in there, I conceived and bore you a child."

' "What happened to him?"

' "Oh, I left him on the edge of the forest. I have a job to do here."

'Some way off stood the djinn, who appeared as a bear to bears and as a man to men. "You were a long time. You were surely not so foolish as to ignore my warnings?"

' "If you had not given me those warnings, I should never have realized that the woman was ready to be seduced or been aware that the drink was there to tempt me."

' "Ah, well," replied the djinn. "That is often the way of things. Let me give you another warning now, though, one that I hope that you will heed better than my previous warnings. Your son lives. He was snatched away by apes from the edge of the forest and reared by them as one of them. It is predicted that he will kill you. It seems to me that your only chance is to identify him and kill him first."

' "But how can I find him? It is impossible, for I know nothing of him."

' "I do not know. I cannot help you. Unless . . . there is an island at the edge of the world, where a Hidden Master is to be found of whom any question may be asked."

207

'With that our interview ended. Years passed before I had amassed a sufficient fortune to charter a ship to take me to my destination. However, I worked hard and, though I saw no more of the djinn, he and his final warning are in my mind all the time, and, of course, I have always the memory of the awful fate of my father to spur me on. The ship I have chartered seems seaworthy enough, though its crew are the dregs of the earth and thoroughly untrustworthy. Only the mate knows anything of my history and the purpose of this voyage; he seems an honest and reliable fellow. I feel in my bones that I am now very close to success. As I write this, I hear the boy in the crow's nest calling out "Land ho! Land ho!" '

'Well, that's that.' And with those words the mate sent the book skimming into the sea and the tides swept it away without trace. I was suspicious and I do not think that I was the only one. Frustrated and annoyed with the mate, we returned to the ship and set sail for home. The mate took over the running of the ship and he was a competent enough master, too competent indeed, for he had only to whistle and a wind would come running up, like an obedient dog, and drive us on towards Sumatra and the lands of the West. Then one day, towards the end of our journey, one of the crew pointed out that we had caught no fish since we had left the island and that every bird avoided the ship.

'What can this mean?'

'It can only mean that this ship is under the guidance of an evil power,' replied another of the crew. He voiced the thought of all of us.

That night we crept down to the captain's cabin, where the mate now slept. As we hesitated we sniffed a smell of singeing that percolated through the door. We burst in and found that the bedclothes were on the verge of igniting from the heat of the mate's body and that the mate was no man but a djinn. We threw ourselves upon him and tried to overpower him, but he reverted to his monstrous natural form and flew off in a storm. Thunder and lightning crashed around the ship. The ship foundered. Death was a cup which came round to all the crew. Only I was spared. I went down in a whirlpool formed in the eddies of the sinking ship, down and down, until it seemed that there was no bottom to this sea, that I should never come up and that my ribcage would be crumpled up like a paper ball by the pressure of the water. I had heard that sometimes a drowning man *in extremis* will see his entire past life pass in review before his eyes. One might well anticipate such an experience with interest. However, I have to tell you that no such thing happened to me and that, if it had, I should have been in far too uncomfortable a condition to pay any attention to it. Such, I believe, were my thoughts at the time, as the whirlpool drew me on to my end, when suddenly the direction of the spiral reversed itself and I was forced like a cork to the top of the waters.

I surrendered myself to the tides and unconsciousness. When I recovered, I found that I had been cast ashore on the Baluchi coast. There I was, naked and half dead, at the very nadir of my fortunes on those same sands where previously I had known my greatest happiness.

Remembering the promises we had made, I walked towards the port. Some way short of my destination, I met a kind citizen who took me in and clothed me and, when I was recovered, answered my questions. He knew of the girl I spoke of, though not the full story and he thought therefore that I ought not to hear it from his lips. I should go instead to a certain *santon* – a holy man – on a hill and he gave me directions with which to find him. Something in the manner in which he spoke of my Baluchi love filled me with apprehension. So, as soon as I could, I hurried to that *santon*.

The *santon* greeted me cordially. He seemed familiar to me. This was the story he told.

'I remember the girl well. She left these parts, but before she did so she came to me with a dream she wished to have interpreted. It was a simple one. She had dreamt repeatedly that she was falling down a bottomless pit. The construction that she put upon it was that she was falling into the Hellish Pit and that she was damned for unspoken sins.

' "Nonsense, my dear girl," I said. "Still, it is true that the dream bodes no good. A dream of falling can have only one meaning. It always means that the dreamer is a fallen woman, but it is the judgement of your family and society you must fear, not God's, for God is merciful and regards these things differently." '

☾

Here Balian interrupted Yoll. 'The *santon*'s interpretation was absurd, for I often dream of falling, but that does not mean that I am a fallen woman!'

Yoll shrugged his shoulders and continued.

ℭ

'I counselled her to leave the places where she was known and flee into the wild forest, where she would be safe from the condemnation of society. She wept for she did not wish to leave her parents, nor did she wish to abandon all hope of seeing her lover again. In the end, though she did not fully understand my advice, she took it and I was never to see her again.'

I turned to leave, but he raised his hand to stop me.

'Stay. There is more. It was obvious to my eye that she was heavily pregnant. Only her innocence had veiled the fact from her. So it was that when her anxious family commissioned a search and that search resulted in the discovery of her body, dead of exposure on the edge of the forest, there were signs that she had given birth, but the searchers found no trace of a baby. There, my tale ends.'

I sobbed. I was distracted. Suddenly I became aware of the source of my distraction – that familiar scorched smell. We fought fiercely (he scratched out my eye), but in the end I could not hold him (for a djinn can slip from form to form) and he readily abandoned the imposture of a *santon* to escape my grasp.

I reflected. She was dead, if the djinn had spoken the truth, yet it was possible that my child lived. 'Only through finding my child can I give some meaning to what has hitherto been meaningless life.' Nevertheless, I was perplexed as to how to prosecute my search. At last I thought of those who had cared for me in my infancy. I returned to the apes. I asked my foster parents for their help and advice. They replied that they would first seek the opinion of their elders.

('And what, I wonder,' inserted Yoll parenthetically, 'is this fascination in stories of talking animals. Perhaps it is the child in us. Children are born under the power of a sort of animal magnetism and give love the form of a furry bear and fear that of a great insect.')

I suspect that those who have not had the privilege of living among them, as I have, will not realize that the society of apes is governed by order and hierarchy and that important decisions are taken by a council of elders. I waited days for the council to convene and a week more before they gave me their answer, and what they gave me was little enough. They gave me a riddle and told me not to abandon my quest until I found someone who could solve it. The riddle was as follows

> *I ask thee for the seven already named.*
> *They err not, cannot be forgotten, are both old and new.*
> *Whoever walks in them walks in both life and death.*

So, an orphan and a stranger, I wander the Earth eternally, asking all men that riddle and looking for my child.

'The djinn had finished reading.

' "I regret now that I killed him," said the boy. "I don't understand, though. Why was he angry, and why did he tip away the water?"

' "The other piece of paper that I gave you, and which you showed to him, had the answer to the riddle. That is why he was angry and also why, when the letter writer had put two and two together, he had you stoned out of the village."

' "I don't understand. I just do not understand."

'Then the djinn, taking back the second document as well, told him the answer to the riddle and affected to turn over and go to sleep.

'The answer to the riddle solved nothing and the wolf-boy remained extremely puzzled, but with that he had to be content. Thinking hard, he retraced his steps and found the royal road that led to the Sultan's palace. There he told his tale to the Sultan and his court very much as I have told it to you. There were many questions and much discussion.

' "This is indeed a puzzle and a wonder!" cried the Sultan of Rucnabad. "What does it all mean?"

' "It means," said the wisest of his courtiers and the only one to follow fully what had been going on, "that this boy is an idiot, the son of an idiot and the grandson of an idiot." Then after a pause he added, "Is he any the wiser for that?"

'The courtier's judgement was decisive and the wolf-boy was banished from the Sultan's palace and lands for ever.'

'I am absolutely baffled,' said the prince, thinking that the porter had finished. 'What has all this to do with anything?'

'You are impatient,' replied the porter. 'You have not heard the end yet. The end of it all was that, after many adventures and mishaps, the banished youth settled in Bagdad and took up portering there. And now I must tell you that I was that youth.'

'You have had a rich and colourful life,' acknowledged the prince and fell to thinking. Then, after a while, he spoke again. 'Now I have heard your story, I realize that you knew the riddle and the answer to the riddle all along, even before you met Washo and the magic Christian and long before you met the lady in the garden.'

'Yes, indeed,' assented the porter smilingly.

'But you did nothing about it?'

'That is right. It never occurred to me that I was supposed to do anything about it.'

'You are indeed an idiot,' concluded the prince. 'Such an idiot that, far from expecting any advancement from me, you are lucky to escape with your life.'

☾

Yoll jerked out these last words convulsively and stopped.

18
The Conclusion of the
Continuation of the Interlude's Conclusion

How embarrassing. I seem to be making a real mess of this story. I feel sick with shame and fatigue and thank God that no rival master from the Qasasyoon was present to witness it all. If only Balian could stop asking questions. I must be polite, but I'm sure that his example is egging the others on. I shall make what must be a final effort. I fear that I do not come out well in the next episode . . .

There was silence. Then: 'But, Yoll, I don't understand at all. The story you have told us does not explain how the monkeys knew the answer to the riddle of "the seven already named".' This was Balian.

The friar agreed. 'Yes, it only provides further evidence that they knew the riddle.'

'And how was it that the Christian in the garden asked the girl that very same riddle?'

This time Yoll beat his head with both his fists. 'Oh, what a double-dyed fool I am! I left out the point of the whole story! Well, let us go back a little.'

Yoll was silent in recollection. He had been dribbling and a drop had reached the bottom of his chin where it was suspended, quivering. Then, as he began to speak, it fell.

'You will recall that, when the man who had been raised among apes started to search for his son, he had recourse to the council of apes. What I should have done was to have made it clear to whom and in what circumstances the apes in their turn had recourse. This I will now try to do.'

'You will recall also that, some time earlier, I endeavoured to tell "The Tale of the Two Dwarves Who Went Looking for Treasure" but was dissuaded on grounds of the tale's excessive length.'

' "The Tale of the Two Dwarves" is not like the rest of your stories – short and simple. It is quite excessively complicated and long; it is known as "The Tongue of the Labyrinth" also. Please don't tell it to us now.'

'I am not going to,' replied Yoll. 'I merely wished to draw attention to that story's length so that you will understand why, when Iblis told the story to the Christian in the desert, there was a pause in the middle for discussion of some of the themes in the story. Being the sort of creatures they were, Iblis and the hermit rapidly moved on to debate theological matters. It was during this exchange of views that Iblis told the Christian that he, Iblis, had created the World and everything in and on it.

' "I, not God, created you." Iblis boasted. "I encompass Man and all his works. I am omnipotent and omniscient."

'The Christian disputed this, and the debate that ensued resulted in Iblis challenging the Christian to set him a riddle or a puzzle that he could not solve, otherwise the Christian would have to acknowledge formally the omniscience of Iblis and the creation of the World by the Evil Principle. Once the challenge had been accepted, Iblis resumed the "Tale of the Two Dwarves". I really think that I ought to give you some idea of that story, since –'

'No, Yoll.' Bulbul's 'no' was a growl almost.

'Well, anyway, when that tale was finally concluded, the Christian returned to playing with the three wishes that Iblis had granted him (in the manner that I have already related). What I omitted to tell you, in the interest of simplicity (always a paramount consideration with me) was that when the Christian left the desert after his first meeting with Iblis, abandoning the career of a hermit for that of a powerful magician, he then spent many months thinking and searching for the problem that would expose Iblis's pretensions. Further, he returned to the desert a year later with what he believed to be the unanswerable riddle that would answer his need to confound Iblis. (It is in this sense that we say, "Every question is the answer to someone else's question.") Before I tell you, however, what happened when the Christian encountered Iblis the second time, I must tell you where he found such a riddle and this involves me in telling you a little of the story of Washo.

'Now, Washo was a magic ape, created by the Christian's enchantments. The Christian was fond of him and allowed him a great deal of freedom, but the ape brooded in his freedom. He knew that he had been created by magic and could be dissolved by magic. His existence was as transient and insubstantial as a soap bubble's. When the Christian had tired of him, he would dissolve him, but Washo did not want to go the way of the fawn that fed on glass or the homunculus who told jokes, yet what prospects did he, the product of a few passes of the enchanter's hand, possess? Preoccupied with such gloomy thoughts, he was swinging from tree to tree one day when he found himself in the orchard of a garden where he had never been before. A young lady sprawled on the lawn below. She whistled at the ape and signalled that he should join her. (Now, lest I raise false expectations, I should say that this lady was not the same person as the girl in the garden that the Christian was later to encounter. No, not at all!) Washo did as he was bid and, descending on to the lawn, bowed low and addressed her with polite words.

'The lady smiled. "I have been looking for a chess partner," she said. "You seem suitable. Won't you sit down and tell me something of your circumstances as we play?"

'Again Washo did as he was bid, and in no time at all he found that he was telling her of his broodings on mortality and his fears of extinction through disenchantment.

'The lady was sympathetic – and helpful. "What you should do," she advised, "is try to make him realize that in creating such a splendid and intelligent ape as yourself he has created more than he was aware of, something that is more than a mere echo of his own mind. Challenge him with an insoluble riddle."

' "I don't know any."

' "I shall give you one." And she did.

'The ape was doubtful, but he went home, squatted before his master and announced that he, Washo the magic Ape, had devised a riddle that his master would never be able to solve. To the ape's surprise, the Christian proved to be very interested in the prospect of an insoluble riddle. Immediately a pact was made. If the Christian could not solve the riddle, he promised that he would never conjure the ape away. Thus Washo would have immortality conferred upon him. Then the ape recited:

"I ask thee for the seven already named.
They err not, cannot be forgotten, are both old and new.
Whoever walks in them walks in both life and death."

'The Christian considered. "This needs thought," he said. "Return here every evening until I shall either have given you the answer to the riddle or given up. By the way, what are you doing with yourself in the daytime?"

' "Every day I go to play chess in a garden with a young lady. Nothing could be more proper. The plants are more passionate than she is," replied the ape.

'The Christian nodded absently and dismissed him.

'Every evening the ape came back to the house of the magic Christian and every evening the Christian sent him away unanswered. This went on for a week. Finally the Christian confessed defeat. "I give up. What is the answer?"

' "I have no idea," the ape admitted (for the lady had not told him the answer). "I thought only of the riddle, not the answer."

' "You idiot!" shrieked the magician. "Any fool can think of a riddle that has no solution at all! And here am I wasting every day this week –"

' "That's it," said the ape quickly. "The seven days of the week."

'He was saved. The Christian, when he had calmed down sufficiently, admitted that the riddle was good. "I have created something cleverer than myself," he cried.'

Here Yoll interrupted himself. 'I do not understand his astonishment, for who has not heard of a storyteller who is stupider than the story he invents?

'What he had created was a monster, for their pact meant that when the Christian renounced his magical powers and later died, the ape survived, and he has since grown extraordinarily in stature and power. As for the Christian, somewhat under a year later he returned to the desert and propounded the riddle to Iblis, who gave the correct answer as quick as a flash. The Christian was devastated and found himself obliged to recognize Iblis's omniscience. Though he still had wishes in hand and many adventures yet to endure, a dark shadow hung over his mind from that moment on. Though the riddle had served him ill twice already – Washo had won his freedom with it and Iblis had won his argument – the Christian was to use the riddle a third time, of course – on the lady in the garden – with similarly unfortunate results. Well, that was the story of the riddling contest between the ape, the Christian and the Devil.'

Yoll looked round triumphantly.

By now Balian was experienced in detecting the shortfall. 'I am still left baffled. Where did the lady in the garden get the riddle? And how did the riddle spread among the apes and monkeys?'

'Aha! Yes, we must backtrack a little if you will insist on every little detail being spelt out. Let us go back to the apes who promised to help the man who was looking for his child. Their elders met in council high in the mountains. It was very cold, cold enough to –'

Here Bulbul let out something between a groan and a yawn, which effectively drowned the next few words.

'– never mind those of an ordinary monkey. Before long

they came to the conclusion that a wiser head than theirs was needed to assist their foster child in his seemingly impossible quest.

'Then one who had travelled widely spoke. "We lack the sophistication and experience of humans, let us admit it. However, when I was in Bagdad, stealing bananas from the orchards, I caught a glimpse of one of our kind, whom I am sure can help us, for he sat in a garden and not only talked to a lady but even played chess with her."

'The others agreed that this must indeed be a remarkable ape, and delegation was dispatched, with all due haste, to Bagdad. They found the ape in the garden without any difficulty and explained the problem to him. As Washo listened, he became more and more convinced that the man's quest was hopeless. However, he wished to appear wise. Therefore, with that fatal oracular obscurity that has plagued so many of the characters in this story, he recited the riddle of "the seven already named" and added, "Tell him to wander through towns and villages asking this riddle of all whom he should meet. Only if he should find someone who can solve the riddle should he abandon the quest. Let his search end then."

'By this Washo meant he will never find his son, for at this time he had only just learnt the riddle from the lady in the garden, and to him both the riddle's solution and the man's quest alike seemed impossible.

'But the apes who listened to him took him to mean that the person to solve the riddle would be that man's son.

'But the man, who listened to the riddle and the message which the apes brought back, took them to mean that if he ever found anyone to answer the riddle, he might as well give up, for it would be a sign that his quest was hopeless. Hence his annoyance and his throwing away of the cup when the riddle was solved by the boy who had been reared among wolves.

'But Iblis, who was behind it all, contrived it to mean that the riddle would be solved and the son found only at the cost of the father's death.

'It was a deadly profusion of meanings.

'Now, let me point to Iblis's role in the story. The djinn in the story were all different manifestations of Iblis, for, though his name and appearance are legion, his evil essence is one. Iblis was the djinn in the toothed cave, the mate on the ship, the djinn fishing at the pool, the *santon* on the hill – all Iblis. He also disguised himself as the chess-playing lady in the garden so as to lead the Christian to his downfall. The reason Iblis solved the riddle was that he set it himself in the first place. The story is all of his contrivance and intervention.'

'So why did Iblis engineer the chain of events that led to Washo passing on the riddle to the council of apes and from them to the man who had been raised among apes, while simultaneously contriving that the wolf-boy should solve his father's riddle? Was it all pure mischief?' asked Balian.

'No, though it is certainly true that Iblis delights to torment mankind. No, the answer has something to do with fatality. Do you know the famous old story of the man who went to Bagdad to avoid his death?'

'Please don't, Yoll,' cut in Bulbul hastily.

'Well, anyway, Iblis wished to illustrate the strangeness of fate. What is fate but pattern? In Iblis's eyes, man's life has no meaning. Therefore Iblis wished to give it at least a pattern. Iblis has a tidy mind and the riddle (which is condensed thought presented in a syllogistic form) appeals to him.

'So, anyway, thus it was that Washo transmitted the Devil's riddle to the council of the apes, and apes and monkeys have treasured it ever since.'

Balian was restless. 'You said that it was a teaching story of the Laughing Dervishes. What message do they get from all of this?'

Yoll ran his fingers through his hair (which was difficult, for his hair was clotted with dirt) before replying. 'Some have taken the moral to be that in some stories there is a penalty for asking the question; in other stories there is a penalty for not asking the question. Therefore both action and inaction have their bad consequences. Others have taken it to be a fable about the child's puzzlement about the sexual act. Myself, I have always felt it to be a rather mysterious parable on the transition from an oral to a written culture, but that is probably just my professional prejudice.'

'This is all very deep, Yoll,' said the friar. Then, after some hesitation, 'However, such a profusion of meanings and interpretations amounts to no meaning at all.'

Balian did not want to ask the question, but in the end he had to. 'Two things still puzzle me, Yoll. What happened to the maiden in the forest, the one who slept with the wolf-boy as he set out on his quest, and should not Iblis have had one more wish?'

Bulbul wept, but Yoll replied, 'Ah, yes, "The Adventures of the Maiden in the Forest and of the Son that She Bore". The story is a trifle intricate, but I must tell it to you.'

And he did. Wonder after wonder unstripped before them – it was a tale of flying horses, haunted castles, captive princesses, sinister flightless birds, intoxicating elixirs and apes, calculating apes, murderous apes, ghostly apes, crowned apes and apes that devoured themselves – but, O God, how Balian longed to sleep!

Finally he did sleep. He dreamt that a face of lined and falling flesh hung over his. With a start he realized that it was Zuleyka, heavily made up to look like a raddled old woman, and that she was waiting for him to get up. 'Come on,' she said. 'We are going to amuse ourselves.'

They stepped out from Zuleyka's kiosk and he noted with surprise that it was early afternoon, there was a lull in trading and the shopkeepers were sprinkling water in the streets to hold down the dust. They hurried on out of the market area towards the villas and pleasure palaces that spread themselves around the Lake of the Elephant.

'Help me up,' said Zuleyka.

Balian gave her bottom a push. She wriggled up, then extended a hand to him, and quite suddenly they were sitting on the wall that surrounded the garden of one of these palaces.

It was deliciously like being naughty children again. He wondered if they were going to rob the orchard. Noiselessly they dropped down into the shrubbery. As they crawled through the tunnels created by the arching of the branches, it began to rain. In the centre of the garden a figure lay sprawled on cushions. Balian recognized the epicene form of the Dawadar.

The rain was so faint that it did not disturb the Dawadar, who lay in blind reverie. Ghostly rainbow webs appeared in the bushes. Steam rose from the brass censer which kept the Dawadar's opium warm and moist.

There was a chattering sound from the trees behind Balian's head. Looking up, he saw a monkey and beside it, on the same branch, the man with the dirty white turban and robe. The man dropped down to join them. He and Zuleyka began to whisper together. From the other side of the garden came the sound of laughter, and after a pause two girls came tiptoeing out from behind a pergola.

Zuleyka pointed to them. 'Khatun and Zamora,' she whispered.

The two girls stole towards the Dawadar's bowl of opium and, snatching handfuls of the stuff, crept stealthily away again, retiring towards the orchard where they ate it. On the edge of the orchard a brief fight for the hammock took place before Zamora installed herself in it and, languorously wriggling, fell asleep. Khatun returned again to the flower garden and went walking by herself along its watercourses. At the crossing of the watercourses was a fish pool. Khatun paused, reflecting over it and watching a fish.

Zuleyka turned to Balian. 'Wait and watch. Your turn will come.'

Then, stepping out from the bushes, she began a self-conscious hobble towards the girl. Khatun was crying and her tears ran down into the basin. Zuleyka advanced until she stood behind the girl's shoulder and bent over looking into the pool.

Khatun did not turn round, but spoke directly to the reflection.

'Old woman, what are you doing here?'

'I have come looking for you or your sister. I am here to satisfy all your desires.'

'You don't look as if you could satisfy all my desires,' said Khatun, looking the squat veiled figure up and down meaningfully.

'I meant that I could procure you all your desires,' came the hasty reply.

'That is different then. You are an opium vision?'

'If you wish. Why do you weep?'

'Our father keeps us captive in this garden. He will never let us marry.'

'It has been well said, "When a girl begins to menstruate, either give her in marriage or bury her." ' Zuleyka recited the proverb in a hoarse croak and made obscene jiggling motions with her fingers.

'It is true. Men and time are passing the garden by.' Khatun lost herself in melancholy thought awhile, then turned to Zuleyka. 'What is it that you are selling or offering to me?'

'I offer you what you desire – men.'

'Does an old crone like you give away men as others give crusts of bread to the indigent and deserving?'

'I offer you seven men. Whomsoever you shall point to up to that number, I shall fetch for you and introduce into the garden while your father sleeps. I can turn this place into a veritable mantrap.'

'Old woman, you promise me all this? Why?'

'I have a friend.' And here Zuleyka whistled and the man in the turban emerged from the bushes. Khatun looked at him suspiciously. 'And he has a friend. His friend is very ugly, hairy, with uneven teeth.'

The man in the turban leered back at the bushes. Revolted, Balian looked up at the ape. The ape looked modestly down.

'And, as payment for sleeping with the seven I desire I must sleep with the one that no one desires?'

'No, that is not our way. We wished to propose a game of forfeits. If the seven are willing and if you can bring them in succession to orgasm, then we shall have worked for you without payment. If you fail, then you shall sleep with our friend.'

'That is ridiculous. They will all sleep with me for I am beautiful.'

'Of course you are.'

'I think that you are djinn. Djinn are addicted to these sorts of game.'

'If you wish.'

'Any man I want!' She clapped her hands. 'Over there is a grille that looks out on the street. I shall make my choice from there.'

The man in the turban settled down on the steps while Zuleyka hurried after Khatun, calling to her as she did so, 'One other thing. Whatever you do, say nothing to these men or the spell is broken. And remember, you have seven choices. Don't hurry.'

The Dawadar stirred uneasily in his sleep. The grille was some distance away, and from then on Balian caught only odd fragments of their excited deliberations.

'One thing is paramount. He must not have a big bottom.'

'I always think hands are the most important thing.'

'It is impossible to tell in advance if he will have hairs on his chest.'

'I should make a representative selection.'

Dizzied by the heat, he sat in the bushes listening. The sun was now low behind the houses, but the day's warmth rose up from the earth. The ape in the tree stolidly munched on a banana. Time passed, the dusk came on and the roses released their scent into the shadows. At length –

'What about that one? If I let that one pass, will I find another as good? That one.' Khatun's first choice was made.

Zuleyka hurried off, letting herself out by a postern gate. Khatun returned to wait by the fish pool. Zuleyka returned, leading a blindfold youth by the hand. The blindfold was lifted and his beautiful gazelle-like eyes revealed. Silently he and Khatun withdrew to the summer house. When the youth re-emerged the man in the turban stood behind him and struck him unconscious with a stick.

The process was repeated. The second of the chosen was an Indian merchant, the third a wiry Bedouin, fresh in from the country. At length Balian, bored, rose from the bushes and stealthily set to exploring the garden. Noctambulos, his lightly padding feet were drowned by the deafening stridulation of the cicada. In the garden, in the half light, his eye was everywhere drawn to and amazed by the spider webs, and threads and cat's cradles of foliage, which seemed to him to descend from the heavens, binding the growing things to the stars. So creepers and vines were drawn up walls and trellises towards the stars, their vegetable passions stirred by unseen conjunctions. The perfumes of the now invisible flowers breathed esoteric virtue at him and he felt himself move through a dark rain of astral influences. The open spaces of the garden were dominated by the waxy mask, the sleeping face, of the Dawadar which, bathed in moonlight, appeared as the dreadful totem of the place. Balian avoided this area but crept from thicket to thicket – chenar, poplar and cypress – towards the orchard.

In the orchard, among the ragged trees with their silvered oranges, the hammock of Zamora was slung. He stood to one side of it with only a profile in light, like a half-man. It was a foolhardy thing to do. What if she should awake?

Khatun was calling for Zuleyka to bring her a black man. Zamora awoke. The eyes did not seem to focus, but the lips parted and spoke. 'Who are you? Where are the servants? Are you an opium vision?'

He felt a flutter of fear, yet he quietened it by reassuring himself that there was nothing to lose in this strange dream. It did not matter what he said. 'If you wish. I am here to satisfy all your desires.'

'I have no desires. I don't want to move or do anything ever again.'

And indeed she looked very comfortable. It seems that I am a failure as a nocturnal apparition, he thought.

Somewhere in the distance Khatun was shouting, 'But I want a Frank! I want an infidel Frank!'

Zamora and Balian shared a smile of enigmatic complicity – that is, Balian smiled with her but he did not know why. Zamora focused on him more clearly.

'You are not an opium vision. Rub your hands together.'

He did so. Threads or worms of dirt appeared in the sweat of his palms.

'I thought so. You are of the earth. Like the vegetables, we are all born of the earth, and share their base needs. Before you woke me I had a real vision, though. A woman stood before me. Her face was white as an asphodel and she carried a knife in her hand. She asked me a riddle. The riddle was this:

> *My sister was my mother.*
> *My father never begot me.*
> *Never an infant, never an adult,*
> *Who am I?*

Can you solve it?'

He shook his head.

'You are not much good at solving riddles,' she murmured.

'Am I a monkey for solving puzzles?' he expostulated, but she was drifting off to sleep again.

He was still standing there, contemplating her cloudy face, when a voice, coming from the direction of the summer house, cried out in English, 'I know you.'

There was a sound of scuffling and a heavy thud. Balian started running towards the wall, but Zuleyka rose up in the darkness before him. 'Stop. All is well.' Yet he thought that her face looked strained. 'She still wants a Frank, though,' she continued. 'This must be your opportunity.'

As they walked towards the summer house, they passed the figure of a man lying deep in the long grass. There was at once something very odd and something very familiar about that figure. Balian was unable to locate the source of his disquiet, for Zuleyka hurried him along and continued to hiss in his ear, 'Don't speak. Remember what I have taught you. Let this be the consummation of your lessons. It is time at last to release the snake.'

The summer house was ablaze with lanterns. They entered and she presented him to Khatun. 'He is thin, I know, but look at the eyes, and he is a student of *imsaak* and uncircumcised!'

Khatun looked troubled, but managed to nod her assent. Close to, he now examined her more closely. She looked like the lady with the peacock fan. The resemblance was there but, frustratingly, not the identity. A half echo. He stepped out of his rags.

'Watch this,' said Zuleyka to the man in the turban. He grunted. She produced an hourglass from the folds of her robe.

After the first embrace, Balian scarcely noticed the girl as he commenced the rituals to uncoil the serpent power. Loop by loop the cobra rises, past the abdomen and through the rib cage, twining itself along the spinal column in painful rhythmic jolts. As it enters the skull, its hood fans out and its jaws open. Its head fills Balian's like a hand inserted in a glove.

He found himself looking out through the snake's eyes at two separate gardens. There was no perspective. He was utterly detached. He was riding the snake. Khatun's eyes were at first dilated in ecstasy, then dropped. The hourglass turned and turned again. Occasionally he heard the ape chatter. He listened to the cries of the night-soil men as they passed in the road outside and the sounds of owls hunting in the garden. Eventually she fainted. He felt the serpent's power growing within him. It forced his back straight, and his mouth opened in an awful rictus.

At length her eyes opened and she screamed as she tried to throw him off, 'O God, will this never stop?'

Then the Dawadar was shouting back to her and there were servants running everywhere. Balian was unable to move of his own accord. The man in the turban half stunned him, and together he and Zuleyka pulled him off the girl. Now the postern gate was guarded. Balian was pushed, almost thrown, over the wall. The man in the turban was the last to come over. He stood on the wall and declaimed, 'The tambourine is broken and the lovers dispersed. Ha! Ha! Ha!' Then, 'That will give His Excellency something to think about,' he said as he dropped down to join them.

The Dawadar's servants were not far behind. The streets were unusually deserted. Once again he was being pursued and running through the streets at night. Again it was a distorted re-enactment, for this time he had two companions in his flight, not counting the ape who loped along beside them. They were running south towards the Citadel. It was only a little distance and they came out at the foot of the Citadel, at the Hippodrome, and the reason for the deserted streets became apparent.

'We are saved,' said Zuleyka. 'They will never find us now.'

Vast crowds had already assembled round the Hippodrome. A fiery ball of slow-burning wood flickered across the pitch. Men on horseback thundered pell-mell through the murk. The Sultan and his officers were playing at polo by torchlight. The Hippodrome was ringed by liveried pages, bearing alternately flambeaux and reserve mallets. At opposite ends of the field, yellow and black spiral-fluted goal posts were topped with pitch, which flared up brilliantly into the night. Every time a goal was scored a gong sounded. Every time the Sultan scored a goal trumpets sounded. At the end of each chukka musicians rode across the field beating on kettledrums. By night the game was dangerous and the crowd feverish.

They were safe in the crowds. The press held him up. To the clack of mallets and music he drifted off into reverie.

Here in Cairo they are specialists in wasting time, he thought. In retrospect the games and stories of the night revolted him. He remembered Emmanuel saying to him, 'In the eastern lands the heat and the idleness breeds among their inhabitants leisured and lethal fantasies.' All of a sudden he realized what was odd about the figure lying in the grass in the Dawadar's garden. It was dead. And what was familiar. It was Emmanuel.

Then he stood alone in Bayn al-Qasreyn. He was surrounded by the crowd, but the crowd slept. Its million eyes were closed. The crowd slept standing, kneeling and sitting. Cairo had stopped. Even the drop of water falling from the water-seller's jar hung in the air, suspended by lethargy. Balian gave the water-seller a nudge. The man stirred uneasily in his sleep and murmured something, but he stayed asleep. Balian moved through the slumberous avenue and falling light, tiptoeing lest he disturb the sleeping throng, heading towards the Citadel. Nothing disturbed them. Crossed pikes, held by nerveless hands, barred the gates of the Citadel and Balian pushed his way past them. At the summit he looked back and saw the city suspended between one act and the next in timeless catatonia. He advanced to the throne room. In the throne room the abandoned postures of the courtiers proclaimed to the creeping Englishman the vulgarity of sleep, defenceless and ignorant.

He tiptoed up to the throne and reached for the crown on Qaitbay's head, intending to take it for himself, when a voice of thunder reverberated through the somnolent halls: 'It's all mine now!'

And a giant hairy hand reached for him, swept him off his feet and raised him over the Citadel. Balian found himself gazing up at the eyes of the Ape of Melancholy.

'Now you have seen them all asleep,' it said. 'They aged without maturing. They wanted to laugh and I made them laugh, but they were a futile people.'

'Were?'

'Were.' The hairy hand set him down on a dusty and ruined road. 'While you idled your time away with enchanted dreams and stories and they slept, millions of years have passed and Cairo has died. Shall these stones speak?'

Balian shook his head mutely.

'The stones will speak.' The guttural voice reverberated in the desolation. 'Nothing has been utterly destroyed. If you will dig deeply enough, you shall discover the origins of Cairo's millennial hysteria. A city is like a mind. The sources of its fall are detectable in past images and words, fragments of columns and half-effaced inscriptions. If you will dig, you shall discover the roads that turn in upon themselves, stone basilisks and gorgons and, everywhere, the arabesque – crystalline patterns of stucco foliage, organic life turning to death – creeping over the buildings like poison ivy. Here the ruins and the causes of those ruins coexist.'

Balian, walking on the dusty horizon, felt panic. 'I want to go back.'

'Of course you shall.'

And so he did, up from the level of the Ape to encounter yet again the sleep-walking funambulist, Karagoz, Shikk and Saatih, Barfi and Ladoo and, finally, Zuleyka. To Zuleyka he observed, 'All my terrors come from never knowing where I shall wake up.'

He awoke in the cellar. Blood marked the end of his passage like a red full-stop.

'– determined that if he could not have him, then nobody should, the magician cast the severed limbs of the boy over the Sultan's battlements.' His mouth now ringed with white foam, Yoll was still talking, but it was Cornu's re-entry into the cellar that had awoken Balian. Cornu's scabbed white fingers rested with apparent affection round Yoll's neck. Then they squeezed. Like a rabbit hypnotized by fear, Balian watched Yoll's strangulation. The eyes stared and the face turned blue. He would have gone to Yoll's rescue but, seeing that Bulbul and the friar did nothing, he did nothing too.

When it was all over Cornu faced Balian challengingly. 'I had to do it. He was a sick animal, truly he was. The Ape had him, and the Ape is the creature of the Father of Cats.'

From under his hood the friar winked at Balian. Balian was too shocked to respond.

'This time he would have talked himself to death,' Cornu continued, 'and held you with him in his thrall, but I have work for you all. The time is imminent. "Watch ye therefore;

for ye know not when the master of the house cometh, at eve or at midnight, or at the cock crowing or in the morning." '

'You have work for me?'

The fierce eyes regarded Balian. 'In a sense. I wish you to go to the Father of Cats and submit yourself to his treatment.'

'I don't want to go back there.'

'You hardly have any choice. Sooner or later the Father or Vane will catch you. The hunt is up. You may tell the Father of Cats that we have examined you and set you free; that may give him something to think about.'

The friar was laying out Yoll. Bulbul continued to write. Balian climbed out of the cellar's darkness into twilight. It was deep night by the time his escort brought him to the House of Sleep. He knocked on the door as loudly as he could, grazing his knuckles, and, since no one answered his knocking, fell to sleep at its foot. The escort left him lying there.

19

The Treasures of Cairo

I wish that the Leper Knight had minded what he was about when he strangled me. It is a maxim among the Qasasyoon that dead men tell no tales and it is unfortunately true that the death of the narrator in the midst of his own narration poses special problems. No one has ever challenged the ruling of the Qasasyoon on this point. Death disqualifies a man from membership of the Guild.

To return to what I was saying when I began this whole story (and I did not intend it to be the story of my death), of late, when I have retired to bed early to read and then to sleep, unaccountable fears have kept me awake. Unaccountable but not indescribable – and in retrospect not so very unaccountable. Now I shall describe the fantasy that held me red-eyed and sleepless on my couch. It was as follows.

The lids grow heavy, the head falls back, the dull book falls from my grasp, the eyes close. The breathing settles into a slow deep rhythm – and then seemingly stops. In the morning when I do not rise at my accustomed hour (usually the cry of the dawn muezzin wakes me) some anxious friend like Bulbul or, more likely, my sister Mary enters and tries to rouse me, shakes me and, finding that I do not respond, listens to my heart and then to my breathing. Both seem to have stopped. The first cry goes out and my face is wet with someone else's tears. Then the ululations of mourning, the funerary rituals, the huddled group looking down on my shrouded figure. Handfuls of dust are cast upon my body, then spadefuls. The sun disappears.

And only now do I awake and feel the weight of the damp earth pressing upon me. Yes. Buried alive! My screams are muffled in the intense confinement of the space. My bloody hands burst free from the winding cloth and claw at the earth with their nails. Oh, who is the man who, envisaging all this, can resign himself to sleep easily? And where is the man who has received a sure guarantee that he will not awaken thus?

Who, indeed, has a guarantee that he will awake at all? That idle phrase 'he passed away easily in his sleep' . . . Closely contemplated, what could be more terrifying than to die from sleep, to die without being conscious of it? But these are deep matters. What I wished to say was that a vividly conceived and morbid fantasy led me to cling to wakefulness. Sometimes whole nights would pass in the company of these imaginings, so that I would rise and leave the house even before the call of the muezzin cut the dawn, and I would walk to the Zuweyla Gate, where I would join the Persians for their first breakfast.

More, it was in the insomniac darkness before the dawn that I meditated on further schemes to instruct my audience – a warning about the dangers of wet dreams, a debate on whether it would be better to have the Arabian Nightmare and not know it or on the other hand to be dead and know it, a visit to Cairo's unique and revolutionary poultry farm, a presentation of Yoll's Great Touchstone – the possibilities seemed endless. Concluded now. Who could have seen that my most morbid and far-fetched fantasy would come true? Not I, certainly. I feared but I did not believe my fears. Almost true. I find some consolation in the fact that strangulation, not sleep, preceded my passage to the grave.

But I digress. Inevitably I am somewhat distracted by my end. The story, though, is not yet concluded. Patience. Patience comes from God; haste comes from Iblis, the Devil. The man who is in a hurry will miss the treasures that Cairo contains . . .

The Father of Cats had gone out that night to the great open space before the Zuweyla Gate. There he had waited for hour after hour. Some time before dawn the temperature dropped sharply, and the entertainers abandoned their booths to gather round a communal bonfire. In the intense cold the steamy breath issued out of their mouths like dead souls. They watched the Father of Cats with an impassivity verging on hostility. Conjurors can never feel anything but mistrust for a magician. The Father of Cats stamped around in circles, trying to keep himself warm.

At last the black man appeared. Habash was not running any more but staggered dispiritedly towards his cage. As he approached, the Father noted that a patch of his head was darkly matted with blood. He observed also that although Habash was muzzy and confused, he was no longer dreaming. Above all, he saw with delight that Habash carried a book in his hand. The Father smiled benignly.

'I see that you have returned battered but triumphant.' He hesitated. Habash had ignored his congratulations and pushed past into the cage. He flopped down on to the straw. Disorientated and drained of all energy, he looked thankful to be in a cage again. The Father followed him in anxiously.

'What happened? Who attacked you? Where did you find the book?'

'I am not sure. It is difficult to remember. I was running through the city looking for your book. An old woman waylaid me and promised me the book if I would do as she said. She led me into a garden. There was a lady, who said that I should sleep with her, and an ape . . .'

'Ah no, not the ape and the lady in the garden again! But at least you have the book . . .'

The Father of Cats prised the tightly sewn manuscript volume from Habash's grip. Something odd about it caught his eye. Incredulously the Father read the dedication on the back: 'This treatise is humbly offered by his Excellency the Dawadar to the Sultan of Sultans, Qaitbay, in the hope that he who rules over the lands of Egypt and Syria and over the hearts and eyes of his subjects with his silver hairs and ageless beauty will . . .' The Father of Cats turned to the front of the book to read its title, *The Key of Embellishment and the Way of Adornment for the Slaves of the Sultan and the Swords of the Faith*.

'You idiot! This is not the book.'

'How should I know that? I can't read.'

'Something has gone wrong. What has gone wrong? We must find out what has gone wrong. You must have another drink and sleep again.'

Habash eyed the cup dubiously.

'Don't be afraid. I'll only question you this time.'

Habash drank and lay back. Meanwhile the Father threw up his hands in stagey despair and declaimed, as if he were intent upon impressing invisible powers, 'I have been thwarted, but I'll find it somehow!'

Habash slept, and as his sleep deepened his breathing became stertorous. It was time to begin the questioning.

'Is there a spirit of the Alam al-Mithal who is ready to speak and answer my questions through the lips of this poor benighted slave of mine?'

'I am.' The voice was so faint that the Father had to put his ear almost to Habash's lips.

'Tell me then who took my book?'

'If dreams wished themselves to be remembered, they would be remembered. If they wished to be understood, they would be understood. The book has been reabsorbed into the Alam al-Mithal. It has ceased to be a book about the dream and has become a dream about the book. Such is paradoxical sleep.'

'But I wrote the book!'

'It was dictated to you in séances. With automatic hand you transcribed the whisperings of the Alam al-Mithal. We study those who study us and we take back what is rightfully ours.'

'My book! My life's work!' The Father wrung his hands.

'You fraud! You bluffer! Your schemes run deeper than that.'

The Father ceased wringing his hands and the voice continued. 'The Chinese box too will be reabsorbed ultimately. You are like your cats. They like to bury their excretions. You hide and hoard your treasures in the House of Sleep, but all are vulnerable. In fact, even at this very moment thieves have entered the House of Sleep. I suggest that you drop this matter of the book and hurry home now to save what you may.'

'I thank you, and may I ask to whom I am indebted for this advice?'

'Why don't you enter the Alam al-Mithal and find out?'

The stertorous breathing stopped and Habash dropped into a softer, natural sleep. The Father turned and hurried away.

A ragged figure lay sleeping across the entrance to the House of Sleep. The Father of Cats turned the body away from the doorway with his foot and hurried in, full of uncertain anticipations.

Earlier that night Barfi and Ladoo had come over the roofs into the House of Sleep. They presented a curious appearance, having oiled their bodies and then coated the surfaces with dust before they set out. Even then, in the small hours of the night, there was a considerable amount of activity in the place: gongs sounded; slaves with torches passed from one level to another; two cats were fighting in the courtyard. Barfi and Ladoo looked down on it all with some dismay. At least in the night, however, they had some chance of shrinking into some dark corner where the torches could not penetrate. Having reached the edge of the roof, they swung themselves over and down into the upper cloister.

Suddenly everything was silent. The cats' fight ended in a flurry of screeching; the tremor of the gongs died; and the slaves disappeared into the cellar. No, almost silent. There was the stridulation of the crickets and both Barfi and Ladoo wondering if it was the other's heart that he could hear beating. There was no moon and only the faintest glimmer of dawn light. Holding hands, they edged their way through the darkness. The geography of the house was mysterious. Barfi tugged at the latch and eased the first of the doors open. In an instant the adventure seemed over. Something hit him in the face, the door swung back with a thud and there was a furious scrabbling in the corner. But for an instant only. They had disturbed a bird trapped in the room. Barfi turned back and pulled the door shut on the otherwise empty room. Then they could hardly hear the flutter of its wings and soon even that faint noise ceased abruptly. That first room was the worst. In one of the other rooms a man lay asleep wrapped up in a carpet. Otherwise the rooms were empty save for boxes of jumble and the odd heap of bedding. It would be necessary to extend the range of their explorations.

It was a cardinal principle with Ladoo that they would discover treasure when they least expected it. He therefore devoutly tried to empty his mind of all expectations, and as he crept and fumbled his way in the dark hunting for treasure he tried not to think of treasure. The mental gymnastics involved took his mind off the terrors of the house to some extent. But still he trembled, even though at times he was so successful in his programme of unawareness that, in the midst of ransacking a chest, he would pause and struggle to remember what it was that he thought he was doing there.

Barfi's thinking was similar, though transposed into a different key. If finding treasure was simply a matter of random searching, then any fool could find hidden treasure. Barfi had observed, however, that the public places of the city were filled with hungry fools. Thought was therefore necessary. Now, treasure would not be hidden in the least likely place in the house, for, as Barfi realized, the least likely was in a sense the most likely. So treasure hunters as cunning as himself, having rejected the least likely place, would turn their thoughts to the second least likely place. So a man as cunning as the Father of Cats would avoid such an obvious spot also. On the same grounds he would avoid the third least likely spot. Fearing cunning and astute men, as he and Ladoo undoubtedly were, the Father of Cats would, stage by stage, be reduced to hiding his treasure in the most obvious place of all – which was in a sense the least obvious place. Or was it? So Barfi, as he searched the rooms with Ladoo, was filled with similarly profitable thoughts.

Occasionally they conferred in whispers, whispers so soft that they could hardly hear one another. This was rarely to exchange sensible suggestions and more often to raise some new image of fear that had occurred to one or the other. Ladoo looked for he knew not what and Barfi searched in places he considered neither particularly likely nor unlikely. Barfi imagined that in the next big chest that they opened they would find the Father of Cats hunched, glaring up at them with accusing eyes. Ladoo was scared witless at the thought of putting his hand unawares on one of the cats that he knew swarmed in the house. Yet the search continued. Such is the power of the dream of money.

Into another room: a splintered box and dust-covered rags lay across the floor. Barfi and Ladoo eyed the debris with hope. Vane's skill and luck as a tomb robber was famous throughout Cairo.

'A sarcophagus from the days of the idolatrous Egyptians – and look,' pointing to the shrivelled human form partly buried by the wood, 'a corpse!'

'There is money for us in this body. It is soaked in jew's pitch.' They prodded it gingerly. 'This where mummy powder comes from. We can sell it.'

'Are you telling me that these disgusting remains will fetch a high price?'

'Yes, such things are highly prized by the apothecaries. The jew's pitch dries round the body and its varnish preserves the liquors of life within the body. It is eaten by those who can afford it, to extend their life and for their health generally.'

'Let us eat some now and take the rest away with us.'

They nodded together excitedly, then paused. Finally Barfi broke off a finger and set to work chewing. Ladoo followed suit. Barfi could not have believed that anything could taste so nasty. It was dry and bitter, and the crumbling stuff clung around the back edges of the teeth. He recollected what it once had been, gagged twice and then it, and more besides, came vomiting out. Ladoo was taken the same way. They coughed and cried.

'When the stomach laughs, the body vomits.'

The Father of Cats was standing in the doorway, towering

above them. They threw themselves into their vomit before his feet.

'Strong stuff for little men. Up! Who are you?'

'Barfi and Ladoo,' one of them replied.

'Yes, I do know you. You run a sweet stall near the Zuweyla Gate.' To their amazement the grim old man began to giggle and then to caper in the doorway. 'And have you been eating *mumia*? It's not so good that way, is it? It tastes better when dissolved in alcohol. And what were you doing here?'

Barfi and Ladoo shuffled on their knees.

'Come on. I'm not angry.' Indeed, he seemed to them to be smiling sweetly.

'Looking for treasure.'

'Looking for treasure! Well, there is none here, but I will give you treasure, if you will work for it.'

Ladoo thought that treasure was not treasure if one had to work for it, but he did not voice this thought. 'We shall do whatever you command.'

'First I want you to try to remember. You have been talking. The word has gone all round Cairo. Some months ago a man came to your stall by night and engaged you in conversation. A strange man, doubtless, and almost certainly behaving very oddly. He told you that he had the Arabian Nightmare. I want you to describe him to me in as much detail as you can.'

'We get a lot of customers late at night. Our sweets are very popular. Our halva is deemed particularly good. People come from other quarters to buy our halva. The fudges, though, are almost as popular –'

Ladoo broke in. 'Some of our customers, it is true, are a little odd, insomniacs who come to talk to us as much as to buy our sweets. We have to talk to them for the sake of our sales, but we don't usually find much of profit to remember in those chats.'

The Father of Cats tapped his foot impatiently.

'But, of course,' Ladoo resumed, 'we do remember being

told by some character that he had the Arabian Nightmare. Don't we?'

'Yes, but I can't remember what he looked like.'

'Neither can I.'

The Father of Cats took this easily enough. 'No matter. These memories can be recovered. I am going to take you downstairs now and put you to sleep. All that I want you to do is tell me what you have dreamed when you wake up, and there will be piles of money waiting beside your beds.'

They descended into the cellars. The Father of Cats took Barfi by the ear and, tweaking it fiercely, forced him down on to one of the beds. Ladoo stood and watched.

'Lie back,' the Father of Cats said to Barfi, 'and think of your toes falling asleep, then your feet and ankles, now your legs are heavy with sleep, your chest . . . your eyelids are too heavy to keep open. You lie there in the dark and you see things. You are near the Zuweyla Gate and you are going to meet a man.'

He continued to whisper.

The chaos of shape and colour adjusted itself. Barfi was near the Zuweyla Gate. It was late and the acrobats and equilibrists were packing up their benches. A few remaining people had gathered round a talking ape who was telling the story of the two *kahins*. Barfi believed that his brother Ladoo was beside him but he could not see him.

A voice came from behind his left shoulder. 'You are Barfi, are you not? Please help me. I think that I have the Arabian Nightmare.'

Barfi turned and stared incredulously. It was the Father of Cats, haggard with pain. The Father's head wavered from side to side for no apparent reason.

In a feeble voice, the Father continued. 'I need your help. Praises to God that you are here, but who sent you?'

'You did.'

The old man seemed unable to concentrate for pain. 'I? But I am only a dream, as are you. Where was I when I sent you here?'

239

Barfi reflected for a long time before replying, 'Outside, outside everything, beyond all this. In your house, the House of Sleep. You sent me here to find the man who suffers the Arabian Nightmare.'

The Father seemed dispirited and at a loss. He mumbled to himself and only slowly did he become audible. 'Yet how do I dream when I never sleep . . .? Well, you won't be much use then. Awake, I could never bear this. No, it would be terrible. No, no, no, no. I must never know and you must never tell. You must swear to me – but no, oaths sworn in dreams are not binding . . . Here is a difficulty. What shall we do then?' He swayed about and contorted his face in indecision and then, with a sad gleam in his eye, produced a little box and continued, 'Those who have the Arabian Nightmare remember nothing. To remember nothing is sweet. Won't you look inside my little box?'

'I think that if I did not have the Nightmare already, you would not be showing the box to me.' And Barfi shook his head violently. Indeed, he found that his whole body was shaking violently, yet he was peering into the little box all the same. Its deep sides shelved downwards steeply and drew the eye inwards. In the centre of the box was a small, dark object that appeared to get nearer and then further, yet the further position was always nearer and nearer. 'If I did not have the Nightmare already, you would not be showing the box to me, me, me, me.' He listened to his voice echo in the box. It was fascinating and repelling. Almost swooning, he peered closer, shaking.

The shaking came from outside. He was being shaken awake in the cellar of the House of Sleep. The Father of Cats and Ladoo stood over him.

'Well?' said the Father of Cats.

'I remember nothing,' said Barfi.

'Nothing at all?' The old man was grim. 'Well, I shall not be thwarted. I have a second string to my bow. Ladoo, take your brother's place on the bed. Relax your toes, your ankles, your feet . . . Your eyes are sealed. Let the visions rise. I want you to go to my house and ask for me or, to be more accurate, my dream image, my *khayal*. My *khayal* shall assist you. Together you and he will go to the market place and meet the man who has the Arabian Nightmare. My *khayal* will tell you what to say when you return to us. You must do better than your brother.'

Ladoo found himself in a street in the Ezbekiyya Quarter by night. The houses appeared a little shaky at first, but soon everything appeared natural. Ladoo drifted towards the House of Sleep. He had no will, for all dreamers lack the power of will, yet he was driven on by his mysterious mission.

He entered the House of Sleep. The door pushed open easily. There was no porter and everywhere there were signs of dilapidation. Still a torch at the gate was lit, and it showed that the courtyard was covered with cockroaches. A few mangy cats continued to inhabit the place. From time to time one of them would pounce on a cockroach, breaking its back with its claws. Ladoo stood there scratching his head.

'Welcome, stranger. I am Saatih.' It flowed across the paving stones and cockroaches towards him. 'Shikk also welcomes you.'

Shikk stood deep in the shadows, only half visible, like a marabout stork in a rigid pose of attention.

'Peace, Masters,' said Ladoo. 'I am sent to find the Father of Cats. Is he here? If not, where can I find him?'

'You are sent? Who sent you?'

'Somebody from outside. It is difficult. I cannot remember.'

'It is difficult to think here. This is the Rat level of dreams. Our thoughts are cramped. Everything is small, very small. See how low the sky is. Since everything here is small, you have not noticed how even your dwarfish frame has shrunk.'

They laughed. Saatih's laugh was low and throaty. Shikk's was shrill.

'You will not find the Father of Cats here,' Saatih went on. 'He has not been here for a very long time. We ask ourselves, is he sick or is he afraid to come? Perhaps he fears that he himself has the Nightmare or, rather, that it has him.'

'I think I have it too,' Ladoo ventured uncertainly.

They laughed again.

'Everybody does, but it is quite a different thing actually to have it. But we should like to see our old friend the Father of Cats again. In fact, if you are a friend of his too, take that message to him. Tell him that we are doing our best to keep his house tidy but that also we are waiting. Remind him too that one of the oldest stories in the Alam al-Mithal is that of the magical monster that escaped its inventor's control. We like company and we are lonely; we like to know what is going on. You don't enjoy our company, though, do you?'

'I am not enjoying this at all,' said Ladoo and struggled to wake. When he opened his eyes, he found himself in the shadow of a wall, staring out on the open wastes of the Tartar Ruins. Everything was light and airy, by comparison at least with the previous scene. A young and ragged foreigner lay sleeping beside him. An ape squatted over him.

'This is the Ape's level of the mind,' said the ape who grinned in welcome.

'I have a message,' said Ladoo. 'Shikk and Saatih wish to see the Master of the House of Sleep and they wish to tell him that one of the oldest stories in the Alam al-Mithal is of the magical monster that escaped its inventor's control.'

'One of the oldest, indeed, but not one of the best,' said the ape. 'Let me tell you better.' And he told Ladoo stories about savage children, sinister infidels, walking heaps of clay and cities at the end of the World.

Ladoo sat listening, his fearful encounter and his mission fast fading from his mind. The stories were enchanting, but, despite the sunlight, Ladoo found himself shivering, shaking, being shaken awake.

He awoke again in the cellar of the House of Sleep. The Father of Cats and a very perturbed Barfi stood beside his bed.

'Well?' said the Father of Cats.

'I had such a beautiful dream. This ape told me stories. There was one about an old Jew who took some clay and –'

The Father of Cats spat. 'You have failed me, both of you,' he said.

Just then a slave ran down the steps and tugged at the sleeve of the Father of Cats. 'Master, come quick. We have the Englishman.'

The Father followed the slave up. Balian's sleeping body had been discovered and brought within the gate.

Later, when Balian awoke, he found himself lying strapped to a bed. It was difficult to see properly. The sun streamed through the shutters and sun-drenched motes of dust danced before his eyes. The lowness of the ceiling signified that it must be an upstairs room. The Father of Cats and his assistants were gathered in a huddle at the far edge of the room, almost beyond the range of his vision, all except Vane who was to explain each stage of the operation as it happened.

For the moment he ignored his surroundings. The actual situation was threatening enough, yet the melancholia that seemed to sit upon him like a fat cat asleep on his stomach was more powerful. He struggled to trace back its origins to the dreams he had been having. The act of recalling a dream brought back to him the vision of fishermen he had seen on the shore at Alexandria, straining at the ropes, drawing in the net. Slowly it surfaced and was hauled on to land. Quite suddenly the water seeped out and thousands of silvery minnows could be seen flickering within.

He had been in the kiosk with Zuleyka. They had been arguing and were angry with one another.

'It's the end. I am bored with your dreams,' she had said.

And he had replied, 'But you are in my head with all my dreams, you and this kiosk!'

'Well, if you wish, I am bored with being in your dreams. I am bored with what you dream.'

'I can walk out of this kiosk and you will vanish for ever.'

'This kiosk fills your head. You can't walk out of your

head. You can't leave me either. I am as much part of you as you are. You thought that you dreamt that you were a man hiding in a garden. Actually you dreamt that you were a garden containing a hidden man.'

'But if I can't leave you, you can't leave me.'

'Of course I can. You can't leave the dream but the dream can leave you.'

'But you can't leave me. I love you.'

'You love the phantasm you have created, the initiatrix, the wise and golden-hearted prostitute who opens her legs and admits you to mysteries. But you don't give me anything. You are passive. You are lying there waiting to be entertained and instructed.'

That was the nastiest part of the dream, but it was not the beginning of their argument. He had awoken in the kiosk, thinking of Khatun, and the first thing he had said was, 'That adventure we had in the garden of the Dawadar was very like an encounter I had previously had with an anonymous lady in Cairo in waking life.'

'That is natural. Dreams are like stories. They both ride on the back of real life. Dreams feed on reality.'

'Why did I see Emmanuel lying dead in the garden? Did you kill him?'

'We killed him. He recognized us. At least he recognized my master.'

'That man with the monkey, your master is –'

'Have you ever heard of a secret book called *The Galleon of the Apes*? I should not expect you to have heard of it. It is guarded closely, we are told, by the devotees of the cult of the Laughing Dervish in Happy Valley. But Emmanuel had heard something of the contents of the book and encountered members of the Order as he travelled along the upper reaches of the Nile, and he recognized one of them that night and guessed our purpose in the garden.

'*The Galleon of the Apes* is in the first instance a study of the building of the pyramids and the Sphinx. It laboriously demonstrates what is obvious – that such marvels could not be built today, and everywhere similar ruins testify to the former greatness of Man. The book teaches that there were once, thousands of years ago, great and elaborate civilizations on Earth and that, with their ingenious mechanical contrivances, they ruled the skies and the seas. The book teaches also the doctrine of the plurality of worlds and holds that there are other stars that are inhabited. Further it holds that millennia ago a fleet of galleons appeared over Earth, carrying apes from another star. They descended to Earth and mated with the humans. Ever since that ill-starred moment civilization has degenerated. The ingenious mechanical devices have been lost. Standards have been abandoned and the ape in Man takes over. Triviality and mass cruelty abound. To speak figuratively, the Ape rules the world.

'The man with us in the garden was a Laughing Dervish who wished to test the doctrine of the book by seeing if apes and humans could indeed breed, for many hold such miscegenation to be impossible. The game of forfeits was proposed for no other purpose. It was our misfortune to have brought on before you Emmanuel, the one man in all Cairo who could detect our design and would try to stop it.'

'Those ideas are absurd. To kill a man for them absurder yet. The doctrine of the Laughing Dervishes is a joke, a parody of true knowledge, which, as the Blessed Niko of Cologne teaches us, should conduct us always to virtue.'

'To discover or invent something is to put two familiar things together in an unfamiliar way, and that is the way of the joke and the riddle too.'

'And how do I know that I too am not the victim of some elaborate joke or experiment designed by your colleague?'

'What sort of answer do you want?'

'I want the truth.'

Her sigh was like a long, slow deflation. 'You ask too many questions.'

And then the argument had become more personal. It all ended up with them returning to the subject of Emmanuel.

'You are looking at me as if I were a murderess, but it was

245

you who wished him dead and the Spirit of the Alam al-Mithal acts always to fulfil your wishes. You knew he would have disapproved of your relationship with me and of what was going on in the garden. Secretly you wished him dead, so you had us kill him covertly in your sleep.'

'But it was only a dream!'

'So it was your truest wish.' All of a sudden she softened. 'You still have the snake between your eyes, haven't you? You never did attain relief that night. There comes a point when it is positively dangerous to delay the climax.'

She ran her fingers down his penis as if it were a flute. 'You know, the penis wishes not so much to discharge as to rest after discharge.'

'My penis has no wishes.'

She ignored this. 'Similarly every story has its death wish, rushing on to become silence. And, similarly again, in reality we desire not what we think we desire but that we should not desire.'

Once more the serpent was uncoiling. The knots were being smoothed away, a painful unwinding of knowledge and sexual frustration. Closer. Closer and closer. The moment was imminent, but as it approached something within him beyond his control recoiled from Zuleyka's manipulation. He tried to cling to her, but it was like clinging to the ropes of the wind. He was waking up. A false climax. He lay there remembering and listened to the Father of Cats sharpen a knife on a whetstone. Vane sat beside him, explaining.

20

The Administration of Justice

Dirty Yoll is Dirty Yoll no longer. While he lived his friends could never persuade him, either by teasing or by bullying, to accompany them to the public baths. It must be admitted that his filthy state was not all the Ape's fault. Now that Yoll is dead his friends have had their way with him. It is the custom in these parts to wash the entire corpse. Both Christians and Muslims do this. Yoll will have been thoroughly washed. I cannot see into the grave, but I am sure that even his fingernails are immaculately clean.

Since his death you have not, I am sure, had dreams of Dirty Yoll creeping up to pester you with his new theory about wet dreams. You have had no visions of Dirty Yoll showing you those miserable, half starved chickens that some rich man is raising at Bulaq. You have heard no mysterious rapping sounds in your house. The dry earth does not crack. No muffled story comes up from underground.

The point I am approaching, in my usual oblique fashion, is that Yoll is not dictating this story. Yoll is dead. What is more, Yoll never was dictating the story. There has been a muddle about identity. It is coming clearer now. I am not yet ready to reveal who I am. I shall do so at the end of the story. Obviously that moment is coming soon. The reader feels with his fingers the diminishing number of pages which remain to be turned and adjusts his expectations accordingly. The reader is warned. As the pages diminish, so do the number of possible solutions. I scratch my head. There is nothing I can do about that. All I can hope is that, to return to the theme with which I opened, finally it will be unclear where the burden of my book ended and the contents of your dreams began.

247

For the moment, though, your sleep and my self-revelation must wait. Sometimes in a dream a man will struggle to do something serious, such as recite a passage from Holy Scripture or cast up accounts. He will never succeed. The denizens of the Alam al-Mithal will lay him low. Read and be instructed . . .

There was a Christian and a Muslim theory behind the operation. Vane used concepts from both to explain the process to Balian. According to Niko of Cologne and the followers of the Rhineland school of Spiritual Medicine, there were five orifices in a man's skin, five wounds which leaked – the penis, the anus, the ears, the mouth and the nose – and from these wounds seeped the biles, black, yellow and white, signifying according to their admixture that all was not well within the body's *terra incognita*. The Arab physicians accepted this on the whole while rejecting the typological analogy which Niko had made between the five orifices and the marks of the Passion of Christ; they pointed out that, more accurately counted, the orifices were six in number (for the Basran school took account of the fact that there were two ears) or seven (for the Kufan school took account of the fact that there were two nostrils also). But the wise men of the Arabs were united in emphasizing the properties of the nose, for 'it is with the nose that one draws in the *rooh*, the breath of life, and within the nose that one sleeps,' according to Ibn Umail.

After much thought, the Father of Cats had come to the conclusion that Balian's post-oneiric loss of blood was due to an excess of pressure in the front ventricle of the brain. As everyone knows, thought rises from the heart as a vapour and condenses in the brain as a thick yellow fluid or snot, which, when it is sufficiently concentrated after, say, some twelve hours or so, regularly produces sleep. According to the Father of Cats, it was this excess snot, yellow bile, which was putting pressure on the blood in the front ventricle.

The Father was ready now. With arms folded he moved to

248

the end of the bed. 'I am going to attempt a very simple cure,' he said.

Balian screamed briefly before a servant covered his mouth with a pad of aromatic smelling cotton. Then another servant passed a red-hot spoon into the gloved hand of the Father. This he applied to Balian's nostrils. At first there was only pain. It felt as though the Father was trying to draw his brains out with a pair of red-hot pincers. Then there was a loosening, and, to the old man's evident pleasure, thick gobs of yellow fluid began to emerge. Balian fainted.

When he came round they showed him the bile neatly bottled and sealed in small glass jars.

'What have you done that for?'

'We shall sell the stuff. There are innumerable reasons why some men cannot sleep. The biggest single reason, though, is fear of boredom. Many insomniacs would envy you your vivid dreams. I shall make your bile into a paste and I shall be surprised if I do not get a good price for it.'

'And am I cured?'

'The symptoms at least are cured. Really, the ultimate cure is up to you. You must make a definite effort in the years to come not to think so much. You have more thoughts than actions and this, as any physician of sleep will tell you, generates enormous pressure inside you.'

'You have been like a kettle boiling on a stove,' Vane put in.

'And I have not got the Arabian Nightmare?'

'By the beard of the Prophet, no! It is one thing to dream that you have the Arabian Nightmare, quite another actually to have it!'

'You know that Jean Cornu and his following have examined me and have told me not only that I do not have the Arabian Nightmare but also that I am not the promised Messiah.'

'Yes, yes. That is very good. I presume that you did not want to have the Arabian Nightmare or be the Messiah?'

'No, of course not. But, for God's sake, why then have you and your familiar been pursuing me across Cairo?'

Vane gave him a lupine grin and the Father of Cats shook his head sorrowfully, saying, 'You are still a child really. You think that the world is enclosed by your vain self-preoccupations and that the sun revolves around you. You thought that Vane and I were hunting you. I assure you, this was not so. How many times have you really met us – outside your dreams, that is? You don't know us at all, I suspect. All that you know is what is projected by your fantasy. It may be hard for you to accept but I assure you that you are of no importance at all in the wider world, simply a man who needed treatment for an illness.'

With that the Father of Cats departed and Vane remained only to hiss, 'Think yourself lucky that you were treated by us. Some physicians, the Jews especially, would have slit your throat first and then cut your skull open to extract your precious snot!'

Balian lay apathetically back on the pillow. They still had not undone his bonds.

The Dawadar was dreaming about two princesses who lived on top of a tower. The tower had no staircase. It had been built that way by order of the Sultan. The Dawadar stood at the foot of the tower and, looking up, discovered that the two princesses were in fact his daughters. Shouting down to him, they explained that they had been imprisoned there because the people had discovered that they had been sharing their souls with the daughters of the Father of Cats. The 'princesses' had done this purely out of kindness, but the people feared them for it and had built the tower under them. By day their souls were their own, but at night the daughters of the Father of Cats took the souls and went walking in the streets with them. The Dawadar received an image of his daughters lying unconscious on the roof of the tower, ghostly music rising from their open mouths. He summoned a water-seller and asked him why he would not help his daughters. The water-seller muttered something obscene.

'My daughters, is all well with my daughters?' The Dawa-dar found himself addressing this question to his deputy and his eunuch of the bed chamber. They were too excited to pay any attention to his drowsy utterance.

'We have caught the murderous lady, just as she was about to take another victim with her knife near the Roda Nilo-meter. Her name is Fatima, and she claims some sort of con-nection with the Father of Cats. The Sultan summons you to the Dar al-Adl within the hour.'

'What time is it?'

'Not yet time for the dawn prayer.'

It was very cold in the Dar al-Adl. Sleepy emirs, pulled out of bed to view Fatima the Deathly, warmed their hands around a ring of braziers, while slaves ran to get cloaks and rugs for the deliberating courtiers. Fatima was already before the Sultan when the Dawadar arrived. She turned her start-lingly white face towards him briefly and the sultan, seeing that his senior officer had arrived, opened the proceedings. At the Sultan's signal an officer narrated the circumstances of Fatima's arrest, then Qaitbay spoke.

'Murderess, you should know that, though the Gate of Jus-tice is now open to you, it would be foolish to pretend that this trial does not have a predetermined end. This afternoon you will be taken out to the Zuweyla Gate to dance with Melsemuth. Now you have the ear of the Sultan and his coun-cil, so speak.'

Fatima spoke with great difficulty and her voice was almost lost in the great *majlis*.

'No. You cannot threaten me with Melsemuth. My sister's madness has already destroyed me. I am Fatima, incestuous daughter of the Father of Cats and his daughter Zuleyka, a whore of the Ezbekiyya Quarter. I have killed many men and women, all customers of the Father of Cats. I killed only his customers and I acted only as a surgeon does who cuts out the buboes from a plague-stricken body. His disciples pass the

Arabian Nightmare round the city in a little box and he plots the ruin of your state.'

'Every day we hear of a hundred plots or more. Who will support your accusation?'

'No one speaks, yet I see several of his customers here.'

Though she spoke slowly and without emphasis, the guards around the Sultan redoubled their vigilance. But she was to say no more. She raised her arm accusingly before the Sultan. The arm dropped off and smashed on the floor in a cloud of dust. Nobody moved as she fell away in a mound of rags and fast disintegrating bones. Finally one of the *khassakiyya* guard beside her turned and tentatively kicked the heap.

'A phantasm.'

'A creation of the Sleep Teacher.'

Courtier sages commented on the miracle, and a halting discussion of what was to be done began. The Sultan was reluctant to act and the Dawadar just shrugged his shoulders.

In the end, however, the Sultan spoke. 'For centuries in Egypt there have been two governments. I hold the sword and staff of visible government in this land, but every man knows that there is an invisible government, though no man knows its nature. Let no man speak of what has happened here this morning. We shall make our preparations, and in the evening we shall go to uncover the mysteries of the House of Sleep. Take that rubbish away and have it burnt.'

They dispersed.

The waters of the fountain ran gurgling over the flagstones in the courtyard of the House of Sleep.

That afternoon Balian was unstrapped from his bed. The Father of Cats motioned him up.

'We have cured the body; perhaps music will heal the spirit. Will you join us in attending a musical interlude?'

'I suppose that I have no choice?'

'It is as you suppose.'

Almost the entire household was there, headed by Vane and Salim the porter. At the end of the room sat the three musicians, flat-faced men from Central Asia, with their instruments, the *ney*, the *rebec* and the frame drum. A dancing boy stood before them. A silk scarf hung suggestively around his silver-trousered hips.

As soon as the *ney* first sounded its sinuous yearnings, those hips began to waggle. Then the *rebec* came in, providing a rhythmic frame through which the strains of the *ney* had to weave. Finally, at no particular point, the drum joined in, its rhythms sometimes emphasizing, sometimes counterpointing, those of the *rebec*. The rhythms were harsh and awful to Balian's ear, from the very first making an impatient rush towards an appointed end, yet delaying themselves in melancholy repetition and refrain, doublings and triplings of structures that turned about and consumed themselves, passionate contradictions and collisions, and through it all the *ney* meandered with reedy complaint. The deaf and visionless boy shimmered and swayed as directed by the third ear, that of balance. He was like the snake which does not hear the music of the snake charmer but, earless, follows the movements of the flute with its eyes. The voices of the orchestra accompanied him in melismatic chant. The plangent note of the *ney* deepened. The boy executed a series of steps, his bare feet slapping against the tiles, and began almost imperceptibly to vibrate as if a thread had been drawn through him from the earth to the sky and plucked.

Conversation broke out and became general. Vane observed that they had been listening to what was really an evening mode. 'It is like a story begun at the hour of the *isha* prayer; those who listen know that the storyteller must conclude before curfew.'

The Father of Cats sat abstracted. He was listening to something else. There were scuffling sounds outside. Conversation stopped and Salim rushed to the window. Balian followed. Down below, the alley was crowded and some of the crowd were looking up curiously. Others were shaking their fists. It was from the other side of the room, however, that trouble came. Suddenly the bolt on the door snapped and the door swung inwards. A pair of Mamluke guards entered and behind them came the Dawadar, looking elegant as ever and very amused at the effect his entry had created. Behind him were perhaps another half-dozen Mamlukes.

'Greetings to the master of this house. Blessings and peace on those here who walk in righteousness. I beg the Father to believe me when I say that I would not willingly inconvenience him or his guests' (and here he saluted them respectfully) 'but I have here a *firman* from the Sultan directing me to escort you to the Citadel and to detain you within its walls for as long as he shall be pleased, and the Sultan's will must be obeyed by you and me alike.' The Dawadar raised his eyebrows in mock commiseration. 'Come with me, please.'

The Father did not move. 'In obeying the will of the Sultan, one follows only one's own true will, so I have always found. An invitation from the Sultan is always welcome.' The Father's voice was silky. 'May I inquire the reason for the Sultan's need of my presence?'

'An officer of the Sultan will never deny a request so courteously made. A certain lady, one Fatima (she is now dead, by the way), was brought before the Sultan this morning charged with many notorious murders. In the course of her short trial she made accusations against you which were doubtless absurd and certainly hard to understand. That is the matter in brief. We look forward to your assistance in interpreting her words.'

'Oh, in that case –' The Father of Cats looked at Salim and snapped his fingers. Salim made a rush at the Dawadar and was fended off by one of the guards. They collapsed in a wrestling heap on the floor. Meanwhile Vane had launched himself on another of the guards. While some of the disciples ran to find arms, the fight spread across the room and into the colonnade. The musicians huddled into a corner. The boy sat among them, trembling, his hands over his face. The Father stood a little to one side of Balian, a staff raised over his head – whether in menace or for magic, it was unclear. No one dared approach him. Balian heard him shout to one of his

254

students to run and fetch help from Jean Cornu and his following.

Balian briefly noted this strange and unexpected instruction without trying to explain it to himself. Perhaps he had misheard the Father? Without a weapon Balian felt that he was powerless to join in the fight (and for whom, he wondered, should he fight anyway?). Vane's long knife had come out from under his ratskin coat and he was the first to claim a victim. Suddenly his free hand dropped to his belt and then he sent an open pouch of pepper flying into the face of his opponent. Then he rushed in to disembowel the blinded Mamluke. Soon there was pepper everywhere, for Vane was not the only disciple of the Father to carry such a purse as protection against footpads. The sounds were awful – a common trick was to close in and slash the enemy's hams, and several men lay or sat screaming in agony on the edge of the conflict. Two swarthy antagonists, having lost their weapons, were engaged rhythmically in trying to smash each other's skulls against the wall. After the first nervous onslaught and savage manoeuvre, the fighting slowed. The struggle was becoming one of stamina, and already some men could hardly lift their weapons and stood cautiously facing one another, bending forward, convulsively trying to regain their breath.

Fresh impetus came to the fight with the arrival of the lepers. The door swung open a second time. For a moment Jean Cornu, in full armour but for a helmet, stood there, filling the doorway. Then, drawing his sword, he entered and behind him thronged a mass of scarred and awful warriors, the leper knights and attendant mendicants. The Mamlukes were exhausted, outnumbered and, above all, terrified of their new opponents. Even the Dawadar, who at first had tried to avoid personal combat, was now hard-pressed and reluctantly fighting to defend his life. It seemed that victory was within the grasp of the Father of Cats – and of Jean Cornu.

Then, quite suddenly, the fighters drew apart. One heard the breath rasp in exhausted men's lungs and the occasional whimper of pain. A third time the gates of the House of Sleep had been forced open, this time by the officers of the Sultan. A hundred or more Mamlukes poured into the courtyard and fanned out through the house. First one emir, then another, elbowed their way into the concert room where the Father of Cats and Jean Cornu now stood side by side. Finally Qaitbay himself entered and the escort behind him poured into the already crowded room. Mamluke guards with drawn swords filed along the walls.

The Sultan just stared at the Father of Cats angrily. Then the Father spoke. 'I bid you welcome. It grieves me that the Sultan should find my house in such disarray.' A dying man moaned. 'We were not prepared for your visit.'

'And we did not expect that you would refuse the invitation that we sent you with the Dawadar.'

'Even so, I now hurry to obey its summons.'

'It is not necessary to inconvenience yourself. We shall hold your trial here.'

'My trial? Who has accused me, and what am I accused of?'

'Fatima, a lady accused of murder, on being brought before us, claimed a connection with you and accused you of conspiring to overthrow the state.'

'Bring forth this witness, so that I may confute her lies.'

'She no longer exists.'

'Then no one accuses me and I am not accused.'

'You are impertinent. There are other charges and we have found other witnesses.' Then, to the Mamluke guards, 'Have these two brought down into the courtyard.'

Everyone trooped down into the courtyard where, surrounded by *khassakiyya* guards, a lady, veiled and robed in black, stood before a black sedan chair borne on the shoulders of Nubian slaves.

The Dawadar pointed to the woman languidly. 'This woman here accuses Jean Cornu, known in the West as the Grand Master of the Poor Knights of St Lazarus, of the murder of Dirty Yoll, a storyteller famous throughout Cairo, but she also accuses the Father of Cats of having "put the ape on Yoll's back", this last expression is, I presume, an obscure piece of criminal argot.'

Balian scrutinized the squat form carefully and identified it as that of Yoll's sister, Mary.

The Dawadar continued, 'Her charges have been corroborated and expanded by another witness, a public-spirited citizen, albeit crippled.'

The slaves had lowered the sedan and one of them now opened the door. Saatih came tumbling down its steps. Saatih squelched and bubbled and cleared his throat. 'Murder and the hunting of men with animals are the least of their crimes,' he said finally. 'These two men before us decided that God's providence moves too slowly and conspired to give it a push –'

Here Vane cried out in anguished confusion, 'But I thought that we and the lepers were on different sides!'

'We were. Utterly.' This was the Father, resigned.

'On different sides and the same side.' This was Cornu.

'On different sides and the same side,' Saatih agreed. 'Made idle by cynicism, these two bored intelligences turned to the study of prophecy and magic. While still young they learned of each other's existence and fame in such arts. They met secretly in Jerusalem and there they made a pact to perform an operation known to occultists as "Raising the Wind". Then they separated and returned to their respective countries, where they patiently set to work preparing the operation. This operation (which has never ever been successfully completed) involves the selection of an ordinary human conflict by powerful magicians who recruit for its armies occult assistance and thereby raise the conflict to a higher power, investing it with apocalyptic significance. Finding Man's story long and wearisome, they wished to force the coming of the Antichrist and, what must follow, the coming of the Messiah and the End of All Things. To slake their boredom they wished to stage Armageddon in front of the pyramids. The Father took the side of Islam, Cornu that of Christendom. The Father recruited healers; Cornu recruited the sick. The Father summoned up assistance from the Alam al-Mithal; Cornu struggled against the phantoms of the dream world.'

'Which one fought for the True God?' This was the friar, who had appeared among the gawping throng around the sedan.

'Their Great Work is and will remain incomplete. No Messiah will come. If one may judge from the signs and portents they did succeed in raising amid us in Cairo, one should judge that the war in the universe is between two equally evil powers. However, the operation has failed. That it has failed is due largely to the excessive cunning and vanity of the Father of Cats. The Father did not trust his adversary. He suborned and corrupted many of Cornu's followers and, in so doing, unbalanced the psychic forces. On the other hand, recently the Father has been unable to control his own legions.' Saatih chuckled. 'Disgusting things have been emerging from the Alam al-Mithal. The Arabian Nightmare is spreading. The Father himself was the source of the nightmare he pretended to cure.'

Saatih gurgled and would have said more, but the Sultan motioned him silent and spoke himself.

'These are incredible charges. I will not lightly accept such bizarre and far-fetched accusations against my old teacher and friend. What have you to say?'

'I will not weary the Sultan's ear or tax his limited powers of understanding. I am eager to be off,' said the Father of Cats.

Qaitbay almost choked. Gesturing furiously, he had Masrur, the Great Eunuch, come forward. Masrur forced the Father of Cats to his knees and, with a fine professional blow of the axe, cut the man's head off. This done, he turned to Cornu, who had already composed himself to die, and cut his head off too.

Saatih's head revolved until it faced the Sultan. 'That was wisely done,' he said.

Vane, Balian, the friar and now Bulbul stood at the front of a crowd of students of Sleep, servants of the house, lepers and mendicants. Qaitbay addressed them all.

'It would seem that, one and all, you have been more dupes than conspirators.' (Vane scowled.) 'My men will escort you to the Citadel, but you are not to regard yourselves as prisoners, for you shall all be my guests at dinner tonight.'

The Sultan's horse was led into the courtyard and he mounted it. Then they all filed out behind him.

21

Eating Well in Cairo

Eat well and farewell! As promised, I shall make my appearance at the end of this final episode, but that will be only to signify the end of our companionship. So if I forget then, let me say now: farewell and sleep well. By the way my vote is cast for the banana . . .

'Consider the banana. Consider its skin, which protects its virtues like a veil. Consider its shape, a muted bow, like a fine arched lady's eyebrows. Consider its trinitarian segmental structure, which faithfully mirrors the threefold dialectic of Nature. Consider how the banana nourishes and cleanses the Third Eye.

'Rice, rather, is the measure of all foods. It occupies the point of equipoise within the scale of taste – only through rice will it be possible to assess the merits of the meal. Without this staple we are adrift on a sea of gastric fantasy.

'The monkey nut has many claims on our attention, not least the polarity within it between nut and shell, but those who speak of such things would do well to remember that the nut is not necessarily truer than the shell.

'The wise men will appreciate the whole meal, taking care to balance its parts. Here we have an evening mode of cooking – the rapid alternation of sweet and sour provides it with the rhythm that intoxicates our senses.'

Light battled against darkness in the cavernous banqueting hall. Pages bearing flambeaux created patterns of reflected light on the tiled arabesques of the walls and the dully glinting, low, bronze tables. Diners and waiters moved through limitless perspectives of horseshoe arches under eternal arcs of stone. The palm grove of marble columns dissolved at their heads into peacock's fan vaulting which, as it ascended, broke into stalactitic ornament; this in turn shattered in its upper reaches into cubes of coloured crystal, which radiated like divine emanations from the centres of the domes. Stars, zodiacal numbers and the Names of God effaced the blankness of the walls and suggested the suspension of time in the Sultan's treasure cave.

The Jashinkir, the Ustudar and a regiment of *sakis* stood to serve at the Sultan's table. On the stone platform behind the Sultan's table were arrayed battle trophies recently won in Anatolia and, in their midst, wrapped in black silk, the heads of the Father of Cats and Jean Cornu reposed on bronze salvers. Convoys of slaves streamed into the hall bearing bowls and panniers – small birds, couscous, khashkhasiya, poppy seed cakes, sheep's tail fat, Persian milk dishes, African fruits and rice. Conversation at the tables was elevated.

'You say that Christ never slept. It is many years now since I made a study of this important question, but my teachers, I recall, maintained this opinion to be notorious heresy and a doctrine capable of rebuttal both in general and in particular!'

The friar was unmoved by the vigour of Vane's onslaught. 'Then rebut it.'

Vane knuckled his forehead in a parody of servile deference. 'First, to raise the general objection, Christ was both God and Perfect Man and, being Perfect Man, must he not have taken upon himself of all Man's qualities and attributes? So it is safest to believe that Christ had two hands, two eyes, a mouth and so forth and that, further, he laughed, cried, slept and dreamt as a man. Then, to take the particular article on which orthodox assent must be fixed, the Gospel tells us that Christ slept, for is it not related in the fourth book of the Gospel of St Mark that Jesus Christ was asleep in the rear part of a ship on the Sea of Galilee when a storm blew up and it was necessary for the disciples to awaken him before he arose to quieten the storm, and, since (as Artemidorus teaches us) sleep is nothing more than a vehicle for dreams, must we not suppose that Christ had dreams on that boat and in other places at other times? So it is certain that Christ slept and likely that he dreamt.'

Vane grinned his wolf's grin.

The friar smiled too. 'You must persevere as a tomb robber, for you will never make your reputation as an exegete. You have put two arguments to me, but a single refutation undermines them both.

'Sleep is not a quality but rather the absence of one, that is, wakefulness. No more is dreaming an attribute but rather the denial of one, that is, rationality. (It is as if one were to call a black man "coloured", which is absurd, for what he actually suffers from is absence of colour for, as the Blessed Niko tells us, black is not a colour.) Like Evil, in that they constitute only absence and negation, sleeping and dreaming are no more to be accounted essential qualities in humanity than are one-leggedness, amentia, blindness or albinism. If Christ slept, then he was not Perfect Man and therefore neither Christ nor God, and, if not God, then the testimony of his disciple Mark might safely be accounted worthless. This would be both absurd and counter to orthodoxy.

'But if we say, as I do, that Christ never slept on that storm-tossed boat, then how can we account for Mark's testimony? In this way. We learn from that very same chapter of Mark that Christ never spoke save in parables. Shall we ascribe fatigue to God? What sane man will rebuke the wind? Should we credit the Galilean Sea with ears? Rather, it is certain that when we read of Christ sleeping we read of the acting out of parable. The sea that they sailed on was no real sea but the Sea of Dreams, and the sense of the parable is that it was not Christ but his Apostles that slept and he stilled their nightmare for them. To sleep is to be unconscious. Can God not be conscious? No. To dream is to be deceived. Can God be deceived? No. Dreaming is deception. Like magic, it is an imposture practised upon reason and the senses, and Christianity rejects dreams and magic alike.'

'You scorn magic?' Saatih dribbled and slobbered. It was horrid to watch him eat.

'Magic is absurd. It is a system of thinking that does not work and does not get one anywhere,' said the friar.

'It works, but it does not get one anywhere,' said Vane.

'But it is very beautiful. Magic is an art which pleases the eye and the ear,' said Bulbul. 'There is poetry in the pentagram and invocation. They seem to promise but cannot fulfil infinite bliss.'

'Like Yoll's stories,' said the friar sighing. 'I shall miss Yoll's stories.'

'Yoll is dead but his stories live,' Bulbul replied. 'I wrote them down at his dictation. I have entitled the manuscript "Alf Layla wa Layla", that is, "One Thousand Nights and One Night".'

Here, a gipsy who was dining at the same table intervened. He was here tonight, he explained, because he understood that something extraordinary was due to happen.

'Even in Saragossa, where I come from, Yoll's stories were known of. Yoll was more than a storyteller, though, and his life signified something more. Each man carries his fate within him. Fate is a story written in his heart, his liver and his bones and it throws out his future before him. Somewhere within the viscera of every man sits his fate, painful like a kidney stone. It is kismet. It is a story which is writing man. Some men's fates make small stories, others great stories, epics. The big stories eat the small stories. We are all here,' he said, glancing round, 'almost all here anyway, episodes in someone else's story.'

'I don't understand,' Balian moaned. 'It's all so horrible and pointless. Things just keep coming round in circles.'

Just then somebody screamed. Everybody turned. The head on one of the salvers was speaking through the sheath of silk.

'It is always a pleasure to be with the Sultan,' the head of the Father of Cats was saying, 'even if only in part.'

'Spirit, may we question you?' demanded the friar.

'You may.'

'Spirit, what is your present state?'

'I longed for sleep, but even in death I have not found it.'

'Even as it is written, "We shall not all sleep, but we shall all be changed",' replied the friar.

'Even so.'

'Tell us now, what is or was the Arabian Nightmare?'

'It is a disease, a curse, a fear and an ogre, these four things equally.'

'That may be so. Yet it can hardly be any of these things in any common sense, for it seems possible to live under its thrall not only with equanimity but with happiness and well-being. Is it not perhaps an idea or a metaphor for a way of existing?'

The head was silent for a moment. Vane had meanwhile risen from the table and begun to creep towards the stone platform on which the head rested.

Then the muffled voice resumed. 'These questions are difficult. You are bold enough to suggest that the nightmare is only an idea. I do not wish to gainsay you. Reflect, however, that it is an idea that has killed – if it is an idea.'

The Sultan trembled. Vane continued to inch forward. The friar returned to the attack.

'Did the Nightmare kill the Venetian painter known as Giancristoforo Doria?'

'The painter you name died at the hands of his callous fellow conspirators. The conditions of his imprisonment in the Arqana destroyed him. He died from a madness inherent within him. He committed suicide. He was killed by sorcery. The Arabian Nightmare took him. His death was determined and more than determined. There are always more causes than events in the Alam al-Mithal. This generates great pressure. Some of the determinations are contradictory. I cannot say more.'

'Why did you have the Englishman known as Balian persecuted and hunted on his arrival in Cairo?'

But the head was silent. Vane had reached the platform now. Removing the silk and raising the head by its wispy hair, he showed it to the hall.

'The dead do not speak. Its lips are sealed.' Then, shouting, 'The old man's really dead!' he booted the head as high as it would go over the heads of the hushed throng into the dark outer reach of the hall. Balian was following its trajectory when something at the corner of his eye attracted his attention. A dirty white turban.

He nudged the friar. 'That man over there in the dirty white turban, he is the ventriloquist of whom Yoll and I spoke.'

The friar did not hesitate. He stood up and bellowed, 'Stop that man! There is the charlatan responsible for this imposture!'

But all was chaos as diners scattered to avoid the descending head and the man easily made his escape. When they sat down again they found that the gipsy had vanished too. The friar was calm.

'Almost certainly a prank of the Laughing Dervishes. Let it pass. Now –'

Here the Dawadar interrupted. 'If we speak of the Laughing Dervishes, my daughter Khatun had the most extraordinary dream the other night. She dreamt that she was made love to by –'

But here the friar interposed smoothly, 'I was always taught that it was bad manners to talk of dreams or indeed to mention a lady's name at table. Now, why should that be, I wonder?'

'It could be that the dreams are boring and women depressing,' growled Vane as he rejoined the company.

The friar turned to Balian. 'Now that your adventures are over, what will you do?'

Somebody on the other side of the table dropped a glass. Balian, distracted, watched the glass intact upon the floor. He was uncomfortable. He did not feel that the climax in his story had been reached. Then, after too long an interval, the glass shattered.

'I shall go and look for Zuleyka and ask her to marry me,' he replied. 'I shall convert to Islam if necessary.'

'Zuleyka is insane. You wouldn't like to marry my daughters instead or as well?' asked the Dawadar hopefully.

'No.'

'A pity.'

His mind was no longer with the Dawadar. Someone was shaking him awake.

The hand that was shaking him felt curiously insubstantial.

'Wake up,' said the Ape. 'I want to tell you another story. But first, give me a drink. I am exhausted.'

Dedalus is the UK's leading publisher of Literary Fantasy.

Titles published include:

The Architect of Ruins - Herbert Rosendorfer £8.99
The History of a Vendetta - Yorgi Yatromanolakis £6.99
The King in Yellow - Robert Chambers £4.95
The Acts of the Apostates - Geoffrey Farrington £6.99
La-Bas - J. K. Huysmans £7.99
Dreams of Roses & Fire - Eyvind Johnson £7.99
Tales from the Saragossa Manuscript - Jan Potocki £6.99
The Golem - Gustav Meyrink £6.99
The Angel from the West Window - Gustav Meyrink £8.99
Torture Garden - Octave Mirbeau £7.99
The Dedalus Book of British Fantasy: the 19th c - ed B.
   Stableford £8.99
The Dedalus Book of Femmes Fatales - ed B. Stableford £7.99
Tales of the Wandering Jew - ed B. Stableford £8.99

forthcoming titles include:

The Limits of Vision - Robert Irwin £5.99
The Book of Nights - Sylvie Germain £8.99
**The Dedalus Book of Austrian Fantasy: the Meyrink Years
   1890–1930** - ed Mike Mitchell £8.99
The Dedalus Book of Dutch Fantasy - ed R. Huijing £9.99
The Dedalus Book of Belgian Fantasy - ed. R. Huijing £8.99

The Limits of Vision - Robert Irwin

'Irwin is an irrepressibly clever writer but never irritating. The book binds together philosophy and mayhem. *The Limits of Vision* ranks as a genuine (and rare) work of the imagination.'

Jeanette Winterson, TLS

'Very funny: it sparkles with brilliance and has a truly superb ending. I confidently predict that there will never be a better novel about housework and that no real housewife will ever imagine a better sequel to *The Brothers Karamazov* than the one Marcia whips up. Robert Irwin is an extremely fine writer who is a sheer joy to read.'

Brian Stableford, Fantasy Review

'*The Limits of Vision* is an immensely intelligent and delightful novel that constantly jumps and turns through level after level of humour and invention. It is a dance of a book.'

Stephen Dobyns, New York Times

'Almost unhesitatingly it is possible to pronounce this novel unique, a ravishing product of pure imagination . . . a writer of rare insight.'

Ruth Rendell, New Statesman

'Weird, hilarious, yet elegantly disciplined, here's a hybrid of satire, fable and reportage. Jaded readers will treasure it.'

Daily Mail

'The most ectopic flight of imagination this month and my own Book of the Month choice . . . some of the best, lurid high-flown prose I've encountered for ages. With an ending, fitted with escape-hatches, Irwin makes an hysterical masterpiece. Your next bout of spring-cleaning might be a great nightmare.'

Ian Parker, Blitz

£5.99 1 873982 10 0 128p B.Format
Forthcoming in the Spring of 1993

Tales of the Wandering Jew – edited by Brian Stableford

'This homage to one of the world great stories collects the Wandering Jew's many English-language manifestations, a fascinating journey down the tangled roads of European Literature, as infinite as those Ahasuerus is still walking. This collection offers you the chance to hitch a lift on the immortal sufferer's back. It's not the sort of offer anybody should turn down.'

City Limits

'Pick your way through classics by the likes of Hawthorn or Kipling or jump straight into the selection of modern interpretations with excellent contributions by Kim Newman, Mike Resnick and Robert Irwin.'

Blast

'Geoffrey Farrington's *Little St Hugh* is a wonderful 13th century tale of fury and repentance, with a touch of *The Monk*. The historical style is impeccable.

Ian McDonald's *Fragments of an Analysis of a Case of Hysteria* is brilliantly written, mixing the early analyses of Freud, the Jew, and an evocative and disturbing foreshadowing of the Holocaust. Scott Edelman provides a bit of bizarre allegory with *The Wandering Jukebox*.

The whopper is the editor's own – Stableford's brilliant, appalling *Innocent Blood*. A heroin addict dying from AIDS, is chained up in a cellar by the Jew, and their relationship is a horror show of uncommunicated pain. Some powerful stuff here.'

Locus

£8.99   0 946626 71 5   384p B.Format

The legend of *The Wandering Jew* appears in several other books published by Dedalus: ***The Architect of Ruins*** – Herbert Rosendorfer; **The Green Face** – Gustav Meyrink; and **The Wandering Jew** – Eugene Sue